OUTPOST

J.G. Austin

OUTPOST

J.G. Austin

© 1st World Library – Literary Society, 2004
PO Box 2211
Fairfield, IA 52556
www.1stworldlibrary.org
First Edition

LCCN: 2003195111

ISBN: 1-59540-436-8

Purchase *"Outpost"*
as a traditional bound book at:
www.1stWorldLibrary.org/purchase.asp?ISBN=1-59540-436-8

1st World Library Literary Society is a nonprofit
organization dedicated to promoting literacy by:

- Creating a free internet library accessible from any
  computer worldwide.
- Hosting writing competitions and offering book
  publishing scholarships.

Readers interested in supporting literacy
through sponsorship, donations or
membership please contact:
literacy@1stworldlibrary.org
Check us out at: www.1stworldlibrary.org

Outpost
contributed by the Charles Family
in support of
1st World Library - Literary Society

CHAPTER I

SUNSHINE

"The last day of October!" said the Sun to himself, "the last day of my favorite month, and the birthday of my little namesake! See if I don't make the most of it!"

So the Sun called to all the winds and all the breezes, who, poor things! had but just gone to bed after a terrible night's work, ordering them to get up directly, and sweep the sky as clear as a bell; and bid all the clouds, whether big white mountains, little pinky islands, sweeping mares'-tails, or freckled mackerel-back, to put themselves out of the way, and keep out of it until November; when, as the Sun remarked with a sigh, they would have it all their own way.

"And as soon as that job's done," continued he, "you may go to bed again in the Mountains of the Moon; for you will only disturb me if you are about."

So the winds, grumbling and sighing a little, went to their work; and the Sun, after a good dip in the Atlantic Ocean, began to roll up the eastern sky, flecking the waves with diamond spray, touching up the gay-colored leaves still clinging to the forest-trees, blazing on the town and city clocks to let every one know how late it was, and finally thrusting his saucy glances into all the windows to see how many persons had needed him.

"Come, come, you city-folks!" cried the Sun. "Your neighbors in the country were up before I was, and have eaten their breakfasts, and half cleared it away by this time; and here are you just beginning to dress yourselves! Hurry up, I say! hurry up! It is the last day of October, don't you know? and to-morrow will be November.

"But, at the corner house of a handsome square, the Sun found himself better satisfied; for through the windows of the dining-room he saw a lady and gentleman seated at the table, having apparently almost finished their breakfast.

"That is better," remarked the Sun: and, thrusting one of his slender golden fingers through the window, he touched the stag's head upon the cover of the silver coffee-pot; glanced off, and sparkled in the cut glass of the goblets and egg-glasses; flickered across the white and gilt china; pierced the fiery heart of the diamond upon the first finger of the lady's left hand, and then, creeping swiftly up her white throat, played joyously in her golden curls, and even darted into her soft blue eyes, making them sparkle as brilliantly as the diamond.

"The sun shines directly in your face, Fanny," said Mr. Legrange, admiring the color in his wife's hair. "Shall I lower the shade?"

"Oh, no! thank you. I never want the sunshine shut out," replied she, moving her chair a little.

"Not to-day of all days in the year, I suppose; not on the birthday of our little Sunshine. And where is she?" asked Mr. Legrange, half turning his chair from the table to the fire, and unfolding the damp newspaper beside his plate.

"I told Susan to send her down as soon as she had done her breakfast. Hark! I hear her." And the Sun, drawing his finger across the mother's lips, helped them to so bright a smile, that her husband said,

"I am afraid we have more than our share of Sunshine, or at least that I have, little wife."

The bright smile grew so bright as the lady bent a little toward her husband, that the Sun whispered, -

"There's no need of sun here, I plainly see," but, for all that, crept farther into the room; while the door opened, and in skipped a little girl, who might have been taken for the beautiful lady at the head of the table suddenly diminished to childish proportions, and dressed in childish costume, but with all her beauty intensified by the condensation: for the blue eyes were as large and clear, and even deeper in their tint; the clustering hair was of a brighter gold; and the fair skin pearlier in its whiteness, and richer in its rosiness; while the gay exuberance of life, glowing and sparkling from every curve and dimple of the child's face and figure, was, even in the happy mother's face, somewhat dimmed by the shadows that still must fall upon every life past its morning, be it never so happy, or never so prosperous.

"Morning, mamma and papa. It's my birthday; and I'm six years old, - six, six years old! One, two, three, four, five, six years old! Susan told them all to me, and Susan said she guessed papa didn't forgotten it. She didn't forgotten it; and see!"

The child held up a gay horn of sugar-plums fluttering with ribbons, and then, hugging it to her breast with one hand, plunged the other in, and offered a little fistful of the comfits, first to her father, and then to her mother. Both smilingly declined the treat, explaining that they had but just done breakfast: and the young lady, dropping some back into the horn, thrust the rest into her own mouth, saying, "So has I; but I like candy all the day."

"Come here, you little Sunshine," said Mr. Legrange, drawing her toward him. "So Susie thought I hadn't forgotten your birthday, eh? Well, do you know what they always do to people on their birthdays?"

"Give 'em presents," replied the child promptly, as she desperately swallowed the mouthful of candy.

"Ho, ho! that's it is it? No; but, besides that, they always pull their ears as many times as they are years old. Now, then, don't you wish I had forgotten it?"

Sunshine's eyes grew a little larger, and travelled swiftly toward her mother's face, coming back to her father's with a smile.

"I don't believe you'd hurt me much, papa," said she, nestling close to his side.

The father folded her tightly in his arms, lifting her to a seat upon his knee.

"I don't believe I would, little Sunshine. Well, then, sometimes, instead of pinches, they give little girls as many kisses as they are years old. How will that do?"

The rosy mouth, gathering for a kiss, answered without words; but Mr. Legrange, taking the dimpled face between his hands, said, -

"No, no! we must go on deliberately. One for the forehead, two for the eyes, - that makes three; one for each cheek makes five; and now the last and best for the lips makes six. Next year, there will be another for the chin, and, after that, one in each ear: won't that be nice?"

"And mamma? Hasn't Sunshine any kisses for her this morning?" asked Mrs. Legrange.

The child slid from her father's knee to the floor, and, with her arms round her mother's neck, whispered, -

"I'll give mamma all these kisses papa just gave me, and some more too."

And for a minute or two it would have been hard to say to which head the showery golden curls belonged, or which pair of lips was the kisser's, and which the kissed; while the Sun fairly danced with delight as he wrapped the two in a beautiful golden mantle woven of his choicest beams.

Mr. Legrange looked on, laughing, for a moment, and then said, -

"So Susan told you people get presents on their birthdays, did she, 'Toinette?"

"Yes, papa;" and the child, half turning from her mother, but still clinging round her neck, looked at her father roguishly.

"And I guess you knew it before, and didn't forgotten about it, did you, papa?" asked she.

"Well, yes, I believe I have heard something of the kind," said Mr. Legrange, gravely considering; "but, dear me! did you expect me to make you a present?"

'Toinette's face grew rather blank; and a sudden impulse turned down the corners of her mouth with a little tremble across the lips. But the instinct of native refinement and delicacy overcame the disappointment; and, coming to her father's side, the child put her hand in his with a brave little smile, saying, -

"It's no matter, papa dear. I've got ever so many pretty things up in the nursery; and Susan gave me the candy."

Mr. Legrange looked at his wife.

"Your own child, Fanny. O Sunshine, Sunshine! what are you coming to by and by? But bless me! what is this in the pocket of my dressing-gown? Let me take it out, lest it should hurt you when I set you in my lap again. Funny-looking little box, isn't it?"

As he spoke, Mr. Legrange laid upon the table a long, flat box of red morocco, with some gilt letters upon the top.

"Yes, papa. What's in the box?" asked 'Toinette, still with a little effort.

"What do you think, Sunshine?"

"I guess it's some cigars, papa."

"It would make a good cigar-case, to be sure; but you know I have one already, and mamma says I ought not to have any. Let us peep in, and see what else the box would be good for besides cigars."

He unfastened the little hooks holding down the cover as he spoke, and placed the casket in 'Toinette's hands. She raised the lid, and uttered a low cry; while her face flushed scarlet with surprise and pleasure.

Upon the white satin lining, lay two bracelets of coral cameos, linked with gold, and fastened by a broad golden clasp.

"Are they pretty?" asked Mr. Legrange, smiling at the eager little face upraised to his.

"Oh! they are lovely pretty. O papa! oh! is they?" -

"Yes they are yours, Sunshine. Mamma said you had been begging for some bracelets like Minnie Wall's; and so, as I had heard that people sometimes liked presents on their birthdays, and as I had not forgotten when Sunshine's came, I thought I would bring her a pair."

The excess of 'Toinette's rapture would not allow of speech; but Mrs. Legrange, peeping over her shoulder, exclaimed, -

"Why, Paul! those are not what I asked you to get. I told you common coral beads, strung on elastic, and fastened with a little snap."

"But these were so much prettier, my dear, and will be of some value when she grows up, as the others would not. At any rate, they are marked: so we must keep them now. See!"

Mr. Legrange touched a tiny spring; and the upper part of the clasp, opening upon a hinge, showed a plate beneath, engraved with the name, "Antoinette Legrange."

"Yes: they are certainly very handsome; and 'Toinette must be as careful of them as possible. They will be just right to loop up her sleeves while she is so little, and, when she is older, to wear as bracelets," said Mrs. Legrange admiringly.

"I may wear them this afternoon at my party, mayn't I, mamma?" asked 'Toinette, trying to clasp one upon her little arm.

"Oh, we are to have a party, are we!" exclaimed Mr. Legrange raising his eyebrows in dismay.

"Just half a dozen children to play with 'Toinette, and to go home after a nursery-tea," explained his wife.

"Oh, well! I shall be a little late to dinner, very likely: so it will all be over when I arrive. Shall I bring Tom Burroughs home with me to dine?"

"I want Cousin Tommy to come to my party, papa. Tell him to come, please, and Sunshine's love."

"Your party, chick? Why! he would be Gulliver among the Liliputians. He would tread on a dozen of the guests at the first step, and never know it."

"I don't think he would, papa; and he's my little wife,

and I want him," persisted 'Toinette.

"No, no, dear," interposed Mrs. Legrange. "Cousin Tom wouldn't want to come, and my little girl mustn't tease."

"No, mamma; but he's my little wife," murmured 'Toinette, going back to her bracelets with a shadow of disappointment in the curve of her pretty mouth.

"If mamma is willing, I will ask Cousin Tom, and he can do as he likes about accepting," said the fond father, watching his Sunshine's face.

Mamma smiled roguishly, murmuring, - "'So long as a woman's possessed of a tear, She'll always have her own way;'" and then, added aloud, -

"Just as you like, of course, papa; but here is Susan, ready to take 'Toinette for her walk."

The dining-room door opened softly, and a fresh, pretty-looking nursery-maid stepped in, saying

"Is Miss 'Toinette ready to come up stairs, ma'am?"

Yes, Susan. You may take the bracelets, pet; but, when you go out, leave them in the drawer of your bureau."

"Yes, mamma. Good-by, mamma and papa; and don't forget my little wife, papa."

"I won't forget, Sunshine," said Mr. Legrange, laughing, as he followed the child and nurse to the door, and watched them up stairs.

CHAPTER II.

THE LITTLE WIFE.

THREE o'clock came at last, although 'Toinette had become fully persuaded it never would; and the little guests arrived as punctually as juvenile guests are apt to arrive. Later on in life, people either expect less pleasure from meeting each other, or are more willing to defer securing it; or perhaps it is that they are willing to allow their friends the first chance of appropriating the happiness in store for all. If none of these, what is the reason, children, that, at grown parties, the struggle is to see who shall arrive last, while at ours it is to see who shall come first?

'Toinette was dressed, and in the drawing-room ready to receive her little friends, by half-past two; and very nice she looked in her light-blue merino frock, with its pretty embroideries, her long golden hair curled in the feathery ringlets Susan was so proud of making, her sleeves looped up with new bracelets, and a little embroidered handkerchief just peeping out of her pockets

Mrs. Legrange, who sat reading by the fire, watched with some amusement and more anxiety the movements of the little beauty, who walked slowly up and down the room, twisting her head to look now at one shoulder and now at the other, now at the flow of her skirts behind, and now at the dainty fit of her bronze cloth gaiter-boots. At last, stopping before the long mirror, Miss 'Toinette began practicing the courtesy she had learned at dancing-school, finishing by throwing a kiss from the tips of her fingers to the graceful little shadow in the mirror.

"She will be spoiled, entirely spoiled, before she is a year older," thought the mother anxiously. "She is so beautiful! and every one tells her of it. What shall I do?"

But sometimes, when our task seems too difficult for us, God takes it into his own hand, and does it in his own way, though that way to us be strange and painful.

While Mrs. Legrange still hesitated whether to speak, and what to say, the doorbell rang, and 'Toinette rushed away to meet her friends, and take them to the dressing room, where they were to leave their outside garments; and the mother laid aside her book, and prepared to help in entertaining the little people.

Another ring at the bell; another troop of little feet, and peal of merry voices; another and another; and, following the last, a firmer step upon the stair, and the appearance in the drawing-room of a tall, fine-looking young man, of twenty two or three years old, who came forward, offering his hand to Mrs. Legrange.

"Why, Tom," said she, "did you really come?"

"As you see, Cousin Fanny. Paul gave me the invitation, with my little wife's love; and how could I decline?"

"I am sure it is very good of you to come and help entertain; but I am afraid it will be a sad bore. Miss

Minnie Wall, the oldest of the young ladies, is but just fourteen; and Bessie Rider, the youngest, is not yet six."

"But I came to visit my little wife," persisted Mr. Burroughs, laughing gayly.

"Here she is, then, with all the rest behind her;" and, as the little hostess caught sight of her new guest, she flew toward him, crying, -

"Oh, my little wife has come! - my little, wife!"

Every one laughed, except the young man thus oddly addressed, who gravely extended his hand, saying, -

"Miss 'Toinette, allow me to wish you many happy returns of this fortunate day."

'Toinette looked at him a moment in surprise, then, glancing at the other guests, said innocently, -

"I guess you talk that way because the girls are here; but I like the way you are always, best."

This time Tom laughed as loud as the rest, and, catching the child in his arms, kissed her a dozen times, saying, -

"That is it, Sunshine. Let us be natural, and have a good time. Get the table-cloth, and make an elephant of me."

CHAPTER III.

CHERRYTOE.

"LET us have a dance!" exclaimed Minnie Wall, when all the games had been played, and the little people stood for a moment, wondering what they should do next.

"O Mrs. Legrange! will you play for us?"

"Certainly. What will you have, Minnie? But, in the first place, can you all dance?"

"Yes'm, every one of us. Even 'Toinette and Bessie have learned at their Kindergarten; and the rest of us all go to Mr. Papanti. O Mrs. Legrange! last Saturday, when you let Susan bring 'Toinette to dancing-school, I told Mr. Papanti what a pretty little dancer she was; and he made her stand up, and she learned the cachuca with half a dozen others of us; and he did laugh and bow so at her, you never saw; and he called her enfant Cherrytoe, or something like that" -

"Cerito," suggested Mrs. Legrange, smiling.

"Yes'm, I guess that was it; and she learned it beautifully. Have you seen her dance it?"

"Yes, the old gentleman called me Cherrytoe; and you must, mamma, and every one, because I dance so pretty, with my little toes. Will you call me Cherrytoe always, mamma?" asked 'Toinette, with such a complacent delight in her own accomplishments, that her mother's smile was sad as it was tender. But she felt that this was not the time or place to reprove the vanity so rankly springing in the child's heart; so she only said, -

"Mr. Papanti was in fun when he called you Cherrytoe, darling. She was a woman who danced better than I hope you ever will. Now, who is ready for Virginia reel?"

Tom Burroughs led Minnie Wall to the head of the set, other children rushed for places, Mrs. Legrange seated herself at the piano, and the merry dance went on; but, when it was over, Minnie Wall returned to Mrs. Legrange's side, followed by two or three more, begging her to play the cachuca, and see how nicely 'Toinette could dance it. Half unwillingly the mother complied, and found really astonished as she noticed the graceful evolutions and accurate time of the child, who went through the intricate motions of the dance without a single mistake, and, at the close, dropped her little courtesy, and kissed her little hand, with the grace and self-possession of a danseuse.

The children crowded around her with a clamor of delight and surprise; but the mother, anxiously watching her darling's flushed face and sparkling eyes, whispered to her cousin, as he playfully applauded, -

"Oh, don't, Tom! The child will be utterly ruined by so much flattery and admiration. I feel very badly about it, I assure you."

"But she is absolutely so bewitching! How can we help

admiring her?" replied he, laughing.

"No: but it is wrong; it won't do," persisted Mrs. Legrange. "Just see how excited and happy she looks because they are all admiring her! You must help me to check it, Tom. Come, you are so famous for stories, tell them one about a peacock, or something, - a story with a moral about being vain, you know, only not too pointed."

"A pill with a very thick sugar-coat," suggested Mr. Burroughs, and, as his cousin nodded, continued, in a louder voice, -

"A story, ladies and gentlemen! Who will listen to the humble attempts of an unfortunate improvisator?"

"Yes, yes, a story; let us have a story!" shouted with one accord both girls and boys; and with 'Toinette perched upon his knee, and the rest grouped about him, Cousin Tom began the story of THE CHILDREN OF MERRIGOLAND.

CHAPTER IV.

THE CHILDREN OF MERRIGOLAND.

ONCE upon a time, in the pleasant country of Merrigoland, all the fathers and mothers, the uncles and aunts, the grandpas and grandmas, in fact, all the grown-up people of every sort, were invited to the governor's house to spend a week; and all the cooks and chambermaids, and nurses and waiters, and coach-men and gardeners, in Merrigoland, were invited to go and wait upon them: so there was nobody left at home in any of the houses but the children; not even the babies; for their mothers had carried them in their arms to the governor's house.

"What fun!" shouted the children. "We can do every thing we have a mind to now."

"We'll eat all the cake and pies and preserves and candies in the country," said Patty Pettitoes.

"We'll swing on all the gates, and climb all the cherry-trees, and chase all the roosters, and play ball against the parlor-windows," said Tom Tearcoat.

"We'll lie down on the sofas, and read stories all day, and go to sleep before the fire at night," said Dowsabelle Dormouse.

"We'll dress up in all our mothers' clothes, and put on their rings and breastpins," said little Finnikin Fine, pushing a chair in front of the looking-glass, and climbing up to look at herself.

"We'll get our stockings dirty, and tear our frocks, and tumble our hair, and not wash our hands at dinner-time, nor put on our eating-aprons," said Georgie Tearcoat, Tom's younger sister.

"Yes, yes: we'll all do just as we like best for a whole week; for father and mother said we might!" shouted all the children in Merrigoland, and then laughed so loud, that the mice ran out of their holes to see what was the matter; and the cats never noticed them, they were so busy sticking the hair straight up on their backs, and making their tails look like chimney-brushes; while all the birds in the pleasant gardens of Merrigoland fluttered their wings, and sung, -

> "Only listen to the row!
> What in the world's the matter now?
> Tweet, tweet! Can't sing a note;
> My heart's just jumping out of my throat.
> Bobolink, bobolink,
> What do you think?
> Is the world very glad,
> Or has it gone mad?"

So the children all did what they liked best, and frolicked in the sunshine like a swarm of butterflies, or like several hundred little kittens, until it came night; and then they went into the houses, and put themselves to bed. But some of them, I am afraid, forgot to say their prayers when their mammas were not there to remind them of it.

The next morning they all jumped up, and dressed very

gayly (for children do not often lie in bed), and came down to breakfast: but, lo and behold! there was no breakfast ready, nor even any fire in the ranges and cooking-stoves, and in some houses not even any shavings and kindling wood to make a fire; and the cows, who were mostly of a Scotch breed, came to the bars, calling, -

"Moo, moo, moo!
Who'll milk us noo?"

and the hens all stuck their heads through the bars of the poultry-yard fence, and cried, -

"Kah-dah-cut, kah-dah-cut!
Are you having your hair cut?
Can you give us some corn
This beautiful morn?"

and the pigeons came flying down to the back door, murmuring, -

"Coo, coo, coo!
Must we breakfast on dew?"

and all the little children began to cry as loud as they could, and call, -

"Mamma, mamma, mamma!
I want you and papa!"

So, altogether, the older children were just about crazy, and felt as if they'd like to cry too. But that never would do, of course; for nobody cries when old enough to know better: so after running round to each others' houses, and talking a little, they agreed they would all work together, and that every one should do what he could do best. So Tom Tearcoat, instead of climbing trees, and smashing the furniture with his hatchet, went and split kindlings in all the wood-houses; and his sister Georgie, who never wanted to be in the house, carried them into the kitchens; and Patty Pettitoes tried her hand at cooking, instead of eating; and Dowsabelle Dormouse made the beds, and beat up the sofa-pillows; and Mattie Motherly, whose chief delight was playing at housekeeping in her baby-house, set the tables, and put the parlors to rights. But there seemed to be nothing that Finnikin Fine could do; for she had never thought of any thing but dressing, in all the gay clothes she could get, and looking into the mirror until she had worn quite a place in the carpet before it. But, at last, someone said, -

"Oh! Finnikin may dress the little children: that will suit her best."

So Finnikin tried to do that. But she spent so much time tying up the little girls' sleeves with ribbons, and parting the little boys' hair behind, that, when breakfast-time came, they were not half ready, and began to cry, -

> "O Finnikin, O!
> Don't spend your time so,
> But put on our dresses,
> And smooth out our tresses;
> We don't care for curls,
> Either boys or girls,
> If we are but neat,
> And may sit down to eat."

So at last Finnikin followed their advice, and, when

she had dressed all the children, was so tired and hungry, that she was glad to sit down and eat her breakfast without even looking in the mirror once while she was at table.

But nobody knew how to milk the cows; and, although Tom and Georgie Tearcoat tried with all their might, they could not manage to get a drop of milk from one of them, and no one else even tried. But, just as the children were all wondering what they should do, little Peter Phinn, who had been listening and looking, with his hands in the pockets of his ragged trousers, and a broad grin on his freckled face, said slowly, -

"I know how to milk."

"You do! Why didn't you say so, Peter Phinn?" cried all the children angrily.

"Oh! I didn't know as you'd want me and Merry amongst you," said Peter.

"Why not? Of course we do," said Patty Pettitoes, who was a very good-natured little girl.

"Because Finnikin Fine told Merry once she wasn't fit to play with her, when her clothes was so poor," said Peter.

"Did Finnikin say that?" asked Patty.

"Yes, she did, sure; and she called her a little Paddy, and said, if she wore such an old, mean gown and bonnet, she'd ought to keep out of the way of folks that dressed nicer, as she did."

Then all the children turned and looked at Finnikin Fine, and said, -

"Oh, shame, Finnikin! for shame to talk so to good little Merry Phinn!"

Then Finnikin hung down her head, and blushed very much, and began to cry; but Merry Phinn went close to her, and whispered, -

"Never mind them, honey. I'll forget it sooner than you will, and I'll come and help you dress the children tomorrow morning."

"And I'll give you my new pink muslin, and my white beads, and my bronze slippers with pink rosettes, and, and," began Finnikin; but Merry put her little brown hand over her mouth, and said, laughing, -

"And, if I get all these fine things, I'd be as bad as yourself, Finny darling. No: I'll wear my calico gown, and my sun-bonnet, and my strong shoes; and you'll see I can get to my work or my play without half the bother you'd make in your finery."

So Finnikin, still blushing, and crying a little, put her arm round Merry's neck, and kissed her; and then she ran and took off the rinses and pins and ribbons and flowers she had found time since breakfast to put on, and changed her blue silk dress for a neat gingham and a white apron, and put her hair into a net, instead of the wreath and curls it had cost her so much trouble to arrange. And, when she came down stairs again, all the children cried, -

"Only see how pretty Finnikin Fine is in her plain

dress! She looks like a little girl now, instead of a wax doll in a toy-shop window."

"Yes," said Tom Tearcoat; "and a fellow could play with her now in some comfort. It used to be, -

"'Dear me, you rude boy! you've gone and torn my flounce!' or, 'You've spoilt my bow!' or, 'Dear me, you troublesome creature! you've made me so nervous!'"

Every one laughed to hear Tom mimic Finnikin, he did it so well; but, when they saw that the little girl herself was troubled by it, they left off directly, and began to talk of other things; and Tom came and tucked a big green apple into her pocket, and a lump of maple-sugar into her hand.

Then Peter and Merry, who had always been used to waiting upon themselves, and doing all the work they were able to do, showed the other children many things which they needed to know, and helped them in so many ways, that the troubles of the morning were soon forgotten; and when, after clearing away the dinner, the little people all came out to play upon the green, they agreed to crown Peter and Merry King, and Queen of Merrigoland from three o'clock in the afternoon until sunset, because they were the only boy and girl in all the land who knew how to do the work that must every day be done to make us all comfortable. But Peter and Merry, who were very sensible as well as very good-natured children, said, -

"No, no, no! There shall be no kings or queens in Merrigoland. We will teach you all that we know, and you shall teach us all that you know, and so we will help each other; and no one shall think himself better than any one else, or forget that none of us can do well without the help of all the rest."

So the children shouted, -

"Hurrah for Peter and Merry, and down with fine ways and fine clothes!"

And then they gave three cheers so loud, that the fathers and mothers, and grandpas and grandmas, and uncles and aunts, and brothers and sisters, heard them, as they sat at dinner in the governor's house; and all came trooping home in a great hurry to see what was the matter.

But when they heard the story, and found how well the children were going on, they said, -

"We could teach them nothing better than what they are learning for themselves. We may let them alone."

So they all went back to the governor's house, and spent the rest of the week, and" -

"Tea is ready, Mrs. Legrange," said James at the parlor-door.

CHAPTER V.

THE RUNAWAY.

TEA was over, and the little guests made ready to go home. Cousin Tom, declining Mrs. Legrange's invitation to dinner on plea of another engagement, delighted Miss Minnie Wall's heart by offering to wait upon her home, but rather injured the effect of his politeness by taking Willy and Jerry Noble upon the other side, and talking pegtop with them as glibly as he talked opera with the young lady.

As for the rest, some went alone, some with their nurses, some with each other. Little Bessie Rider was the last; and, when the nurse did not come for her as had been promised, Mrs. Legrange bid Susan lead her home, leaving 'Toinette in the drawing-room till her return.

"And I must go and lie down a little before I dress for dinner," continued she to 'Toinette. "So, Sunshine, I shall leave you here alone, if you will promise not to touch anything you should not, or to go too near the fire."

The little girl promised; and, with a lingering kiss, her mother left her.

Alone in the twilight, 'Toinette sat for a while upon the rug, watching the bright coals as they tinkled through the grate, or rushed in roaring flame up the chimney.

"I wish I was a fire-fairy, and lived in that big red hole right in the middle of the fire," thought 'Toinette. "Then I would wear such a beautiful dress just like gold, and a wreath on my head all blazing with fire; and I would dance a-tiptoe away up the chimney and into the sky: and perhaps I should come to heaven; no, to the sun. I wonder if the sun is heaven for the fire-fairies, and I wonder if they dance in the sunset."

So 'Toinette jumped up, and, running to one of the long windows, put her little eager face close to the glass, and looked far away across the square, and down the long street beyond, to the beautiful western sky, all rosy and golden and purple with the sunset-clouds; while just above them a great white star stood trembling in the deep blue, as if frightened at finding itself out all alone in the night.

"No," thought 'Toinette; "I don't want to be a fire-fairy, and dance in the sunset: I want to be a - a angel, I guess, and live in that beautiful star. Then I'd have a dress all white and shining like mamma's that she wore to the ball. But mamma said the little girl in the story was naughty to like her pretty dress, and she weared a gingham one when she was good. Guess I won't be any fairy. I'll be Finnikin Fine, and wear a gingham gown and apron. I'll tell papa to carry away the bracelets too. I'm going to be good like Merry that weared a sun-bonnet."

Eager to commence the proposed reform, 'Toinette tugged at the bracelet upon her left shoulder until she broke the clasp and tore the pretty lace of her under-sleeve.

"Dear, dear, what a careless child!" exclaimed the little

girl, remembering the phrase so often repeated to her. "But it ain't any matter, I guess," added she, brightening up; "for I shan't have any under-sleeve to my gingham dress. Susan's aunt doesn't."

'Toinette paused, with her hand upon the other bracelet trying to remember whether Susan, or the little girl who came to see her, was the aunt. The question was not settled, when the sound of music in the street below attracted 'Toinette's attention. Clinging to the window-ledge so as to see over the iron railing of the balcony, she peeped down, and saw a small dark man walking slowly by the house, turning the crank of a hand-organ which he carried at his side. Upon the organ was perched a monkey, dressed in a red coat with gilt buttons, a little cocked hat, and blue trousers. He was busily eating a seed-cake; pausing now and then to look about him in a sort of anxious way, chattering all the while as if he thought some one wanted to take it away from him.

'Toinette had never before seen a monkey; and she stared at this one in great surprise and delight, taking him for a little man, and his inarticulate chattering for words in some foreign language such as she had sometimes heard spoken.

The music also suited the little girl's ear better than the best strains of the Italian opera would have done; and altogether she was resolved to see and hear more both of the monkey and the music.

"Mamma's asleep, and Susan gone out; so I can't ask leave, but I'll only stay a little tiny minute, and tell the little man what is his name, and what he is saying," reasoned the pretty runaway, primly wrapping herself in her mother's breakfast-shawl left lying upon the sofa, and tying her handkerchief over her head.

"Now I's decent, and the cold won't catch me," murmured she, regarding herself in the mirror with much satisfaction, and then running softly down stairs. Susan, thinking she should be back directly, had left the catch-latch of the front-door fastened up: so 'Toinette had only to turn the great silver handle of the other latch; and this, by putting both hands to it and using all her strength, she finally succeeded in doing, although she could not close the door behind her. Leaving it ajar, 'Toinette ran down the steps, and looked eagerly along the square until she discovered the hand-organ man with his monkey just turning the corner, and flew after him as fast as her little feet would carry her. But, with all her haste, the man had already turned another corner before she overtook him, and was walking, more quickly than he had yet done, down a narrow street. He was not playing now; but the monkey, who had finished his cake, was climbing over his master's shoulders, running down his arms and back, chattering, grinning, making faces, and evidently having a little game of romps on his own account.

'Toinette, very much amused, tripped along behind, talking as fast as the monkey, and asking all manner of questions, to none of which either monkey or man made any reply; while all the time the beautiful rosy light was fading out of the west, and the streets were growing dark and crowded; and as the organ-grinder, followed by 'Toinette, turned from one into another, each was dirtier and narrower and more disagreeable than the last.

All at once, the man, after hesitating for a moment,

dashed across the street, and into a narrow alley opposite. Two or three dirt-carts were passing at the same time; and 'Toinette, afraid to follow, stood upon the edge of the sidewalk, looking wistfully after him, and beginning to wonder if she ought not to be going home.

While she wondered, a number of rude boys came rushing by; and, either by accident or malice, the largest one, in passing the little girl, pushed her so roughly, that she stumbled off the sidewalk altogether, and fell into the gutter.

A little hurt, a good deal frightened, and still more indignant, 'Toinette picked herself up, and looked ruefully at the mud upon her pretty dress, but would not allow herself to cry, as she longed to do.

"If I'd got my gingham dress on, it wouldn't do so much harm," thought she, her mind returning to the story she had that afternoon heard; and then all at once an anxious longing for home and mother seized the little heart, and sent the tiny feet flying up the narrow street as fast as they could move. But, at the corner, 'Toinette, who never had seen the street before, took the wrong turn; and, although she ran as fast as she could, every step now led her farther from home, and deeper into the squalid by-streets and alleys, among which she was lost.

CHAPTER VI.

MOTHER WINCH.

IN a narrow court, hardly lighted by the one gas-light flaring at its entrance, 'Toinette stopped, and, looking dismally about her, began at last to cry. At the sound, a crooked old woman, with a great bag on her back, who had been resting upon the step of a door close by, although the little girl had not noticed her, rose, and came toward her.

"What's the matter, young one?" asked the old woman harshly.

"I don't know the way home, and I'm lost!" said 'Toinette, wiping her eyes, and looking doubtfully at the old woman, who was very dark and hairy as to the face, very blinking and wicked as to the eyes, and very crooked and warped as to figure, while her dress seemed to be a mass of rags held together by dirt.

"Lost, be you?" asked this unpleasant old woman, seizing Mrs. Legrange's beautiful breakfast-shawl, and twitching it off the child's shoulders. "And where'd you git this 'ere pretty shawl?"

"It's my mamma's, and you'd better not touch it; you might soil it, you know," said 'Toinette anxiously.

"Heh! Why, I guess you're a little lady, ain't you? B'long to the big-bugs, don't you?"

"I don't know. I want to go home," stammered 'Toinette, perplexed and frightened.

"Well, you come right in here along o' me, and wait till I get my pack off; then I'll show you the way home," said the woman, as, seizing the little girl's hand, she led her to the bottom of the court, and down some steps into a foul-smelling cellar-room, perfectly dark, and very cold.

"You stop right there till I get a light," said the woman, letting go the child's hand when they reached the middle of the room. "Don't ye budge now."

Too much frightened to speak, or even cry, 'Toinette did as she was bid, and stood perfectly still until the old woman had found a match, and, drawing it across the rusty stove, lighted a tallow candle, and stuck it into the mouth of a junk-bottle. This she set upon the table; and, sinking into a chair beside it, stretched out a skinny hand, and, seizing 'Toinette by the arm, dragged her close to her.

"Yes, you kin let me have that pooty shawl, little gal, cause - Eh, what fine clo'es we've got on!" exclaimed the hag, as, pulling off the shawl 'Toinette had again wrapped about her, she examined her dress attentively for a moment, and then, fixing her eyes sternly upon the child, continued angrily, -

"Now look at here, young un. Them ain't your clo'es; you know they ain't. You stole 'em."

"Stealed my clothes!" exclaimed 'Toinette in great indignation. "Why, no, I didn't. Mamma gave them to me, and Susan sewed them."

"No sech a thing, you young liar!" returned the old woman, shaking her roughly by one arm. "You stole 'em; and I'm a-going to take 'em off, and give you back your own, or some jist like 'em. Then I'll carry these fine fixings to the one they b'long to. Come, now, no blubbering. Strip off, I tell yer."

As she spoke, she twirled the little girl round, and began to pull open the buttons of her dress. In doing this, her attention was attracted by the bracelet looping up the right sleeve; 'Toinette having, it will be remembered, pulled off the other, and left it at home.

"Hi, hi! What sort o' gimcrack you got here?" exclaimed she, pulling at it, until, as 'Toinette had done with the other, she broke the links between two of the cameos, without unclasping the bracelet.

"Hi! that's pooty! Now, what a young wretch you be for to go and say that ere's yourn!" added she severely, as she held the trinket out of reach of the little girl, who eagerly cried, -

"It is, it is mine! Papa gave me both of them, 'cause it's my birthday. They're my bracelets; only mamma said I was too little to wear them on my arms like she does, and she tied up my sleeves with them."

"Where's t'other one, then?"

"It's at home. I pulled it off 'cause I was going to be like Merry, that weared a sun-bonnet, and didn't have any bracelets."

"Sun-bonnet! What d'ye want of a sun-bonnet, weather like this? I'll give you my old hood; that's more like it,

I reckon," replied the hag, amused, in spite of herself, by the prattle of the child. 'Toinette hesitated.

"No," said she at last: "I guess you'd better give me my own very clo'ses, and carry me home. Then mamma will give me a gingham dress and a sun-bonnet; and maybe she'll give you my pretty things, if you want them."

"Thanky for nothing, miss. I reckon it'll be a saving of trouble to take em now. I don't b'lieve a word about your ma'am giving 'em to you; and, more'n all, I don't b'lieve you've got no ma'am."

So saying, she rudely stripped off, first the dress, then the underclothes, and finally even the, stockings and pretty gaiter-boots; so that the poor child, frightened, ashamed, and angry, stood at last with no covering but the long ringlets of her golden hair, which, as she, sobbing, hid her face in her hands, fell about her like a veil.

Leaving her thus, the old woman rummaged for a few moments in a heap of clothes thrown into the corner of the room, - the result, apparently, of many a day's begging or theft. From them she presently produced a child's nightgown, petticoat, and woolen skirt, a pair of coarse shoes much worn, and an old plaid shawl: with these she approached 'Toinette.

"See! I've got your own clo'es here all ready for you. Ain't I good?"

"They ain't my clothes: I won't have 'em on. Go away, you naughty lady, you ain't good a bit!" screamed Toinette, passionately striking at the clothes and the hand that held them.

"Come, come, miss, none o' them airs! Take that, now, and mend your manners!" exclaimed the old woman with a blow upon the bare white shoulder, which left the print of all her horny fingers. It was the first time in all her life that 'Toinette had been struck; and the blood rushed to her face, and then away, leaving her as white as marble. She cried no more, but, fixing her eyes upon the face of the old woman, said solemnly, -

"Now the Lord doesn't love you. Did you know it was the bad spirits that made you strike me? Mamma said so when I struck Susan."

"Shut up! I don't want none of your preaching, miss," replied the woman angrily. "Here, put on these duds about the quickest, or I'll give you worse than that. Lor, what a mess of hair! What's the good on't? Maybe, though, they'd give some'at for it to the store."

She took a large pair of shears from the table-drawer as she spoke, and, grasping the shining, curls in her left hand, rapidly snipped them from the head, leaving it rough, tangled, and hardly to be recognized.

'Toinette no longer resisted, or even cried. The blow of that rough hand seemed to have stunned or stupefied her, and she stood perfectly quiet, her face pale, her eyes fixed, and her trembling lips a little apart; while the old woman, after laying the handful of curls carefully aside, dragged on the clothes she had selected, in place of those she was stealing, and finished by trying the plaid shawl around the child's shoulders, fastening it in a great knot behind, and placing a dirty old hood upon the shorn head.

"There, now, you'll do, I guess; and we'll go take you home: only mind you don't speak a word to man, woman, nor child, as we go; for, if you do, I'll fetch you right back here, and shut you up with Old Bogy in that closet."

So saying, she bundled up 'Toinette's own clothes, slipped the bracelet into her pocket, then, with the parcel in one hand, grasped the child's arm with the other, and led her out into the street.

"Will you really take me home?" asked 'Toinette piteously, as they climbed the broken steps leading from the cellar to the pavement.

"There, now! What did I tell yer?" exclaimed the woman angrily, and turning as if to go back. "Now come along, and I will give you to Old Bogy."

"No, no! oh, please, don't! I will be good. I won't say a word any more. I forgotten that time, I did;" and the timid child, pale and trembling, clung to the wretch beside her as if she had been her dearest friend.

"Well, then, don't go into fits, and I'll let you off this time; but see that you don't open your head agin, or it'll be all up with yer."

"Yes'm," said the poor child submissively; and, taking her once more by the hand, the old woman led her rapidly along the filthy street, now entirely dark except for the gaslights, and more strange to 'Toinette's eyes than Fairy-land would have been. As they turned the corner, a tall, broad-shouldered man, dressed in a blue coat with brass buttons, and a glazed cap, who stood leaning against the wall, looked sharply at them, and called out,

"Hullo, Mother Winch! What's up to-night?"

"Nothing, yer honor, - nothing at all. Me and little Biddy Mahoney's going to leave some duds at the pawnbroker's for her mother, who's most dead with the fever."

"Well, well, go along; only look out you carry no more than you honestly come by," said the policeman, walking leisurely up the street.

Mother Winch turned in the opposite direction, and, still tightly grasping 'Toinette's arm, led her through one street after another, until, tired and bewildered, the poor child clung with half-closed eyes to the filthy skirts of the old woman, and stumbled along, neither seeing nor knowing which way they went.

"Hold up, can't ye, gal!" exclaimed Mother Winch, as the child tripped, and nearly fell. "Or, if you're so tired as all that, set down on that door-stone, and wait for me a minute." Pushing her down upon the step as she spoke, Mother Winch hurried away so fast, that, before 'Toinette's tired little brain could fairly understand what was said, she found herself alone, with no creature in sight all up and down the narrow street, except a cross-looking dog walking slowly along the pavement toward her. For one moment, she sat wondering what she had better do; and then, as the cross-looking dog fixed his eyes upon her with a sullen growl, she started to her feet, and ran as fast as she could in the direction taken by Mother Winch. Just at the corner of the alley, something glittering upon the sidewalk attracted her attention; and, stooping to pick it up, she uttered a little cry of surprise and pleasure. It was her own coral bracelet, which had traveled round in Mother Winch's pocket until it came to a hole in the bottom, and quietly slipping out, and down her skirts to the pavement, lay waiting for its little mistress to pick it up.

'Toinette kissed it again and again, not because it was a bracelet but because her father had given it to her; and it seemed somehow to take her back a little way toward him and home. It must have been this she meant, in saying as she did, -

"I guess you have come after me, pretty bracelet, hasn't you? And we'll go home together."

And so, hugging the toy as close to her heart as she would have liked herself to be hugged to her mother's heart, 'Toinette wandered on and on through the dark and lonely streets, her little face growing paler and paler, her little feet more and more weary, her heart swelling fuller and fuller with fright and desolation; until at last, stopping suddenly, she looked up at the sky, all alive now with the crowding stars, and with a great sob whispered, -

"Pretty stars, please tell God I'm lost. I think he doesn't know about it, or he'd send me home."

And then, as the wild sob brought another and another, 'Toinette sank down in the doorway of a deserted house, and, covering her face with her hands, cried as she had never cried in all her little life.

CHAPTER VII.

TEDDY'S LITTLE SISTER.

"THERE, honey!" said Mrs. Ginniss, giving the last rub to the shirt-bosom she was polishing, and setting her flat-iron back on the stove with a smack, - "there, honey; and I couldn't have done better by that buzzum if ye'd been the Prisidint."

Mrs. Ginniss was alone, so that one might at first have been a little puzzled to know whom she addressed as "honey;" but as she continued to talk while unfolding another shirt, and laying it upon her ironing-board, it became evident that she was addressing the absent owner of the garments.

"And sure it's many a maner man they've made their prisidints out on, and sorra a better one they'd find betune here and Canady. It's yees that have the free hand and the kind way wid yees, for all your grand looks. The good Lord save and keep ye all the days of yer life!"

A wrinkle in the wristband here absorbed the attention of the laundress; and, while smoothing it out, she forgot to continue what she had been saying, but, as she once more ironed briskly upon the sleeve, began upon a new subject.

"And it's late ye're agin, Teddy Ginniss, bad 'cess to yees! And thin it's mesilf that should take shame for saying it; for niver a b'y of them all is so good to his ould mother, and niver a one of 'em all that his mother's got so good a right to be proud on, as Ted. But where is the cratur? His supper's cowld as charity wid stannin."

At this moment a heavy step was heard upon the stairs, as of some one climbing slowly up with a heavy burden in his arms. Mrs. Ginniss paused to listen, holding the iron suspended over the collar she had just smoothed ready for it.

"Murther an' all!" muttered she. "And what's the crather got wid him anyhow? Shure an it's him; for, if it wor Jovarny with his orgin, he'd ha' stopped below."

The heavy steps reached the top of the stairs as she spoke, and clumped along the narrow passage to the door of Mrs. Ginniss's garret. She was already holding it open.

"Teddy, b'y, an' is it yersilf?" asked she, peering out into the darkness.

"Yes, mother, its meself," panted a boy's voice, as a stout young fellow, about fifteen years old, staggered into the room, and sank upon a chair.

"Saints an' angels, child! and what have ye got there?" exclaimed his mother, bending over the something that filled Teddy's arms and lap.

"It's a little girl, mother; and I'm feared she's dead!" panted Teddy.

"A little girl, an' she's dead! Oh, wurra, wurra, Teddy

Ginniss, that iver I should be own mother to a murderer! An' is it yersilf that kilt the purty darlint?"

"Meself, mother!" exclaimed the boy indignantly. "Sure and it wasn't; and I wouldn't 'a thought you'd have needed to ask. I found her on a doorstep in Tanner's Court: and first I thought she was asleep, and so I shook her to tell her to go home before the Charley got her; and then, when she wouldn't wake up, I saw she was either fainted or dead; and I fetched her home to you, - and it's you that go for to call me a murtherer! Oh, oh!"

As he uttered these last sounds, the boy's wide mouth puckered up in a comical look of distress, and he rubbed the cuff of his jacket across his blinking eyes. Mrs. Ginniss gave him a slap, on the shoulder, intended to be playful, but actually heavy enough to have thrown a slighter person out of the chair.

"Whisht, honey, whisht!" said she. "And it's an ould fool I am wid me fancies an' me frights. But let us looks at the poor little crather ye've brought home to me. Sure and it was like yees, Teddy, b'y."

As she spoke, she took from Teddy's arms the little lifeless form, with its pale, still face, and laid it gently upon her own bed.

"Oh thin! an' it's a shame to see the party darlint lay like that and I'm 'feared, unless the breath's in her yet, she's dead intirely," muttered the good woman, rubbing the little hands in her own, and gently feeling for the beating of the heart.

"Maybe it's only the cold and the hunger that's ailing

her, and she'll come to with the fire and vittels. She can have my supper and my breakfast too, and a welcome with it," said Teddy eagerly.

"The cowld, maybe, it is; for her clothes is nixt to nothing, an' the flesh of her's like a stone wid the freezing: but she's got enough to ate, or she never'd be so round an' plump. It's like she's the child of some beggar-woman that's fed her on broken vittels, an', whin she got tired ov trampin' wid her, jist dropped her on the doorstep where yees got her. - Howly mother! what's this?"

Mrs. Ginniss, as she spoke, had taken the little lifeless form upon her lap close to the stove, and was undressing it, when, among the folds of the old shawl crossed over the bosom, she found a bracelet of coral cameos, set in gold, and fastened with a handsome clasp.

She held it up, stared at it a moment, and then looked anxiously at Teddy.

"An' where did this splindid armlit come from, Teddy Ginniss?" asked she sharply.

"Sorra a bit of me knows, thin; an' is it a thafe ye'll be callin' me as well as a murtherer!" exclaimed the boy, falling, in his agitation, into the Irish brogue he was generally so careful to avoid.

"Whisht, ye spalpeen! an' lave it on the mantletry till we see if the breath's in her yit. Sure an' sich a little crather niver could have stole it."

Teddy, with an air of dignified resentment, took the

bracelet from his mother's hand, and laid it upon the mantlepiece; while Mrs. Ginniss, with a troubled look upon her broad face, finished stripping the little form, and began rubbing it all over with her warm hands.

"Power some warm wather into the biggest wash-tub, Teddy, an' I'll thry puttin' her in it. It's what the Yankee doctor said to do wid yees, whin yees had fits; an' it niver did no harm, anyways."

"Is it a fit she's got?" asked Teddy, with a look of awe upon his face.

"The good Lord knows what's she's got, or who she is. Mabbe the good folk put her where yees got her. Niver a beggar-brat before had a skin so satin-smooth, an' hands an' feet like rose-leaves and milk. An' look how clane she is from head to heel! Niver a corpse ready for the wakin' was nater."

"The water's ready now," said Teddy, pushing the tub close to his mother's side, and then walking away to the window. For some moments, the gentle plashing of the water was the only sound he heard; but then his mother hastily exclaimed, -

"Glory be to God an' to his saints! The purty crather's alive, and lookin' at me wid the two blue eyes av her like a little angel! Han' me the big tow'l till I rub her dhry."

Teddy ran with the towel; and as his mother hastily wrapped her little charge in her apron, and reseated herself before the fire, he caught sight of two great bright eyes staring up at him, and joyfully cried, -

"She's alive, she's alive! and she'll be my little sister, and we'll keep her always, won't we, mother?"

"Wait, thin, till we see if it's here she is in the morning, said his mother mysteriously.

"And where else would she be, if not here?" asked Teddy in surprise.

"If it war the good folks, Meaning the fairies, whom the Irish people call by this name. that browt her, it's they that will fetch her away agin 'fore the daylight. Wait till mornin', Teddy darlint."

But, in spite of her suspicions, Mrs. Ginniss did all for the little stranger that she could have done for her own child, even to heating and giving to her the cupful of milk reserved for her own "tay" during the next day, and warming her in her own bosom all through the long, cold night.

CHAPTER VIII.

THE FAYVER.

"AND is she here, mother?" asked Teddy, rushing into his mother's room next morning as soon as there was light enough to see.

"Yis, b'y, she's here; but it's not long she'll be, savin' the mercy o' God. It's the heavy sickness that's on her the morn."

"And will she die, mother?"

"The good Lord knows, not the likes of me, Teddy darlint."

"And you'll keep her, and do for her, mother, won't you?" asked the boy anxiously.

"Sure and it wouldn't be Judy Ginniss that'd turn out a dying child, let alone sending her to the poor'us. Thim that sint her to us will sind us the manes to kape her," said the Irish woman confidently; and leaving her little moaning, feverish charge dozing uneasily, she rose, and went about the labors of the day.

"Here's the masther's shirts done, Teddy; and ye'd betther take thim to his lodgings before yees go to the office. More by token, it's him as u'd tell us what we'd ought to be doin' wid the darlint, if she lives, or if she dies. Tell the masther al l ye know uv her, Teddy; an' ax him to set us sthraight."

"No, no, mother!" exclaimed Teddy eagerly; "I'll be doing no such thing: for it's ourselves wants her, and any thing the master would say would take her away from us. Sure and how often I've said I'd give all ever I had for a little sister to be my own, and love me, and go walking with me, and be took care by me; and, now one is sent, if it's the good folks or if it's the good God sent her, I'm going to keep her all myself. Sure, mother, you'll never be crossing me in this, when it's yourself never crossed me yet; and more by token, it'll keep me out of the streets, and such."

"Thrue for ye, Teddy; though it's you was alluz the good b'y to shtop at home, an' niver ax fur coompany savin' yer poor owld mother," said the washerwoman, looking fondly at her son.

"And you'll keep the child, and say nothing to nobody but she's our own; won't you, mother?" persisted Teddy.

"Yis, b'y, if it's yer heart is set on it."

"It is that, mother; and you're the good mother, and it's I always knowed, I mean knew it. And will I bring home a doctor to the little sister?"

"No, Teddy; not yit. Faix, an' it's hard enough to live when we're well; but it's too poor intirely we are to be sick. Whin the time cooms to die, it's no doctherin' 'll kape us."

Teddy looked wistfully at the little burning face upon the coarse, clean pillow: but he knew that what his mother said was true; and, without reply, he took up the parcel of clothes, and left the room.

All through the long day, Mrs. Ginniss, toiling at her wash-tubs, found a moment here and another there to sit upon the edge of the bed, and smooth her little patient's hair, or moisten her glowing lips and burning forehead, trying at intervals to induce her to speak, if even but one word, in answer to her tender inquiries; but all in vain: for the child already lay in the stupor preceding the delirium of a violent fever, and an occasional moan or sigh was the only sound that escaped her lips.

Toward night, Teddy, returning home an hour earlier than usual, came bounding up the stairs, two at a time, but, pausing at the door, entered as softly as a cat.

"How is the little sister now, mother?" asked he anxiously.

"Purty nigh as bad as bad can be, Teddy," said his mother sorrowfully, standing aside as she spoke that the boy might see the burning face, dull, half-closed eyes, and blackening lips of the sick child, and touch the little hands feebly plucking at the blanket with fingers that seemed to scorch the boy's healthy skin as he closed them in his palm.

Teddy looked long and earnestly, - looked up at his mother's sad face, and down again at the "little sister" whom he had taken to his heart when he first took her to his arms; and then, shutting his lips close together, and swallowing hard to keep down the great sob that seemed like to strangle him, he turned, and rushed out of the room. Mrs. Ginniss looked after him, and wiped her eyes.

"It's the luvin' heart he has, the crather," murmured she. "An' if the baby wor his own sisther, it's no more he could care for her. Sure an' if the Lord spares her to us, it's Teddy's sisther she shall be, forever an' aye, while me two fists hoold out to work fer 'em."

An hour later, Teddy returned, conducting a stranger. Rushing into the room before him, the boy threw his arms around his mother's neck, and whispered hastily, in his broadest brogue, -

"It's a docther; an' he'll cure the sisther; an' it's not a cint he'll be afther axin' us: but don't let on that she's not our own."

Mrs. Ginniss rose, and courtesied to the young man, who now followed Teddy into the room, saying pleasantly, -

"Good evening, ma'am. I am Dr. Wentworth; and I came to see your little girl by request of Teddy here, who said you would like a doctor if you could have one without paying him."

Mrs. Ginniss courtesied again, but with rather a wrathful look at Teddy, as she said, -

"And it's sorry I am the b'y should be afther beggin' of yees, docther. I thought he'd more sinse than to be axin' yees to give away yer time, that's as good as money to yees."

"But my time is not as good as money by any means," said Dr. Wentworth, laughing as he took off his hat and coat; "for I have very little to do except to attend patients who cannot give more than their thanks in payment. That is the way we young doctors begin."

"An' is that so indade! Sure an' 'Meriky's the place fur poor folks quite an' intirely," said Mrs. Ginniss admiringly.

"For some sorts of poor people, and not for others. Unfortunately, bakers, butchers, and tailors do not practise gratuitously; so we poor doctors, lawyers, and parsons have to play give without take," said the young man, warming his hands a moment over the cooking-stove.

"An' sure it was out of a Protistint Bible that I heard wonst, 'Him as gives to the poor linds to the Lord:' so, in the ind, it's yees that'll come in wid your pockets full, if ye belave yer own Scripter," said Mrs. Ginniss shrewdly.

The young doctor gave her a sharp glance out of his merry brown eyes, but only answered, as he walked on to the bedside, -

"You have it there, my friend."

For several moments, there was silence in the little room while Dr. Wentworth felt his patient's pulse, looked at her tongue, examined her eyes, and passed his hand over the burning skin.

"H'm! Typhoid, without doubt," said he to himself, and then to Mrs. Ginniss, -

"Can you tell the probable cause of the child's illness,

ma'am? Has she been exposed to any sudden chill, or any long-continued cold or fatigue?"

Mrs. Ginniss was about to reply by telling all she knew of the little stranger; but catching Teddy's imploring look, and the gesture with which he seemed to beg her to keep the secret of his "little sister's" sudden adoption, she only answered, -

"Sure an' it's the cowld she took last night but one is workin' in her."

"She took cold night before last? How was it?" pursued the doctor.

"She was out late in the street, sure, an' the clothes she'd got wasn't warm enough," said the washwoman, her eyes still fixed on Teddy, who, from behind the doctor, was making every imploring gesture he could invent to prevent her from telling the whole truth. The doctor did not fail to notice the hesitation and embarrassment of the woman's manner, but remembering what Teddy had told him of his mother's poverty, and her own little betrayal of pride when he first entered, naturally concluded that she was annoyed at having to say that the child had been sent into the street without proper clothing, and forbore to press the question.

Ah Teddy and Teddy's mother! if you had loved the truth as well as you loved little lost 'Toinette, how much suffering, anxiety, and anguish you would have saved to her and her's!

But the doctor asked no more questions, except such as Mrs. Ginniss could answer without hesitation; and pretty soon went away, promising to come again next day, and taking Teddy with him to the infirmary where medicine is furnished without charge to those unable to pay for it.

Before the boy returned, 'Toinette had passed from the stupid to the delirious stage of her fever; and all that night, as he woke or dozed in his little closet close beside his mother's door, poor Teddy's heart ached to hear the wild tones of entreaty, of terror, or of anger, proving to his mind that the delicate child he already loved so well had suffered much and deeply, and that at no distant period.

Toward morning, he dressed, and crept into his mother's room. The washerwoman sat in the clothes she had worn at bed-time, patiently fanning her little charge, and, half asleep herself, murmuring constantly,

"Ah thin, honey, whisht, whisht! It's nothin' shall harm ye now, darlint! Asy, now, asy, mavourneen! Whisht, honey, whisht!"

"Lie down and sleep, mother, and let me sit by her," whispered Teddy in his mother's ear; and, with a nod, the weary woman crept across the foot of the bed, and was asleep in a moment.

CHAPTER IX.

THE NIGHT-WATCH.

TEDDY, waving the old palm-leaf fan up and down with as much care as if it had carried the breath of life to his poor little charge, sat for some time very quiet, listening to her wild prattle without trying to interrupt it; until, after lying still for a few moments, she suddenly fixed her eyes upon him, and said, -

"Oh! you're Peter Phinn, sister to Merry that weared a sun-bonnet, ain't you?"

The question seemed so conscious and rational, that Teddy answered eagerly, -

"No, honey; but I'm Teddy Ginniss; and I'm going to be your brother forever and always. What's your name, sissy?"

"I'm Finny; no, I'm Cherrytoe, - I'm Cherrytoe, that dances. Want to see me dance, Peter?"

As she spoke, she started up, and would have jumped out of bed; but Teddy laid his hand upon her arm, and said soothingly, -

"No, no, sissy; not now. Another day you shall dance for Teddy, when you're all well. And you mustn't call me Peter, 'cause I'm Teddy."

"Teddy, Teddy," repeated 'Toinette vaguely, and then, with a sudden shrill laugh, shouted, - "'Taffy was a Welshman, Taffy was a thief; Taffy came to my house and stole a piece of beef.' Guess you're Taffy, ain't you?"

"No: I'm Teddy. I'm your brother Teddy," repeated the boy patiently; and then, to change the subject, added coaxingly, "And what's the pretty name you called yourself, darlint?"

"I'm Cherrytoe, - Cherrytoe that dances so pretty. Don't you hear, you great naughty lady? - Cherrytoe, Cherrytoe, Cherrytoe!"

The wild scream in which the name was repeated woke even tired Mrs. Ginniss, who started upright, crying, -

"What's it, what's it, Teddy? Ochone! what ails the crather?"

"It's only her name she's telling, mother; and sure it's a pretty one. It's Cherrytoe."

"And what sort of a quare name is that for a christened child? Sure we'll call it Cherry; for wunst I heerd of a lady as was called that way," said Mrs. Ginniss.

"Yes, we'll call her Cherry, little sister Cherry," said Teddy, delighted with the promise implied in his mother's words of keeping the child for her own. "And, mother," added he, "mind you don't be telling the doctor nor any one that she ain't your own, or maybe they'll take her away to the 'sylum or somewheres, whether we'd like it or not: and, if they do, I'll run off to sea; I will, by ginger!"

"Whisht, thin, with your naughty words, Teddy Ginniss! Didn't I bate ye enough whin ye wor little to shtop ye from swearin'?"

"Ginger ain't swearing," replied Teddy positively. "I asked the master if it wor, and he said it worn't."

"Faith, thin, and he says it hisself, I'm thinkin'," half asked the mother, with a shrewd twinkle of her gray eyes. Teddy faltered and blushed, but answered manfully, -

"No, he don't; and he said it was low and vulgar to talk that way; and I don't, only by times."

"Well, thin, Teddy, see that yer don't, only thim times whin yer hears the masther do it forninst ye: thin it'll be time enough for ye. And don't ye be forgettin', b'y, that ye're bound to be a gintleman afore ye die. It was what yer poor daddy said when yer wor born, a twelvemonth arter we landed here. 'There, Judy,' says he, 'there's a native-born 'Merican for yees, wid as good a right to be Prisidint as the best ov 'em. Now, don't yer let him grow up a Paddy, wid no more brains nor a cow or a horse. Make a gintleman, an' a 'Merican gintleman, of the spalpeen; an' shtrike hands on it now.'

"'Troth, thin, Michael alanna, an' it's a bargain,' says I, an', wake as I wor, give him me fist out ov the bed; an' he shuk it hearty. An', though Michael died afore the year wor out, the promise I'd made him stood; an' it's more ways than iver ye'll know, Teddy Ginniss, I've turned an' twisted to kape ye dacent, an' kape ye out ov the streets, niver forgittin' for one minute that Michael had towld me there was the makin's of a gintleman in yees, an' that he'd left it to me to work it out."

To this story, familiar as it was, Teddy listened with as much attention as if he had never heard it before, and, when it was ended, said, -

"And tell about your putting me to the squire, mother."

"Yis, b'y; an' that wor the biggest bit of loock that iver I wor in yet. Two twelvemonth ago come Christmas it wor, an' iver an' always I had been thinkin' what 'ud I do wid ye nixt, when Ann Dolan towld me how her sisther's son had got a chance wid a lawyer to clane out his bit ov an office, and run wid arrants an' sich, an' wor to have fifty dollars a year, wid the chance ov larnin' what he could out ov all thim big books as does be in sich places. Thin it somehow kim inter my head so sudden like, that it's sartain sure I am it was Michael come out ov glory to whishper it in my ear: 'There's Misther Booros'll mebbe do as much for your Teddy.' I niver spoke the first word to Ann Dolan, but lapped my shawl about me, an' wint out ov her house with no more than, 'God save ye, Ann!' an' twenty minutes later I wor in Misther Booros's office.

"'Good-evenin', Mrs. Ginniss,' says he, as ginteel as yer plaze. 'An' how is yer health?'

"'Purty good, thank ye kindly, sir,' says I; 'an' its hopin' you have yours the same, I am.'

"'Thank you, I am very well; and what can I do for you this evening? Pray, be sated,' says he, laning back in his chair wid sech a rale good-natured smile on the handsome face of him, that I says to myself, 'It's the lucky woman you are, Judy Ginniss, to put yer b'y wid sech a dacent gintleman: an' I smiled to him agin, an' begun to the beginnin', and towld him the whole story, - what Michael said to me, an' what I said to Michael; an' how Mike died wid the faver; an' how I'd worked an 'saved, an' wouldn't marry Tom Murphy when he axed me, an' all so as I could kape my b'y dacent, an' sind him to the school, an' give him his books an' his joggerphy-picters" -

"Them's maps, mother," interposed Teddy.

"Niver yer mind, b'y, what they be. Yer had 'em along wid the best of yer schoolmates; an' so I towld the squire. 'An' now,' says I, 'he's owld enough to be settlin' to a thrade; an' I likes the lawyer thrade the best, an' so I've coom to git yer honor to take him 'printice.'

"At that he stared like as he'd been moonsthruck; an' thin he laughed a little to hisself; and thin he axed mighty quite like, 'How do you mane, Mrs. Ginniss?' So I towld him about Ann Dolan's sisther's son, an' what wor the chance he'd got; an' thin I made bowld to ax him would he take my b'y the same way, on'y I'd like he'd larn more, an' I wouldn't mind the fifty dollars a year, but 'ud kape him mesilf, as I had kep' him since his daddy died, if the wuth uv it might be give him in larnin'."

"And what did the master say to that, mother?" asked Teddy, with a bright look that showed he foresaw and was pleased with the answer.

"Sure and he said what a gintleman the likes uv him should say, and said with his own hearty smile that's as good as the goold dollar uv another man, -

"'My good 'oman,' says he, 'sind along your b'y as soon as you plaze; an' if he's as - as' - what's that agin, Teddy, darlint?"

"Amberitious," pronounced Teddy with a grand sort of air; "and it means, he told me, wanting to be something more than you wor by nater."

"Faith, and that's it, Teddy: that's the very moral uv what I wants to see in yees. Well, the masther said if the b'y was as amberitious an' as 'anest as his mother afore him (that's me, yer see, Teddy)," -

"Yes, yes, mother, I know. Well?"

"That he'd make a man uv him that should be a pride an' a support to the owld age uv me, an' a blissin' to the day I med up my mind to eddicate him. That wor two year ago, Teddy Ginniss; an', so far, hasn' the gintleman done by yees as niver yer own daddy could? Hasn' he put yees to the readin' an' the writin' an' the joggerphy - picters, an' the nate figgers that yees puts on me washin' - bills, till it's proud I am to hand 'em to the gintlefolks, an' say, 'If ye plaze, the figgers is pooty plain. It's me b'y made 'em'? Now till me, Teddy, hasn' the shquire done all this by yees, an' give yees the fifty dollars by the year, all the same as if he give ye nothin' else?"

"He has so, mother."

"An' whin I wanted to wash for him widout a cint uv charge, an' towld him it was jist foon to rinshe out his bit things, bekase he is that good - natered an' quite that there's niver the fust roobin' to do to 'em, he says, -

"'An' if I let yees do 'em widout charge, I'd as lieve wear the shirt of Misther Nessus;' an' more by token, Teddy Ginniss, I told ye iver and oft to look in the big books an' see who was Misther Nessus, an' what about his shirt."

"Faith and ye did, mother; but I never could find him yet. Some day I'll ask the master," said Teddy with a puzzled look.

"An' so he pays me what I ax, an' it isn' for the likes uv him to be knowin' what the others ud charge; an', whin he gives me forty cints the dozen, he thinks, the poor innercint! that it's mooch as I would ax uv any one. Now, Teddy b'y, isn' all I've towld ye God's truth? and haven't ye heerd it as many times as yees are days owld out uv yer own moother's lips?"

"Faith and I have, mother."

"An' wud yer moother till yees a lie, or bid yees do what wasn't plazin' to God, Teddy?"

"Sure she wouldn't; and I'll lick the first fellow that'll say she would, if he was as big as Goliah in the Bible," said Teddy, doubling up his fist, and nodding fiercely.

"Thin, Teddy Ginniss, we cooms to this; an' it's not the first time, nor yet the last, we'll coom to it. If iver ye can do yer masther a service, be it big or be it little; if iver the stringth, or the coorage, or the life itself, of yees, or thim as is dear to yees, ud sarve him or plaze him, - I bid yees now to give it him free an' willin' as ye'd give it to God. An' so ye mind me, it's my blissin' an' the blissin' uv yer dead father that's iver wid ye; an' so ye fail me, it's the black curse uv disobedience, an' yer moother's brukken heart, that shall cling to yees for iver and iver, while life shall last. Do ye mind that, b'y?"

"I mind it, and I'll heed it, mother, as I've promised you before," said Teddy solemnly; and mother and son exchanged as tender and as true a kiss as young Bayard and his lady-mother could have done when she gave him to be a knight and chevalier.

All through this long conversation, which had been carried on in a low tone of voice, and frequently interrupted when it seemed to disturb her, 'Toinette had slept feverish and restlessly; but as the washwoman crept away to begin her daily labors, and Teddy lingered for a moment more to look at the poor little sister whose beauty was to him an ever-new delight, her great blue eyes suddenly opened, and fixed upon him, while with an airy little laugh she said, -

"We're King and Queen of Merrigoland, Peter; isn't we? Does you love me, Peter?"

"I couldn't tell how well I love you, Cherry dear; but it's Teddy I am, and not Peter," said the boy, bashfully kissing the little hot hand upon the outside of the bed.

To his dismay, the delirious child snatched it from him with a wild cry, and burst into a storm of tears and sobs, crying, -

"Go away, wicked lady! go away, I say! God won't love you when you strike me, you know. He won't: my mamma said so. Oh, oh, oh!"

Her cries brought Mrs. Ginniss to her side in a moment

, who, tenderly soothing her, turned upon Teddy.

"Bad 'cess to yees, ye spalpeen! An' what ud ye be afther vexin' her for, an' her in a faver? What did yees say to her?"

"I said my name was Teddy, and not Peter; and then she said I was a lady, and struck her," replied the boy, bewildered, and a little indignant.

"And sure ye'r Peter or Paul, or Judas hissilf, if so be she likes to call ye so while she's this way; an', if ye shtrike her, it's the weight uv my fist ye'll feel; mind that, young man! - Whisht, thin, darlint! asy, mavourneen!"

'Toinette, hushed upon the motherly bosom of the good woman, soon ceased her cries, and presently fell again to sleep; while Teddy, with rather an injured look upon his uncouth face, and yet pleased to see the little sister in his mother's arms, crept softly from the room, with his breakfast in his hand.

CHAPTER X.

THE EMPTY NEST.

WHEN Susan returned from carrying Bessie Rider home, she was quite surprised to find the front-door ajar, as she thought she had been sure of latching it in going out; but, without stopping to make any inquiries of the other servants, she ran up the stairs, took off her shawl and hood, and then went to the drawing-room for 'Toinette. The room was empty; and Susan at once concluded that Mrs. Legrange had taken the child to her own chamber while she dressed for dinner, as 'Toinette often begged to be present at this ceremony, and was often indulged.

"I'll just ready up the nursery a bit before I fetch her," said Susan, looking round the littered room; and so it was half an hour before she knocked at Mrs. Legrange's chamber-door with, "I came for Miss 'Toinette, ma'am."

"Come in, Susan. Miss 'Toinette, did you say? She is down in the drawing-room by herself, and you had better put her to bed at once. She must be very tired."

Alas! the tender mother little guessed how tired!

Without reply, Susan closed the door, and ran down stairs; an uneasy feeling creeping over her, although she would not yet confess it even to herself.

The drawing-room was still empty; but James had lighted the gas and stirred the fire, so that every corner was as light as day. In every window-recess, under every couch and sofa, behind every large chair, even in the closet of the ,tagŠre, Susan searched for her little charge, hoping, praying to find her asleep, or roguishly hiding, as she had known her to do before. But all in vain: no merry face, no sunny curls, no laughing eyes, peeped out from recess or corner or hiding place; and Susan's ruddy face grew pale even to the lips.

She flew to the dining-room, and searched it as narrowly as she had done the drawing-room.

No: she was not there!

The library, the bath-room, the chambers, the nursery again, the servants' chambers, the kitchen, laundry, pantries, the very cellar!

No, no, no! 'Toinette was in none of them. 'Toinette was not in any nook of the whole wide house, that, without her, seemed so empty and desolate. Standing in one of the upper entries, mute and bewildered, Susan heard a latch-key turn in the front-door lock, and presently Mr. Legrange's pleasant voice speaking in the hall. A sudden hope rushed into Susan's heart. The child might possibly have gone to meet her father, and was now returned with him. She rushed down stairs as fast as her feet could carry her; but in the hall stood only Mr. Legrange, talking to James, who had some message to deliver to him.

As Susan flew down the stairs, the master turned and looked at her in some surprise.

"Be careful, Susan: you nearly fell then. Is any thing the matter?"

"Miss 'Toinette, sir: I can't find her, high nor low!" gasped Susan.

"Can't find her! Good heavens! you don't mean to say she's lost!" exclaimed the father, turning, and staring at the nurse in dismay.

"Oh! I don't know, sir, I'm sure; but I can't find her," cried Susan, wildly bursting into tears.

"Where is her mother? Where is Mrs. Legrange, James?"

"I don't know, sir, I'm sure," said the footman blankly.

"She's in her own room, sir; and I'm afraid to go to tell her, she'll feel that bad. And indeed it wasn't any fault of mine: I only went" -

"Hush!" exclaimed Mr. Legrange, who had heard his wife close her chamber-door and begin to descend the stairs, and did not wish her to be frightened.

"Wait here a moment, Susan," added he, and, running up stairs, entered the drawing-room just after his wife, who stood before the fire, looking so pretty and so gay in her blue silk-dress, with a ribbon of the same shade twisted among her golden curls, that her husband shrunk back, dreading to ask the question that must so shock and startle her. But Mrs. Legrange had caught sight of him, and, running to the door, opened it suddenly, crying, -

"Come in, you silly boy! Are you playing bo-beep? I don't do such things since my daughter is six years old, I would have you to understand."

Mr. Legrange, forcing a laugh and a careless tone, came forward as she spoke, and, stooping to kiss her, asked, -

"And where is your daughter, my love?"

"'Toinette? Oh! I suppose she is with Susan," began Mrs. Legrange carelessly; and then, as something in her husband's voice or manner attracted her attention, she drew back, and hurriedly looked into his face, crying, -

"O Paul! what is it? What has happened? Is 'Toinette hurt? Where is she?"

"Be quiet, darling; don't be alarmed. Wait till we know more. - Susan, come up here," called Mr. Legrange; and Susan, with her face buried in her apron, and sobbing as if her heart would break, crept timidly up the stairs and into the room.

At sight of her, Mrs. Legrange turned pale, and clung to her husband for support.

"O Susan! what is it? Tell me quick!"

"She's gone, ma'am, and I don't know where!" sobbed the nurse.

"Gone! What, 'Toinette gone! Lost, do you mean?" cried the mother wildly, while her pale cheeks flushed scarlet, and her soft eyes glittered with terror.

"Oh! I don't know, ma'am; but I can't find her."

"Lost! What, 'Toinette lost!" repeated the mother in the same wild tone, and trying to tear herself away from her husband's detaining arms. But, soothing her as he would a child, Mr. Legrange, by a few calm and well-directed questions, drew from both mistress and maid all that was to be known of 'Toinette's disappearance, and, when the whole was told, said, -

"Well, Susan, you are not to blame. You merely obeyed your mistress's directions, and need not feel that this misfortune is at all your fault. No doubt 'Toinette has gone out by herself, and is, for the moment, lost, but, I trust, will soon be found. You may go at once to the houses of the neighbors whose children she has been in the habit of visiting. Be as quick as you can about it; and, if you do not find her, come directly home, and I will warn the police. Send James up to me as you go down."

"Yes, sir," said Susan, a little comforted; and, as she closed the door, Mr. Legrange returned to his wife, and, clasping her tenderly in his arms, kissed the burning cheeks and glittering eyes that frightened him, until the dangerous calm broke up in a gracious flood of tears and wild sobs of, "My child! - O my little child!"

"Hush, darling, hush! You must be calm, or I cannot leave you, - cannot go to look for her. I will not leave you so, even to search for her."

"Yes, yes, go! I will try - O Paul, Paul! do go and look for her!"

"When I see you calmer, love; not till then;" and the tender-hearted man could himself have wept to see the heroic efforts of that delicate nature to control itself and put his fears to rest. He still was soothing her, when, with a tap at the door, entered James, followed by Susan, who hurriedly announced that 'Toinette was not to be heard of at any of the neighbors, and asked where she should go next.

"Nowhere! Stay here and attend to Mrs. Legrange until I return. I shall go at once to the police-station. James, you know where Mr. Burroughs lives?"

"Yes, sir."

"Go to him. Or stay: he is dining with a friend to-day. Here is the direction. Go to this house at once; see Mr. Burroughs; tell him that 'Toinette is lost, and beg him to come up here directly. Keep your eyes open as you go: you may possibly meet her yourself. Hurry, man; hurry for your life!"

"Yes, sir," replied the man heartily; and Mr. Legrange returned to his wife, who was walking quickly up and down the room, her hands clasped tight before her, her lips rigid, and her eyes set.

"There, darling, I have sent for Tom to help us; and no one could do it better than he will. I am going to the police myself. Take courage, dearest, and hope, as I do, that, before morning, we shall have our pet back, safe and sound. But you - O Fanny! how can I leave you so? Try, try, for my sake, for 'Toinette's sake, to be calm and hopeful."

"Yes - I - will - try!" sobbed the poor mother; and Mr.

Legrange, not daring to trust himself to look at her again, lest he also should break down, hastened from the room.

But morning came, and night, and yet another morning and as the father, the mother, the cousin who was almost brother to both, the assistants, and poor broken-hearted Susan, looked into each other's wan, worn faces, they found nothing there but discouragement, and almost hopeless despair.

Mrs. Legrange who had not eaten or slept since 'Toinette's disappearance, was already too ill to sit up, but insisted upon remaining dressed, and waiting in the drawing-room for the reports that some one of those engaged in the search brought almost hourly to the house. Her husband, looking like the ghost of his former self, wandered incessantly from his own home to the police-office and back again, each time through some new street, and peering curiously into the face of every child he met, that more than one of them ran frightened home to tell their mothers that they had met a crazy man, who stared at them as if he would eat them up.

And yet no clew, no faintest trace, of the little 'Toinette, who lay tossing in her fever-dreams upon good Mrs. Ginniss's humble bed, while the young doctor day by day shook his head more sadly over her, and said to his own heart that it was only by God's special mercy she could ever rise from that cruel illness.

CHAPTER XI.

A TRACE AND A SEARCH.

THREE weary nights and two days had passed, when as Mr. Legrange, bending over his wife's sofa, entreated her to take the food and drink he had himself prepared for her, a sharp peal at the bell, followed by a bounding step upon the stair, startled them both.

"It is Tom, and he has news!" exclaimed Mrs. Legrange in a low voice, as she pushed away the tray and rose to her feet.

The door opened, and the young man entered, his tired face glowing with hope and satisfaction. In his hand he held a little bundle; and sitting down, with no more than word of greeting, he hastily untied it upon his knee.

"Aren't these her clothes?" asked he breathlessly, as he held up by one sleeve a little sky-blue merino-dress, with a torn lace undersleeve hanging from the shoulder, and in the other hand a pair of dainty little boots of bronze cloth.

Mrs. Legrange, with a wild cry, darted forward, and, grasping the pretty dress, buried her face in it, covering it with kisses, while she cried, -

"Yes, yes! O Tom! where is she? Tell me quick, before my poor heart breaks with joy!"

Mr. Burroughs remained silent. How could he say that he knew as little as ever how to answer this appeal?

"Where did you get them, Tom?" asked Mr. Legrange hurriedly.

"Billings found them in a pawn-broker's shop. You know we gave all the detectives a list of the clothing, and full description of the child. Billings has been all over the city, examining at every pawn-broker's shop all the children's clothes brought in since we lost her, you know" -

"Yes, yes! And when" -

"Last night he found this in a little out-of-the-way place (I didn't stop to ask where), and, thinking they looked like the right thing, brought them to me. I was asleep, and the people stupidly would not wake me: so he waited; and this morning, when I rose, there he was.

I snatched the bundle, and came right along with it. Now, of course, they'll soon find who left them: only, unluckily, they weren't pawned, but sold outright; so they didn't take the name; but the man thinks it was an old woman who sold them to him. He is in custody; and we will go down and hear the examination, Paul."

"Certainly, at once." And Mr. Legrange nervously buttoned his coat, and moved toward the door.

"It is to be at ten, and it is now half-past nine. I suppose we had better go at once. Good-by, dear cousin Fanny!" said Mr. Burroughs, looking sorrow-fullly at the wan face upraised to his, as the poor mother replied, -

"Good-by, Tom! and oh, pray, do every thing, every thing, that can be done! I cannot tell" -

She was unable to finish, and the two men hurried away from the sight of a sorrow as yet without remedy.

The examination of the blear-eyed and stupid old pawn-broker resulted in very little satisfaction. He believed that it was a woman who had sold him the bundle of child's clothing. He was not sure if it were an old or a young woman, but rather thought it was an old woman. It might have been a week ago that he bought them; it might have been more, or it might have been less: he didn't set it down, and couldn't say.

This was all; and, as nothing could be proved or even suspected of him in connection with 'Toinette's disappearance, he was discharged from custody, although warned to hold himself in readiness to appear at any moment when he should be summoned.

He had not yet, however, left the room, when one of the audience, a policeman off duty, stepped forward, and, intimating that he had something to say, was sworn, and went on to tell how he had been leaning against a lamp-post at the extreme of his beat, just resting a bit, in the edge of evening before last, when he saw an old woman that they call Mother Winch come up the street, carrying a bundle, and leading a little girl. He knew she hadn't any child of her own; and the child was dressed very poor; and Mother Winch called her Judy or Biddy, or some Paddy-name or other; and maybe it was all right, and maybe it wasn't. It could be worked up easy enough, he supposed.

So supposed the detective in whose hands the clew was immediately placed; but when, an hour later, he descended the steps into Mother Winch's cellar, he found that a keener and a swifter messenger than himself had already called the wretched old woman to account; and she lay across the rusty old stove, quite dead, with a broken bottle of spirit upon the floor beside her, and all the front of her body shockingly burned. The coroner who was called to see her decided that she had fallen across the stove, either in a fit, or too much intoxicated to move, and had died unconscious of her situation. She was buried by public charity, and in her grave seemed hidden every hope of tracing the lost child.

"She must have been carried from the city," said the detectives; and the search was extended into the country, and to other towns and cities, although not neglected at home.

CHAPTER XII.

TEDDY'S TEMPTATION.

TEDDY GINNISS sat alone in his master's office, feeling very sad and forlorn: for Dr. Wentworth had that morning said that the chance of life for his little patient was very, very small; and it seemed to Teddy heavier news than human heart had ever borne before. His morning duties over, he had seated himself at his little table, and tried to study the lesson given him by Mr. Burroughs upon the previous day; but a heavy heart makes dim eyes, and the page where Teddy's were fixed seemed to him no better than a crowd of disjointed letters swimming in a blinding mist.

A hasty step was heard upon the stair; and, passing the sleeve of his jacket across his eyes, the boy bent closer over the book as his master entered the room.

"Any one been in this morning, Teddy?" asked Mr. Burroughs, passing into the inner office.

"No, sir."

"I am going out of town for a day or two, Teddy, - going to New York; and Mr. Barlow will be here to attend to the business. You will do whatever he wishes as you would for me. You understand?"

"Yes, sir."

The good-natured young man, struck by the mournful tone of Teddy's usually hearty voice, turned and looked sharply at him.

"Aren't you well, Teddy?"

"Yes sir, thank your honor."

"Not 'your honor' until I'm a judge, Teddy. But what's amiss with you, my boy?"

"I wouldn't be troubling your - you with it, sir. It's nothing as can be helped."

"No, no; but what is it, Teddy?" insisted the lawyer, who saw that Teddy could hardly restrain his tears.

"Nothing, sir; but the little sister is mortal sick, and the doctor says he's afeard she won't stand it."

"Your little sister, Teddy?"

"Yes, sir."

"I didn't know you had one. You never spoke of her before, did you?"

"Maybe not, sir."

"What is the matter with her?"

"The faver, sir."

Mr. Burroughs knew that this phrase in an Irish mouth means but one disease, and replied, in a sympathizing voice, -

"Typhus! I'm sorry for you, Teddy, and sorry, too, for your mother, who is an excellent woman; but the little girl may yet recover: while there is life, there is hope, you know. Even if she dies, it is not so bad as - I am going to New York, Teddy, to look for a little cousin of mine whose parents do not know if she is living or dead, suffering or safe: that is worse than to have her ill, but under their care and protection, isn't it?"

"Yes, sir, perhaps. Is the little girl in New York, sir, do you think?"

"We hear of a child found astray there, who answers to the description; and I am going to see her before we mention the report to her mother. Have you never seen Mr. Legrange here, Teddy? It is his little girl. I wonder you haven't heard us talking of the matter."

"I don't mind the name, sir; and I haven't heard of the little girl before. Is she long lost?"

"Ten days yesterday. I have been busy all the week in the search for her. The clothes she had on when lost were found in a pawn-broker's shop; but we have no trace of her yet."

"What looking child was she, if you please, sir?" asked Teddy after a short pause, in which he seemed to study intently; while Mr. Burroughs went on glancing at the newspapers in his hand.

"'Toinette? Here is a description of her in 'The Journal,' and I have a photograph in my pocket-book. Here it is. It is well for you to study them both; for possibly you may discover her. I didn't think of it before; but you are just the boy to put upon the search. If you should find her, Teddy, Mr. Legrange will make your fortune. He is rich and generous, and this is his only child. Eleven o'clock. Shall be in at one."

As he spoke, Mr. Burroughs threw the paper and photograph upon Teddy's table, and hastily left the office. The boy took up "The Journal," and read the following advertisement: -

"Lost, upon the evening of Oct. 31, a little girl, six years of age, named Antoinette Legrange; of slight figure, round face, delicate color, large blue eyes, long curled hair of a bright-yellow color, small mouth, and regular teeth. She was dressed, at the time of her disappearance, in a blue frock and brown boots, with a lady's breakfast-shawl; and wore upon the sleeve of her dress a bracelet of coral cameos engraved under the clasp with her name in full. A liberal reward will be paid for information concerning her. Apply at the police-station."

When he had studied this, Teddy took up the photograph, and examined it earnestly. The dress, the long curled hair, the joyous expression, were very different from the pale face, wild eyes, and cropped head of the little sister at home; but Teddy's heart sank within him as he traced the delicate features, the curved lips, and trim little figure. He dropped the picture, and, leaning his face upon his arm, sobbed aloud.

"I'll lose her anyway, if she dies or if she lives; and it's all the little sister ever I got."

But presently another thought made Teddy lift his head, and look anxiously about him to make sure that his emotion had not been seen by any one. He was still alone; and, with a sigh of relief, he dashed away the tears from his eyes, muttering, -

"It's the big fool I am, entirely! Sure and mightn't she have picked up the bracelet in the street, where maybe the little lady they've lost dropped it? And, if she looks like the picture, so does many a one beside; and it's no call I have to be troubling the master with telling him about her anyway. She's my own little sister, and I'll keep her to myself."

A sudden sharp recollection darted through the boy's mind, and he grew a little pale as he added, -

"Leastways, I'll keep her if God will let me; and sure isn't he stronger nor me? If it isn't for me to have her, can't he take her, if it's by death, or if it's by leading them that's searching for her to where she is? And more by token, that's the way I'll try it. If God means she shall stay and be my little sister, she'll live, and I'll take her, and say nothing to nobody about it: but, if it's displasin' to him, she'll die; and then I'll tell the master all about it, and he may do what he's a mind to with me. That's the way I'll fix it."

And Teddy, well satisfied with his own bad argument, took comfort, and went back to his books.

When Mr. Burroughs returned to the office, he was accompanied by Mr. Barlow, the gentleman who was to occupy it during his absence; and he did not speak to Teddy, except to give him a few directions, and bid him a kind good-by. The paper and picture he found lying upon his desk, and hastily put in his pocket without remark or question.

For the first time in his life, Teddy avoided meeting his master's eye, but watched him furtively over the top of his book, raising it so as to screen his face whenever Mr. Burroughs looked his way, and trembling whenever he spoke to him; and, for the first time in his life, he secretly rejoiced at seeing him leave the office, knowing that he was to be gone for some time.

The long day was over at last; and, so soon as the hour for closing the office had begun to strike, Teddy locked the door, sprang down stairs, and ran like a deer towards home, feeling as if in some manner the little sister was about to be taken away from him, and he must hasten to prevent it.

At the foot of the stairs, however, he checked himself, creeping up as silently and cautiously as possible, and stopping at the head to listen for the clear voice, frightfully clear and shrill, of the delirious child, which usually met him there. No sound was to be heard except the deep voice of the Italian organ-grinder in the room below, talking to himself or his monkey as he prepared supper; and Teddy, creeping along the entry to his mother's door, softly opened it, and went in.

At one side of the bed stood Mrs. Ginniss; at the other, Dr. Wentworth: but Teddy saw only the little waxen face upon the pillow between them, - the little face so strange and lovely now; for all the fever flush had passed away, the babbling lips were folded white and still, the glittering eyes were closed, and the long dark lashes lay motionless upon the cheek, - the little face so strange and terrible in its sudden, peaceful beauty.

As Teddy softly entered, Dr. Wentworth turned and held a warning finger up; then bent again above the little child, his hand upon her heart.

The boy crept close to his mother, down whose honest face the tears ran like rain; although she heeded the earnest warning of the physician, and was almost as still as she little form she watched.

"Is she dead, mother?" whispered Teddy.

"Whisht, darlint! wait till we know," whispered she in return; and the young doctor glanced impatiently at both out of his strained and eager eyes. Had it been his own and only child, he could not have hung more earnestly about her: and here was the strange, sweet charm of this little life, - that all who came within its influence felt themselves drawn toward it, and opened wide their hearts to allow its entrance; feeling not alone that they loved the lovely child, but that she was or should be their very own, to cherish and fondle and bind to them forever.

So the coarse, hard-working woman, who two weeks before had never seen her face, now wept as true and bitter tears as she had done beside the death-bed of the child she had lost when Teddy was a baby; and the young doctor, who had watched the passage of a hundred souls from time to eternity, hung over this little dying form as if all life for him were held within it, and to lose it were to lose all. And Teddy-ah! poor Teddy; for upon his young heart lay not only the bitterness of the death busy with his "little sister's" life, but the heavy burden of wrong and deception, and the proof, as he thought, of God's displeasure in taking from him at last what he had tried so hard to keep.

He sank upon his knees beside the bed, and hid his

face, whispering, -

"O God! let her live, and I will give her back to them as I kept her from."

Over and over and over again, he whispered just these words, clinching tight his boy-hands to keep down the agony of the sacrifice; while in the very centre of his heart throbbed a hard, dull pain, that seemed as if it would rend it asunder.

His face was still hidden, when, like an answer to his petition, came the softest of whispers from the doctor's lips, -

"She will live, with God's help, and the best of care from you."

"An' it's the bist uv care she'll git, I'll pass me word for that," whispered back Teddy's mother, so earnestly, that the doctor answered, -

"Hush! She is falling asleep. Do not wake her, for her life!"

He sank into a chair as he spoke. Mrs. Ginniss crept round to the stove, and, crouching beside it, covered her head with her apron, and remained motionless. As for Teddy, he never stirred or looked up, but with his face hidden upon the bed, repeated again and again those words, to him so solemn and so full of meaning, until in the silence and the waiting he fell asleep, and gradually sank upon the floor.

And so the night went on: and the careful eyes of the young physician marked how a faint tinge of color crept into the death-white cheek upon the pillow; and how the still lips lost their hard, cold line, and grew human once more, though so pale; and how the eyelids stirred, moving the heavy lashes; and a faint pulse fluttered in the slender throat.

At last, with a long, soft sigh, the lips lightly parted; the eyelids opened slowly, showing for a moment the blue eyes, dim and languid, but no longer wild with delirium; and then they slowly closed, and the breath came softly and regularly from the parted lips.

Dr. Wentworth heaved an answering sigh of mingled weariness and relief, and, rising, went to Mrs. Ginniss's side, touching her upon the shoulder, and whispering, -

"She is doing well. Keep her as quiet as possible. I will be in at nine."

Hushing the murmured blessings she would have poured upon his head, the young man stole softly from the room and down the stairs into the street, where already the first gray of dawn struggled with the flaring gas-lights.

CHAPTER XIII.

THE CACHUCA.

TEN days more, and beside the fire in Mrs. Ginniss's attic-room sat a little figure, propped in the wooden rocking-chair with pillows and comfortables; while upon a small stand close beside her were arranged a few cheap toys, a plate with some pieces of orange upon it, a sprig of geranium in a broken-nosed pitcher of water, and a cup of beef-tea.

But for none of these did the languid little invalid seem to care; and lying back in the chair, her head nestled into the pillow, her parched lips open, and her eyes half closed, she looked so little like the bright and glowing 'Toinette who had danced at her birthday-party not a month before, that it is a question if any one but her own mother would have believed her to be the same.

Mrs. Ginniss, hard at work upon the frills of a fashionable lady's skirt, paused every few moments to look over her shoulder at the little wasted face with the wistful look of some dumb creature who sees its off-spring suffering, and cannot tell how to relieve it.

Suddenly setting the flat-iron she had just taken back upon the stove, the washwoman came and bent over the child, looking earnestly into her face.

"An' it's waker an' whiter she gits every day. Sure and

I'm afther seeing the daylight through the little hands uv her; and her eyes is that big, they take the breath uv me whin I mate 'em. See, darlint! - see the purty skipjack Teddy brought ye!"

She took from the table the toy she named, and, pulling the string, made the figure of the man vault over the top of the stick and back several times, crying at the same time, -

"Hi, thin! - hi, thin! See how the crather joomps, honey!"

But, although the languid eyes of the child followed her motions for a moment, no shadow of a smile stirred the parched lips; and presently the eyes closed, as if the effort were too much for them.

Mrs. Ginniss laid the toy upon the table, and took up the cup of beef-tea.

"Have a soop of yer dhrink, darlint?" said she, tenderly holding the cup to the child's lips, and raising her head with the other hand; but, with a moan of impatience or distress, the weary head turned itself upon the pillow, and the little wasted hand half rose to push away the cup.

"An' what is it I'll plaze ye wid, mavourneen? Do yees want Teddy to coom home?" asked the poor woman in despair.

A faint murmur of assent crept from between the parched lips; and the eyes, slowly opening, glanced toward the door.

"It's this minute he'll be here, thin," said the washwoman joyfully. "An' faith yees ought to love him, honey; for he'd give the two eyes out of his head to plaze yees, an' git down on his knees to thank yees for takin' 'em. Now, thin, don't ye hear his fut upon the stair?"

But the heavy steps coming up the stairs were not Teddy's, as his mother well knew; and although, when they stopped upon the landing below her own, she pretended to be much surprised, she would, in reality, have been much more so if they had not stopped.

"And it's Jovarny it wor that time, honey," said she soothingly: "but Teddy'll coom nixt; see if he doun't, Cherry darlint."

But Cherry, closing her eyes, with no effort at reply, lay as motionless upon her pillow as if she had been asleep or in a swoon.

Suddenly, from the room below, was heard a strain of plaintive music. The organ-grinder, for some reason or other, was trying his instrument in his own room; although, remembering the sick child above, he played as softly and slowly as he could. It was the first time he had done so since Cherry had been ill; and Mrs. Ginniss anxiously watched her face to see what effect the sounds would have.

The air was "Kathleen Mavourneen;" and, as one tender strain succeeded another, the watchful nurse could see a faint color stealing into the child's face, while from between the half-closed lids her eyes shone brighter than they had for many a day.

"If it plazes her, I'll pay him to grind away all day, the

crather," murmured she joyfully.

The song ended, and, after a little pause, was succeeded by a lively dancing-tune.

"She'll not like that so well, thought Mrs. Ginniss; but, to her great astonishment, the child, after listening a moment, started upright in her chair, her eyes wide open and shining with excitement, her cheeks glowing, and her little hands fluttering.

"Mamma, mamma! I'm Cherritoe! and I can dance with that music, and mamma can play it more" -

The words faltered upon her lips, and she sank suddenly back upon the pillows in a death-faint. At the same moment, Teddy came bounding up the stairs and into the room.

"Go an' shtop that fool's noise if yees brain him, an' ax him what's the name o' that divil's jig he's playing!" exclaimed Mrs. Ginniss as she caught sight of the boy; and Teddy, without stopping for a question, hastily obeyed.

In a moment he was back.

"It's the cachuca, mother; but what's the matter with the little sister?"

"Whist! She's swounded wid the noise he's afther making," replied his mother angrily, as she laid the wasted little figure upon her bed, and bathed the temples with cold water.

Teddy stood anxiously looking on. Ever since the night

when the little sister's fever had turned, and the doctor had promised that she should live, a struggle had been going on in the boy's heart. He could not but believe that God had given back the almost-departed life in answer to his earnest prayer and promise; and he had no intention of breaking the promise, or withholding the price he felt himself to have offered for that life. But, like many older and better taught persons, Teddy did not see clearly enough how little difference there is between doing right and failing to do right, or how much difference between promising with the lips and promising with the heart.

While his little sister, as he still called her, lay between life and death, Teddy said to himself that the excitement of seeing her friends might be fatal to her, and that, if she should die, their grief in this second loss would be greater than what they were now suffering.

When she began slowly to recover, he said that they would only be frightened at seeing her so wasted and weak, and that he would keep her until she had recovered something of her good looks; and, finally, he had begun to think that it would be no more than fair that he should repay himself for all the sorrow and anxiety her illness had given him by keeping her a little while after she was quite well and strong, and could go for a walk with him, and see the beautiful shops, with their Christmas-wares displayed.

"New Year's will be soon enough. I'll take her to the master for a New-Year's gift," Teddy had said to himself that very night as he came up the stairs; and a sort of satisfaction crept into his heart in thinking that he had at least fixed a date for fulfilling his promise.

But New-Year's Day found 'Toinette, or Cherry as we must learn to call her, more unlike her former self than she had been when he formed the resolution. The strange emotion that had overcome her in listening to the organ-grinder's music had caused a relapse into fever, followed by other troubles; and spite of Dr. Wentworth's constant care, Mrs. Ginniss's patient and tender nursing, and Teddy's devotion, the child seemed pining away without hope or remedy.

"I'll wait till the spring comes, anyway," said Teddy to himself. "Maybe the warm weather will bring her round, and I'll hear her laugh out once, and take her for just one walk on the Commons before I carry her to the master."

CHAPTER XIV.

GIOVANNI AND PANTALON.

IT was April; and the bit of sky to be seen between two tall roofs, from the window of Mrs. Ginniss's attic, had suddenly grown of a deeper blue, and was sometimes crossed by a great white, glittering cloud, such as is never seen in winter; and, when the window was raised for a few moments, the air came in soft and mild, and with a fresh smell to it, as if it had blown through budding trees and over fresh-ploughed earth.

Cherry was now well enough to be dressed, and to play about the room, or sew a little, or look at pictures in the gaudily painted books Teddy anxiously saved his coppers to buy for her: but, more than once in the day, she would push a chair to the bed, and climb up to lie upon it; or would come and cling to her foster-mother, moaning, -

"I'm tired now, mammy. Hold me in your lap."

And very seldom was the petition refused, although the wash-tub or the ironing-table stood idle that it might be granted; for so well had great-hearted Mrs. Ginniss come to love the child, that she would have been as unwilling as Teddy himself to remember that she had not always been her own.

Sitting thus in her mammy's lap one day, Cherry suddenly asked, -

"Where's the music, mammy?"

"The music, darlint? And what music do ye be manin'?"

"The music I heard one day before I went to heaven. Didn't you hear it?"

"An' whin did ye go to hivin, ye quare child?"

"Oh! I don't know. When I came back, I was sick in the bed. I want the music, mammy."

"It's Jovarny she manes, the little crather," said Mrs. Ginniss, and promised, that if Cherry would lie on the bed, and let her "finish ironing the lady's clothes all so pretty," she should hear the music as soon as Teddy and the organ-grinder came home.

To this proposal, Cherry consented more willingly than her mammy had dared to expect; and when, after finishing the ironing of some intricate embroideries, the laundress turned to look, she found the child had dropped quietly asleep.

"An' all the betther fur yees, darlint," said she. "Whin ye waken, ye'll think no more uv the music that wellnigh kilt yees afore."

An hour later, Teddy's entrance aroused the sleeper, who, rolling over upon the bed with a pretty little gape, smiled upon him, saying, -

"Where's the music, Teddy? Mammy said you'd get it for me."

"It's Jovarny she's afther wantin' to hear play on his grind-orgin; an' I towld her he'd coom whin yees did," explained Mrs. Ginniss: and Teddy, delighted to be asked to do any thing for his little sister, lost no time in running down stairs, and begging the Italian, who had just returned home, to play one of the prettiest tunes in his list, but on no account to touch the one that had so strangely affected the little invalid upon a former occasion.

The Italian very willingly complied, and was already in the midst of a pretty waltz when Teddy re-appeared in his mother's room. Cherry's delight was unbounded; and when the whole list of tunes, with the exception of the cachuca, had been exhausted, she put her arms round Teddy's neck, and kissed him, saying, -

"Thank you, little brother. I'll eat my supper for you now."

And this, as Cherry had hardly been willing to eat any thing since her illness, was considered, both by Teddy and herself, as a remarkable proof of amiability and affection.

The next day, before Teddy went away in the morning, he was obliged to promise that he would bring the music at night; and, as he ran down stairs, he stopped to beg the organ-grinder to come home as early as possible, and to come prepared to play for the little sister's benefit.

"Let her come down and see the organ and Pantalon," said the Italian in his broken English; and Teddy eagerly cried, -

"Oh! may she?" and ran up stairs again with the invitation. But Mrs. Ginniss prudently declared that Cherry
must not think of leaving her own room at present,
while the stairs and entries were so cold; and "Thin
agin," said she, "maybe the bit moonkey ud scare her
back into the fayver as bad as iver."

So, for a week or two longer, Cherry was obliged to
content herself with an evening-concert through the
floor; and upon these concerts the whole of the day
seemed to depend. Very soon the little girl began to
have her favorites among the half-dozen airs she so
often heard, and, little by little, learned to hum them
all, giving them names of her own. "Kathleen Mavourneen" she always called "Susan," although quite unable
to give any reason for so doing; and Teddy, who
watched her constantly, noticed that she always
remained very thoughtful, wearing a puzzled, anxious
look, while hearing it. After a time, however, this dim
association with the almost-forgotten past wore away;
and although Cherry still called the air "Susan," and
liked it better than any of the rest, it seemed to have
become a thing of the present instead of the past.

At last, one warm day in April, when Giovanni had
returned home earlier than usual, and Teddy again brought an invitation to the bambina, as he called Cherry,
to visit him, Mrs. Ginniss reluctantly cones-nted; and
the little girl, wrapped in shawls and hood, with warm
stockings pulled over her shoes, was carried in Teddy's
arms down the stairs as she had been brought up in
them six months before. The boy himself was the first
to think of it, and, as he stooped to take the little figure
in his arms, said, -

"You haven't been over the stairs, sissy, since Teddy

brought you up last fall."

"Teddy didn't bring me up. I never came up, 'cause I never was down," said Cherry resolutely; and the boy, who dreaded above all things to awaken in her mind any recollection of the past, said no more, but carefully wrapping the shawl about her, and promising his mother not to stay too long, carried her gently down the stairs, and to the door Giovanni opened as he heard them approach.

"Welcome, little one!" said the Italian in his own language as they entered; and Cherry smiled at the sound, and then looked troubled and thoughtful.

The truth was, that 'Toinette's father and mother had often spoken both Italian and French in her presence; and although the terrible fever had destroyed her memory of home and parents, and all that went before, the things that she had known in those forgotten days still awoke in her heart a vague sense of pain and loss, - an effort to recall something that seemed just vanishing away, as through the strings of a broken and forsaken harp will sweep some vagrant breeze, wakening the ghosts of its forgotten melodies to a brief and shadowy life, again to pass and be forgotten.

So 'Toinette, still clinging to Teddy's neck, turned, and fixed her great eyes upon the Italian's dark face so earnestly and so piteously, that he smiled, showing all his white teeth, and asked, -

"Does the little one know the language of my country?"

"No: of course she don't. I don't," said Teddy, looking

a little anxiously into Cherry's face, and wondering in his own heart if she might not have known Italian in that former life, of whose loves and interests he had always been so jealous.

Giovanni looked curiously at the two children. Cherry, in recovering from her illness, was regaining the wonderful beauty, that, for a time, had seemed lost. The remnant of her golden hair spared by Mother Winch's shears had fallen off after the first attack of fever, and was now replaced by thick, short curls of a sunny brown, clustering about her white forehead with a careless grace far more bewitching than the elaborate ringlets Susan had been so proud of manufacturing; while long confinement to the house had rendered the delicate complexion so pearly in its whiteness, so exquisite in its rose-tints, that one could hardly believe it possible that flesh and blood should become so etherealized even while gaining health and strength.

The subtle eye of the Italian marked every point of this exquisite loveliness, ran admiringly over the outlines of the graceful figure, the delicate hands and little feet, the classic curve of the lips, the thin nostrils and tiny ears; then returned to the clear, full eyes, with their pencilled brows and heavy lashes, and smiled at the earnestness of the gaze that met his own. Then, from this lovely and patrician face, the Italian's eyes wandered to Teddy's coarse and unformed features, and figure of uncouth strength.

"Nightingales are not hatched from hens' eggs," muttered Giovanni in his native tongue.

"Speak that some more; I like it," said Cherry softly.

"Yes; and you are like it, and, like all that belongs to my Italian, beautiful and graceful," said Giovanni, dropping the liquid accents as lovingly from his lips as if they had been a kiss. Then, in the imperfect English he generally spoke, he asked of Teddy, -

"Where did the child come from?"

"She's my little sister," replied the boy doggedly.

The Italian shrugged his shoulders and raised his eyebrows, muttering in his own tongue, -

"I never heard or saw any child above there in the first weeks of my living here. But what affair is it of mine? The child I have lost is safe with the Holy Mother!"

He crossed himself, and muttered a prayer; then from behind the stove, where he lay warming himself, pulled a little creature, at sight of whom Cherry uttered a scream, and clung to Teddy.

"It's the monkey, sissy; it's Jovarny's monkey; and his name is Pantaloons," explained Teddy.

"Pantalon," corrected the monkey's master; and snapping his fingers, and whistling to the monkey, he called him to his shoulder, and made him go through a number of tricks and gestures, - some of them so droll, that Cherry's terror ended in peals of laughter; and she soon left Teddy's side to run and caper about the room in imitation of the monkey's antics.

"Does she dance, the little one?" asked Giovanni, watching the child's lithe movements admiringly.

"Sure, and every step she takes is as good as dancing," said Teddy evasively.

"Let us see, then."

And the Italian, arranging the stops of his organ, played the pretty waltz Cherry had so often heard from it, and liked so well.

The child continued her frolicsome motions, unconsciously adapting them to the music, until she was moving in perfect harmony with it, although not in the step or figure of a waltz.

"She was born to dance!" exclaimed Giovanni with enthusiasm; and, moving the stops of the organ, he passed, without pause, into the gay and airy movement of the cachuca.

As the first tones struck the child's ear, she faltered; then stopped, turned pale, and listened intently.

"Whisht! That's the tune I told you not to play!" exclaimed Teddy. But Giovanni, his eyes fixed upon the child, did not hear or did not heed him, but played on; while Cherry, trembling, pale, her hands clasped, lips apart, and eyes fixed intently upon the musician, seemed shaken to the very soul by some strange and undefined emotion. Suddenly a scarlet flush mounted to the roots of her hair, her eyes grew bright, her parted lips curved to a roguish smile; and, pointing her little foot, she spun away in the graceful movements of the dance, and continued it to the close, finishing with a courtesy, and kiss of the hand, that made Giovanni drop the handle of his organ, clasp his hands, and cry in Italian, -

"Bravo, bravo, picciola! Truly you were born to dance!"

But the child, suddenly losing the life and color that had sparkled through every line of face and figure, ran with a wild cry to Teddy, and, clasping him tight round the neck, burst into a flood of tears, crying, -

"Take me home, Teddy! - quick, quick! I want mamma!"

Mrs. Ginniss had taught her to say "mammy;" and Teddy remembered with dismay that she had never used the name "mamma," except in the delirium of her fever, when she was evidently addressing some distant and beloved object. But still he chose to understand the appeal in his own way; and, hastily wrapping the shawls about the little figure, he raised it in his arms, saying soothingly, -

"Come, then; come to mammy, little sister. You didn't ought to have danced and get all tired."

"Good-by, little one," said Giovanni somewhat ruefully. The child raised her head from Teddy's shoulder, and, smiling through her tears, said sweetly, -

"Good-by, 'Varny. It wasn't you made me cry, but because" -

"'Cause you was tired, little sister," interposed Teddy hastily; and Giovanni looked at him craftily.

"I'll come and see you another day, 'Varny; but I must go lie down now," continued Cherry, anxious to remove any wound her new friend's feelings might have received. And the organ-grinder smiled until he showed all his white teeth, as he replied, - "Yes, and again and again, - as often as you will, picciola."

But Teddy, shaking his head disapprovingly, muttered, as he carried his little sister away, -

"No: it isn't good for you, sissy, to get so tired and worried."

CHAPTER XV.

THE PINK-SILK DRESS.

BUT, spite of Teddy's disapproval and his mother's doubts, neither of them could resist the earnestness of Cherry's entreaties, day after day, to be allowed to "go down and see the music in 'Varny's room;" and it finally became quite a regular thing for Teddy, upon his return home, to find his little sister ready shawled and hooded, and waiting for him to accompany her.

As the summer came on, and whole streets-full of his patrons left the city, Giovanni became less regular in his hours of leavings or returning home; often remaining in his room several hours of the day, smoking, sleeping, or training Pantalon in new accomplishments.

So sure as she knew him to be at home, Cherry gave her foster-mother no peace until she had consented to allow her to visit him; and Mrs. Ginniss said to herself, "Sure, and it's no harm the little crather can git uv man nor monkey nor music; an' what's the good uv crossin' her?"

So it finally came about that Cherry spent many more hours in the company of Giovanni, Pantalon, and the organ, than Teddy either knew, or would have liked, had his mother thought fit to tell him.

At first, the conversation between the new friends was carried on in the imperfect English used by both; but, very soon, Giovanni, noticing the facility with which the child adopted an occasional word of Italian, set himself to teach her the language, and succeeded beyond his expectations. Indeed it seemed to him that the soft and liquid accents of the beloved tongue had never sounded to him so sweet beneath Italian skies as now, when they fell from the rosy lips and pure tones of the charming child whom he, with all who approached her, was learning to love with the best love of his nature.

Besides the Italian lessons, Giovanni taught his little pupil to sing several of the popular songs of his native city of Naples, and to perform several of his national dances; watching with an ever-new delight the grace and ease of her movements, and the quickness with which she caught at his every hint and gesture.

Occasionally, Cherry insisted upon making Pantalon join in the dance; and the somewhat sombre face of the Italian would ripple all over with laughter as he watched her efforts to subdue the creature's motions to grace and harmony, and to cultivate in his bestial brain her own innate love of those divine gifts.

"You will never make him dance as if of heaven, as you do, picciola," said he one day; and Cherry suddenly stood still, and, dropping the monkey's paws, came to her teacher's side, asking eagerly, -

"Have you been to heaven too? and did you see me dance there?"

"Padre Johannes says we all came from heaven; so I suppose I did, and perhaps Pantalon also," said the Italian with a comical grimace: "but, if so, I have long forgotten what I saw there. Do you remember heaven, picciola?"

"Yes; I don't now," slowly replied the child with the weary and puzzled look she so often wore. "Sometimes I do. I used to dance; and mamma-that wasn't mammy-was there: but there was a naughty lady that slapped me; and there was a little man-why, it was Pantalon, wasn't it? Did Pantalon eat some cake that I - no, that some one gave him? Oh! I don't know; and I am so tired! I guess I'll go see mammy now, and lie down on the bed."

Giovanni did not try to detain the child, but, after closing the door behind her, remained looking at it as if he still saw the object of his thoughts, while an expression of perplexity and doubt clouded the careless good-humor of his face. Presently, however, it cleared; and, with a significant gesture of the head, he muttered, -

"What then? Is it my business or my fault? Come, Pantalon: we shall sup."

When Cherry appeared the next day in Giovanni's room, it was with as gay and untroubled a face as if no haunting memories had ever vexed her; and Giovanni, who liked her sunny mood much the best, was careful not to awaken any other. He played for her to dance; he sang with her; he told her stories of Italy, and the merry life he had lived there with his wife and child.

"And my little Julietta, like you, loved music and dancing, and sang like the angels," said he, smoothing Cherry's shining curls.

"Did she? Then she sings in heaven, and is happy: and by and by, when we go there, we'll see her; won't we?"

The Italian shook his head.

"You may, picciola; but the good God, if he takes me to heaven, must make me so changed, that Julietta could no longer know me, or I her. We men are not as little maidens."

Then, with a sudden change of mood, the Italian snatched from its case his cherished violin, and drew from it such joyous strains, that the child, clapping her hands, and skipping round the room, cried, -

"It laughs! the music laughs, and makes me laugh too! And Pantalon-see poor Pantalon try to laugh, and he can't!"

Giovanni stopped suddenly, and laid down his violin. A new thought, a sudden plan, had entered his head, and made his breath come quick, and his eyes grow bright. He looked attentively at the child for a moment, and then said, -

"Julietta used to wear such a beautiful dress, and go with me to the houses of rich people to dance; but you dance better than she did, picciola."

"Oh! let me go, and wear a beautiful dress. I don't like this dress a bit!" said Cherry, plucking nervously at the coarse and tawdry calico frock Mrs. Ginniss had thought it quite a triumph to obtain and to make up.

"I have saved two of Julietta's dresses for love of her.

You shall see them," said the Italian; and from the box where he kept his clothes he presently brought a small bundle, and, unfolding it, shook out two little frocks, - one of pink silk, covered with spangles; the other a gay brocade, upon whose white ground tiny rosebuds were dotted in a graceful pattern. Some long silk stockings, and white satin boots with red heels, and blue tassels at the ankle, dropped from the bundle; and from one of the latter Giovanni drew a wreath of crushed and faded artificial roses.

"All these were given her by the beautiful march,sa for whom she was named. Many times we have been to play and dance before her pal zzo; and she, sending for us in, has given the little one a dress or a wreath, or a handful of confetti, or a silver-piece in her hand. It was when the march,sa died that our troubles began; and in three months more the little Julietta followed her, and Steph na (that was my wife) went from me, and - But see, picciola! is it not a pretty dress? Let us put it upon you, and it shall dance the Romaika with you as it once did with her."

Nothing loath, Cherry hastened, with the help of the Italian, to array herself in the pink-silk frock, and to exchange her coarse shoes for the silken hose and satin boots of the little lost Julietta. Although somewhat large, the clothes fitted better than those Cherry had taken off; and when, seizing the violin, Giovanni drew a long, warning note, the little dancer took her position, and pointed her tiny foot with so assured and graceful an air, that the Italian, nodding and smiling, cried with enthusiasm, -

"Ah, ah! See the little Taglioni! Why is she not upon the boards of La Sc la?"

What this might mean Cherry could not guess, nor greatly cared to know. She understood that her friend was pleased, and her little heart beat high with vanity and excitement. She danced as she had never danced before; and at the end, while Giovanni still applauded, and before she had regained her breath, the child was panting, -

"I want to go and dance for the rich ladies, like Julietta used to do, and wear her beautiful dresses, and have a wreath."

"Why not, then?" exclaimed the Italian eagerly. "Only you must never say so to the woman above there or the boy: they will not allow it."

"Won't mammy and Teddy like it? Then I can't go. Oh, dear! Why won't they like it, 'Varny?"

"Because they can't dance, and they don't want you to be different from them; and they will be afraid you will tire yourself. They don't know that it makes you well and happy to dance, and hear music, as it does me to make it. They are not like us, these people above there."

Cherry looked earnestly in his face, and her own suddenly flushed while she replied indignantly, -

"They're real good, 'Varny; and I love them same as I do you and Pantalon. Don't you love them?"

"Oh! but I adore them, picciola; and I like well that you should place me and Pantalon beside them. But surely they do not dance, or love music, as we do."

Cherry shut tight her lips, and shook her head with an uneasy expression.

"Mammy says she don't believe they dance in heaven: and Teddy says it wasn't there I used to learn; for I never went anywhere but to mammy's room since I was borned."

"But they do dance in heaven, and sing, and listen to music; and it is because you came from heaven so little while ago that you remember, and they have forgotten," said Giovanni positively. "And it is right that you should love these things; and it is right that you should go with me, and say nothing to them till we come back. I will ask the good woman that I may take you for a walk in a day or two and I will carry the pretty dress and the violin; and, when we are away from the house, you shall put it on, and we will go and dance for the rich people a little while; and some one shall give you beautiful things, and much money, as they did Julietta; and then we will come home, and bring it all to the mammy, and she will be so happy, and see that it is a good thing, after all, to dance."

"Yes, yes; that will be splendid!" cried Cherry, clapping her hands and jumping up and down. "I will save every bit of the candy, and all the beautiful dresses, and the roses, and every thing, and bring them to mammy."

"And the money, that she may buy bread and clothes and wood, and not have to work so hard for them herself," suggested Giovanni artfully.

"Yes, Teddy gives her money; and she calls him her brave, good boy. So she'll call me too, pretty soon;

won't she?"

"Truly will she; but remember always, picciola, that she nor Teddy must know any thing of this, or they will prevent it all. You won't tell them?"

"No; I won't tell," said Cherry, shuttling her lips very tight, and shaking her head a great many times. "Only we must go very quick, or else I might forget; and, when I opened my mouth, it might jump out before I knew."

"We will go to-morrow if it is fine," said Giovanni, after a moment of consideration; and Cherry, after changing her clothes, returned home so full of mystery and importance, that unless Mrs. Ginniss had been more than usually busy, and Teddy obliged to hurry with his supper and go directly out again, one or the other must have suspected that something very mysterious was working in the mind of their little pet.

CHAPTER XVI.

BEGINNING A NEW LIFE.

As if to favor Giovanni's plot, it chanced, that, in the morning of the next day, Mrs. Ginniss received a sudden summons to the bedside of Ann Dolan, the friend whose advice had led to Teddy's being placed in his present situation.

The messenger had reported that Ann was "very bad wid her heart, an' the life was knocked out intirely, sure:" and Mrs. Ginniss felt herself bound to hasten to the help of her friend, should she still be alive; or to see that she was "waked dacent" if dead. Just as she was wondering if it was best to take Cherry with her, or to leave her locked up alone until her return, Giovanni appeared at the door, his face disposed in its most winning smile, and his manner as respectful as if he had been addressing the march,sa who had been his own and his daughter's patron.

"Will my good neighbor allow that the little girl go for a walk with me this fine morning?" asked he. "I would like to show her the flowers and the swans in the gardens of the city."

"An' will you take the monkey an' the grind-orgin the day?" asked Mrs. Ginniss doubtfully.

"Indeed, no ! I go to a walk to enjoy the fine time, and to see the flowers and the swans," explained Giovanni in his best English, and with a proportion of bows and smiles; while Cherry stood by, her little face full of surprise and mystery, not unmingled with a little shame as she felt that her good mammy was being deceived and misled by the wily Italian.

"Faith, thin, Mr. Jovarny, it's very perlite ye are iver an' always; but I don't jist feel aisy wid the child out uv my sight. Mabbe she'd better wait till night, when Teddy can take her out."

"Oh, let me go, mammy! I want to go with 'Varny, and I'll bring you" -

"Yes; we'll get the pretty flowers to bring to mammy, she would say," interrupted the Italian hastily; and Mrs. Ginniss, looking down at the little anxious face and pleading eyes, found her better judgment suddenly converted into a desire to please her little darling at any rate, and to see her smile again in her own sunny fashion.

"Sure, an' ye shall go, 'vourneen, if it's that bad ye're wantin' it," said she, stooping to take the child in her arms; and, as Cherry kissed her again and again, she added, -

"An' it's well ye don't ask the heart out uv me body; for it's inter yer hand I'd have to give it, colleen bawn."

Giovanni looked on, his half-shut, black eyes glittering, and a wily smile wrinkling his sallow cheek.

"Every one has his day," muttered he in Italian, "Your's to-day, good woman; mine to-morrow."

Half an hour later, Cherry, dressed as neatly as her foster-mother's humble means and taste would allow, and her face glowing with pleasure and excitement, skipped out of the door of the tenement-house, looking like the fairy princess in a pantomime as she suddenly emerges from the hovel where she has been hidden.

Giovanni followed, carrying a bundle, and his violin wrapped in papers. These, he explained to Mrs. Ginniss, were only some matters he had to leave with a friend as he went along; but he should not go into any house, or take the little girl anywhere but for the walk he had mentioned.

"Faix, an' it's mighty ginteel ye are, anyway, Misther Jovarny," said the Irishwoman, watching the pair from the window of her attic as they walked slowly up the street. "But I'm afther wishin' I'd said no whin I said yis. Nor yet I couldn't tell why, more than that Teddy'll be mad to hear she's been wid him. But the b'y hasn't sinse whin it's about the little sisther he's talkin'. He thinks the ground isn't good enough for her to walk on, nor goold bright enough for her to wear."

So saying, Mrs. Ginniss closed the window, and, throwing a little shawl over her head, locked the door, leaving the key underneath, and hurried away to her sick friend, with whom she staid till nearly night.

Giovanni and Cherry, meantime, walked gayly on, chatting, now of the wonderful things about them, now of the yet more wonderful scenes they were to visit. At a confectioner's shop, in a shady by-street, they stopped to rest for a while; and the Italian provided his little guest with ice-creams, cakes, and candies, to her heart's content.

"I like these better than potatoes and pork-meat. I used to eat these in heaven," said the little girl, pausing to look at a macaroon, and then finishing it with a relish.

The Italian laughed.

"Canary-birds do not feed with crows," said he. "When we are rich, picciola, you shall never eat worse than this."

"Shall we be rich soon, 'Varny?" asked the child eagerly.

"Upon the moment almost, if you will dance and laugh, and look so pretty as you can, always."

"But we needn't stop to be very rich before we go and carry some of the nice things to mammy," rejoined Cherry anxiously.

"No, no, indeed! We will but make a little turn in the country, and come back princes. But mind you this, picciola: I am to be your father now, or all the same; and I shall tell every one that you are my own little girl: so you must never say, 'Not so.'"

"But mammy said my father was dead, and Teddy said so too. He was Michael darlint."

"I doubt not that Signor Michaelli died, and has gone to glory; but I strangely doubt if he were thy father, picciola," said the Italian with a grave smile. "However that may be, forget that you have ever had other father than me, and call me so always: 'Mio padre,' you must say, and no more 'Varny. Also, too, you must speak in Italian, as I shall to you; and never, as you do now, in English."

"But mammy and Teddy don't know Italian," said Cherry, beginning to look a little troubled.

"'In Rome, do as the Romans do.' When you are again with the woman and boy, speak as they speak: with me, speak as I speak."

Giovanni said this more decidedly than he had ever spoken before, and Cherry looked quickly up at him.

"Is that the way you talk because you want to make believe you are my father?" asked she.

A sudden smile shot across the Italian's face, lighting its dark features like a gleam of sunshine sweeping across a pine-clad mountain-land.

"Shame were it to me, dear little heart, if to be thy father were to make thee less happy than thou hast been with those others," said he softly in Italian, and using the form of address, which, in almost every language but the English, marks a different and more tender relation from that indicated by the more formal plural pronoun.

"You will be happy with me if we do not soon revisit these people we leave behind?" asked he.

The child's eyes grew large and deep as she fixed them upon his face, and presently asked, -

"Are you going with me to try to find heaven again?"

"Perhaps: who knows, picciola? The heaven you miss

may come to you more easily if you go to seek it. At any rate, I will carry thee no farther from it. But come: we must get to our journey."

Leaving the confectioner's shop, Giovanni lingered no longer in the gay streets, or even upon the fresh green grass of the Common, where Cherry would have staid to play all day. Hurrying across it, and through some crowded streets, the Italian entered a large station-house, where stood the train of cars, already half filled with passengers; while the engine, puffing and panting with impatience, seemed unwilling to wait a moment longer.

Leaving Cherry in the ladies' room, the Italian bought his tickets, and reclaimed from the baggage-room, where he had left it, his organ, with Pantalon chained to the top of it. Then, calling the child, he hurried with her into the cars, and selected a seat behind the door, in the evident wish of being seen as little as possible.

"Now, then, Ciriegia mia, we go to seek our fortune," said he, as the train left the station, and began to rush through the suburbs of the city, scattering little dirty children, vagrant dogs, leisurely pigs, and dawdling carriages driven by honest old ladies, from its track.

Cherry never had ridden in the cars before; and she clung tight to the sleeve of her companion, afraid to move, or even to speak, until he laughingly asked, -

"It does not fear, the poor little one, does it?"

"No, I guess not, 'Varny," replied the child doubtfully; but the Italian sharply said, -

"What is this 'Varny you say? I am mio padre."

"I forgot. Won't I tumble out of this carriage, my father, it goes so quick?"

"Fear nothing, figlia mia. You are safe with me and with Pantalon," said the Italian, drawing the little girl close to his side; while the monkey, crouching upon the organ at their feet, chattered his own promises of protection and comfort.

With 'Toinette, to live was to love and trust; and, clinging close to her new guardian's side, she laid her little shining head upon his breast, clinging with one hand to the lappet of his coat; and, laughing down at Pantalon, she fell presently asleep.

At night the Italian left the train, and took lodgings at a hotel near the centre of a large town. His little charge-tired, hungry, and sleepy-was very glad to have supper, and to be allowed to go to bed, where she slept soundly until summoned the next morning by Giovanni, who brought her some breakfast with his own hands, and, placing it upon the table, laid a bundle of clothes beside it.

"Rise and eat, carissima," said be gayly; "and then make thyself as beautiful as the morning with these fine clothes. See, here are roses from the garden for a wreath! They are better than the others. When thou art ready, come out to me."

He left the room; and 'Toinette, rising, made a hasty breakfast; and then, putting on the brocade-silk dress, and placing upon her head the wreath Giovanni had twisted of natural flowers for her, she peeped into the glass, and laughed aloud at the fanciful and beautiful image that met her eyes.

"I am glad I look so pretty," murmured she, with an innocent delight at her own beauty, that was not vanity, although, it might, if untrained, lead to it.

"Come, Ciriegia, are you never ready?" called Giovanni from the other side of the door; and Cherry, running to open it, exclaimed in Italian, -

"Oh, see, my father! am I not beautiful?"

"Truly so; but you should not say it, bambina. The charm of a maiden is her modesty," said the Italian gravely.

"But, if it is true, why mustn't I say so?" asked Cherry positively.

"Many things that we know are never to be said, Ciriega. But come, now: you are to dance first for these people, and they will make no charge for our beds and the miserable provender they have given us."

As he spoke, Giovanni led the way to the lower hall of the hotel, where a number of men were lounging, smoking, or talking; while through the open doors of the parlor and office were to be seen some ladies and gentlemen, idling away the hour after breakfast, before proceeding to their business, their journey, or their amusement.

Placing himself in the center of the hall, Giovanni, with a bow to the company, played a little prelude, and then struck into the lively strains of the cachuca.

Cherry, who had stood looking at him, her head slightly bent, her lips apart, eyes and ears alert to catch the signal to begin, pointed her little foot at the precise moment, and, holding her dress in the tips of her slender fingers, slid into the movement with a grace and accuracy never to be attained except by vigorous practice, or a temperament as sensitive to time and tune, limbs as supple, and impulses as graceful, as were those of this gifted and unfortunate child.

"See there! - the poor little thing!" exclaimed one of the ladies, who came to the door of the drawing-room to see the performance.

"How can you say poor little thing?" asked another. "Don't you see how she enjoys it herself? That smile is not the artificial grimace of a ballet-dancer; and no eyes ever sparkled so joyously to order."

"Perhaps she does enjoy it; but all the more 'Poor little thing!' say I," rejoined the first speaker, adding thoughtfully, "What sort of training for a woman is that?"

"Oh, well! but it is very pretty to see her; and she would probably be running in the streets, or doing worse, if she did not dance; and so little as she is! It is equal to the theatre."

The speaker drew out her purse as she spoke, and carelessly threw a dollar-bill towards the child, who had finished her dance, and stood looking round with an innocent smile, as if asking for applause rather than reward.

"Go and take it, carissima; and then hold your hand to the others; each will give you something," said

Giovanni in a low voice.

"How much we shall have to carry to mammy!" exclaimed the child eagerly; and, as she gathered in her harvest, she chattered away, always in Italian, -

"And more, and more, and more! O my father! how many cents they give me! What nice people they are! Let me dance some more for them; and let Pantalon come down, and let them see him."

" No, no, child! These are not of those who would care for Pantalon. While you rest by and by, I shall take him and the organ, and go about the streets; but your little feet are worth many Pantalons to me. Come, we will give them the tarantella as they have done so well."

Skipping to his side, with a childish grace more attractive than the studied movements of the most accomplished actress, Cherry stuffed the proceeds of her first attempt into the pocket of her guardian, and then, throwing herself into position, went through the wild and grotesque movements of the tarantella, with a life and freshness that drew from the spectators a burst of applause and surprise.

"That will do. We must not give them too much at once, lest the wonder come to an end. Make the pretty kiss of the hand, figlia mia, and run up the stairs to your own little room."

Cherry obeyed, calling back, as she disappeared, "Tell them I will dance some more for them by and by if they want me to."

CHAPTER XVII.

WHOLESALE MURDER.

IN the course of that day, Giovanni and his little danseuse visited all the principal public places in the town, and also several of the best private houses; and, at all, the performances of the child called forth the surprise, delight, and admiration of those who witnessed them. Nor were more substantial proofs of their approval wanting; so that at night, when Giovanni counted up his gains, he found them so large, that he cried, while embracing poor weary little Cherry, -

"O blessed, blessed moment when thou didst cross my path, Ciriegia carissima!"

"Now can't we go home to mammy? I am so tired, and my head feels sick!" moaned the child, laying the poor aching little head upon his shoulder.

Giovanni looked down at the pale face, and, meeting the languid eyes, felt a pang of conscience and pity.

"Thou art tired, bambȷna povera mia," said he kindly. "Another day, we will be more careful. Lie down now, and sleep for a while. We go again in the steam-carriage to-night."

Cherry climbed upon the bed without reply, and in a moment was fast asleep. The Italian drew the coverings about her, and stooped to kiss the pale cheek, where showed already a dark circle beneath the eye, and a painful contraction at the corner of the mouth.

"Poveracita!" murmured he. "But soon we will have money enough to go home to the father-land, and then all will be well with her as with me."

Three hours later, he came to arouse the child, and prepare her to renew the journey.

"Oh, I am so tired! I want to sleep some more so bad, 'Varny!-no, my father, I mean. I don't want to go somewhere," said she piteously, closing her eyes, and struggling to lay her head again upon the pillow. Giovanni hesitated for a moment; and then, never knowing that the decision was one of life and death, the question of a whole future career, he determined to pursue his plan in spite of that plaintive entreaty, and, hastily wrapping a shawl about the child, took her in his arms, and carried her down stairs. The organ and Pantalon waited in the hall below; and Giovanni, setting Cherry upon her feet, shouldered the organ and, taking the little girl by the hand, led her out into the quiet street, where lay the light of a full moon, making the night more beautiful than day. Cherry's drowsy eyes flew wide open; and, looking up in Giovanni's face with eager joy, she cried, -

"Oh! now we're going back to heaven; aren't we, my father? It was bright and still like this in heaven; and I saw a star, and-and then the naughty lady struck me" -

"Peace, little one! I know not of what you speak, nor any thing of heaven," said the Italian in a troubled voice; and the child, hurrying along at his side, raised her face silently to the summer sky, seeking there, perhaps, the answer to the questions forever stirring in her struggling soul.

A little later, and the swift train, flying through the sleeping land, bore away the travellers; while Giovanni, settling himself as easily as possible, laid the head of his little Ciriegia upon his breast, tenderly smoothed down her silky curls, and laid his hand upon the bright eyes, that frightened him with the intensity of their gaze.

"Sleep, carissima mia, sleep," murmured he soothingly; "sleep, and forget thy weariness and thy memories."

"I can't sleep now, my father. It seems to me that we are going to heaven; and I want to be awake to see-the lady" -

The words faltered, and died upon her lips. The beautiful image of her mother, fading slowly from her memory, seemed already a vision so vague, that to name it were to lose it, - an idea too precious and too impalpable to put in words. The past, with all its love and joy and beauty, was becoming for our 'Toinette what we may fancy heaven is to a little baby, whose solemn eyes and earnest gaze seem forever attempting to recall the visions of celestial beauty it has left for the pale, sad skies, and mournful sounds of earth.

On rushed the train through the quiet night, waking wild echoes in the woods, and leaving them to whisper themselves again to sleep when it had passed; lighting dark valleys that the moonlight left unlighted, with its whirling banner of flame and sparks, and its hundred blazing windows; moving across the holy calm of midnight like some strange and troubled vision, some ugly nightmare, that for the moment changes peace and rest to horror and affright, and then passes again to the dim and ghostly Dreamland, whose frontier crowds our daily life on every hand, and whence forever peep and beckon the mysteries that perplex and haunt the human mind.

On and on and on, through misty lowland and shadowy wood, and over shining rivers, and through sleeping hamlets, and winding, snake-like, between great round hills and along deep mountain-gorges, until the wild, bright eyes that watched beneath Cherry's matted curls grew soft and dim; and at last the white lids fell, and the curve of the sad lips relaxed beneath the kiss of God's mildest messenger to man, - the spirit of sleep.

As for Giovanni, he long had slumbered heavily; and even Pantalon, whose bright eyes were seldom known to close, was now curled up beneath the organ-covering, dreaming, perhaps, of the nut-groves and spice-islands where he had once known liberty and youth.

Just then it came, - a crash as if heaven and earth had met; a wild, deep cry, made up of all tones of human agony and fright; the shriek of escaping steam; the rending and splintering of wood and iron; destruction, terror, pain, and death, all mingled in one awful moment. Then those who had escaped unhurt began the sad and terrible task of withdrawing from the ruin the maimed and bleeding bodies of those who yet lived, the crushed remains and fragments of those who had been killed in the moment of the encounter: and, in all the bewildering confusion of the scene, none had eyes for the little childish figure, that, hurled from the splintered car, lay for a while stunned and shaken among the soft grass where it had fallen, and then, staggering to its feet, fled wildly away into the dim forest-land.

CHAPTER XVIII.

DORA DARLING.

THE sun was setting upon the day succeeding that of the great railroad accident, that, for weeks, filled the whole land with horror and indignation, when a young girl, driving rapidly along a country-road at a point about five miles distant from the scene of the disaster, met a child walking slowly toward her, whose disordered dress, bare head, and wild, sweet face, attr-acted her attention and curiosity.

Checking her spirited horse with some difficulty, the young girl looked back, and found that the child had stopped, and stood watching her.

"See here, little girl!" called she. "Are you lost? Is any thing the matter with you?"

The child fixed her solemn eyes upon the face of the questioner, but made no answer.

"Come here, sissy! I want to talk to you; and I can't turn round to come to you. Come here!"

The little girl slowly obeyed the kind command, and stood presently beside the wagon, her pale face upraised, her startled eyes intently fixed upon the clear and honest ones bent to meet them.

"What is your name, little girl?"

"Sunshine," said the child vaguely; and her eyes dropped from the face of her questioner to fix themselves upon the far horizon, where hung already the evening-star, pale and trembling, as it had hung upon the evening of 'Toinette Legrange's birthday ten months before. Was it a sudden association with the star and the hour that had suggested to the heart of the desolate child this name, so long forgotten, once so appropriate, now so strange and sad?

"Sunshine?" replied the young girl wonderingly. "You don't look like it a bit. Where do you belong? and where are you going?"

The child's eyes travelled back from Dreamland, and rested wistfully upon the kind face above her.

"I don't know," said she sadly. "I want to go to heaven; but I've forgot the way."

"To heaven! You poor little thing, have you no home short of that?"

"I don't know. I wish I had some water."

"You had better jump into the wagon, and come home with me, Sunshine, if that is your name. Something has got to be done for you right away."

The child, still looking at her in that strange and solemn manner, asked suddenly, -

"Who are you?"

"I? Oh! I'm Dora Darling; and I live about five miles from here. Jump in quick; for It is growing dark, and we must be at home for supper."

As she spoke, she leaned down, and gave a hand to the little girl, who mechanically took it, and clambered into the carriage. Dora lifted her to the seat, and held her there, with one arm about her waist, saying kindly,-

"Hug right up to me, you poor little thing! and hold on tight. We'll be at home in half an hour, or less. - Now, Pope!"

The impatient horse, feeling the loosened rein, and hearing his own name, darted away at speed; whirling the light wagon along so rapidly, that the child clung convulsively to her new protector, murmuring, -

"I guess I shall spill out of this, and get kilt."

"Oh, no, you won't, Sunshine! I shall hold you in. You're not Irish, are you?"

"What's that?"

"Why, Irish, you know. You said 'kilt' just now, instead of 'killed,' as we do."

The child made no reply; but her head drooped upon Dora's shoulder yet more heavily, and her eyes closed.

"Are you sick, little girl? or only tired?" asked Dora, looking anxiously down into the colorless face, over which the evening breeze was gently strewing the tangled curls, as if to hide it from mortal view, while the poor, worn, spirit fled away to peace and rest.

"Sunshine!" exclaimed Dora, gently moving the heavy

head that still drooped lower and lower, until now the face was hidden from view.

"She has fainted!" said Dora, looking anxiously about her. No house and no person were in sight, nor any stream or pond of water; and the young girl decided that the wisest course would be to drive home as rapidly as possible, postponing all attempt to revive her little patient until her arrival there.

Without checking the horse, she dragged from under the seat a quilted carriage-robe, and spread it in the bottom of the wagon, arranging a paper parcel as a pillow. Then, laying poor Sunshine upon this extemporized couch, she took off her own light shawl, and covered her; leaving exposed only the face, white and lovely as the marble statue recumbent upon a little maiden's tomb.

"Now, Pope!" cried Dora, with one touch of the whip upon the glossy haunch of the powerful beast, who, at sound of that clear voice, neighed reply, and darted forward at the rate of twelve good miles an hour; so that, in considerably less than the promised time, Dora skilfully turned the corner from the road into a green country lane, and, a few moments after, stopped before the door of an old-fashioned one-story farm-house, painted red, with a long roof sloping to the ground at the back, an open well with a sweep and bucket, and a diamond-paned dairy-window swinging to and fro in the faint breeze. Around the irregular door-stone, the grass grew close and green; while nodding in at the window, and waving from the low eaves, and clambering upon the roof, a tangle of white and sweet-brier roses, of woodbine and maiden's-bower, lent a rare grace to the simple home, and loaded the air with a cloud of delicate perfume.

A young man, lounging upon the doorstep, started to his feet as the wagon came dashing up the lane, and was going to open the gate of the barn-yard; but Dora stopped before the open door, and called to him, -

"Karl! Come here, please."

"Certainly. I was running out of the way for fear of being ground to powder beneath your chariot-wheels; for I said to myself, 'Surely the driving is as the driving of Jehu, the son of Nimshi.'"

"I shouldn't have driven so fast; but-see here!"

She pulled away the shawl as she spoke, and showed to the young man, who now stood beside the carriage, the still inanimate form of the little waif at her feet.

"Phew! What's that? and where did you get it?"

"A little girl that I met; lost, I think. I took her into the buggy, and then she fainted, and I laid her down," rapidly explained Dora; adding, as she raised the little figure in her arms, -

"Take her in, and lay her on the bed in the rosy-room."

"Poor little thing! She's not dead, is she, Dora?" asked the young man softly, as he took the child in his arms and entered the house, followed by Dora.

"Oh, no! I think not; only fainted. I suppose there's hot water, for a bath, in the kitchen."

As she spoke, they entered the sitting-room, - a cool, shady apartment, with a great beam crossing the ceilings, and deep recesses to the windows, with seats in them.

At the farther side, Dora threw open the door of a little bedroom, whose gay-papered walls and flowered chintz furniture, not to speak of a great sweet-brier bush tapping and scratching at the window, with all its thousand sharp little fingers, gave it a good right to be called the rosy-room. Dora hastily drew away the bright counterpane, and nodded to Karl, who laid the little form he carried tenderly upon the bed.

At this moment, another door into the sitting-room opened; and a girl, somewhat older than Dora, put in her head, looked about for a moment, and then came curiously toward the door of the rosy-room.

"I thought I heard you, Dora," said she. "What are you doing in here? Why! - who's that?"

"O Kitty! can you warm a little of that broth we had for dinner, to give her? She's just starved, I really believe. And is there any ammonia in the house? - smelling-salts, you know. Didn't aunt have some?" asked Dora rapidly.

"I believe so. But where did you get this child? Who is she?"

"Run, Kitty, and get the salts first. We'll tell you afterward."

"What shall I do, Dora?" interposed the young man; and Kitty ran upon her errand, while Dora promptly replied, -

"Open the window, and bring some cold water; and then a little wine or brandy, if we have any."

"Enough for this time, at any rate," said Karl, hurrying away, and returning with both water and wine just as Kitty appeared with the salts; but it was Dora who applied the remedies, and with a skill and steadiness that would have seemed absolutely marvellous to one unacquainted with the young girl's previous history and training.

"She's coming to herself. You'd better both go out of sight, and let her see only me. Kitty, will you look to the broth?" whispered Dora; and Karl, taking his sister by the sleeve, led her out, softly closing the door after them.

"Dora does like to manage, I must say. Now, do tell me at last who this child is, and where she came from, and what's going to be done with her," said Kitty as they reached the kitchen. "Why shouldn't she like to manage, when she can do it so well? I can tell you, Miss Kitty, if she hadn't man aged to some purpose on one occasion, you wouldn't have had a brother to-day to plague you."

The girl's dark eyes grew moist as she turned them upon him, saying warmly, -

"I know it, Charley; and I would love her for that, if nothing else: but I can't forget she's almost a year younger than I am, and ought not to expect to take the lead in every thing."

"Pooh, Kit-cat, don't be ridiculous! Get the soup, and put it over the fire; and I'll tell you all I know about our little guest."

"I let the fire go down when tea was ready, it is so warm to-night," said Kitty, raking away the ashes in the open fireplace, and drawing together a few coals.

"That will do. You only want a cupful or so at once, and you can warm it in a saucepan over those coals."

"Dear me! I guess I know how to do as much as that without telling. Sit down now, and let me hear about the child."

So Karl dropped into the wooden arm-chair beside the hearth, and told his story; while Kitty, bustling about, warmed the broth, moved the tea-pot and covered dish of toast nearer to the remnant of fire, waved a few flies off the neat tea-table, and drove out an intrusive chicken, who, before going to roost, was evidently determined to secure a dainty bit for supper from the saucer of bread and milk set in the corner for pussy.

"If the broth is ready, I'll take it in," said Karl, as his sister removed it from the fire.

"Well, here it is; and do tell Dora to come to supper, or at least come yourself. I want to get cleared away some time."

"I'll tell her," said Karl briefly, as he took the bowl of broth, set it in a plate, and laid a silver spoon beside it.

"How handy he is! just like a woman," said Kitty to herself as her brother left the room; and then, going out into the sink-room, she finished washing and putting away the "milk-things," - a process interrupted by the arrival of Dora with her little charge.

CHAPTER XIX.

A CHAMBER OF MEMORIES.

"How is she now, Dora?" asked Karl, softly opening the door of the rosy-room.

"Better. You can come in if you want to. Have you got the broth?"

"Yes: here it is."

"That's nice. Now hold her up, please, this way, while I feed her. See, little Sunshine! here is some nice broth for you. Take a little, won't you?"

The pale lips slightly opened, and Dora deftly slipped the spoon between them. The effect was instantaneous; and, as the half-starved child tasted and smelled the nourishing food, she opened wide her eyes, and, fixing them upon the cup, nervously worked her lips, and half extended her poor little hands, wasted and paled by even two days of privation and fatigue.

"I tell you what, Dora, this child has had a mighty narrow chance of it," said Karl aside, as Dora patiently administered the broth, waiting a moment between each spoonful.

"Yes," replied she softly. "I am so glad I met her! it was a real providence."

"For her?"

"For me as much," returned Dora simply. "It is so pleasant to be able to do something again!"

"You miss your wounded and invalid soldiers, and find it very dull here," said Karl quickly, as he glanced sharply into the open face of the young girl.

"Hush, Karl! don't talk now: it will disturb her. Is tea ready?"

"Yes, and Kitty sent word for you to come. Run along, and I will stay with the chick till you come back."

"No: I can't leave her yet. You go to supper, and perhaps, when you are done, I will leave you with her; or Kitty can stay, and I will clear away."

"Won't you let me stay now?" asked the young man hesitatingly.

"No. Here, take the bowl, and run along."

"'Just as you say, not as I like,' I suppose," said Karl, laughing; and, taking the bowl, he went softly out.

"Now, little girl, you feel better, don't you?" asked Dora cheerily, as she laid the heavy head back upon the pillow, and tenderly smoothed away the tangled hair.

"Si, signora," murmured Giovanni's pupil.

"What's that? I don't know what you mean. Say it again, won't you?"

But the child only fixed her dreamy eyes upon the face of the questioner, with no effort at reply; and then the lids began slowly to close.

"Now, before you go to sleep, Sunshine, I am going to take you up stairs, and put you in my own bed, because I sha'n't want to leave you alone to-night; and no one sleeps here. Wait till I fold this shawl round you, and then pull your arms about my neck. There: now we'll go."

She lifted the child as she spoke, and carried her again into the front entry, and up the square staircase to a cottage-chamber with white, scoured floor, common pine furniture, the cheapest of white earthern toilet-sets, and nothing of expense or luxury to be found within its four whitewashed walls, and yet a room that gave one a feeling of satisfaction and peace not always inhabiting far wider and more costly chambers: for the little bed was artistically composed, and covered with snow-white dimity, as was the table between the windows, and the cushion of the wooden rocking-chair; while curtains of the same material, escaped from their tri-colored fastenings, floated in upon the soft breeze like great sails, or the draperies of twilight spirits departing before mortal presence.

In the fireplace stood a large pitcher, filled with common flowers, fresh and odorous; and upon the high mantle-shelf, and all around the room, was disposed a collection of the oddest ornaments that ever decked a young girl's sleeping-chamber. Among them we will but pause to mention two muskets, the one bent, the other splintered at the stock; four swords, each more or less disabled; an officer's sash; three sets of shoulder-straps; a string of army-buttons, each with a name written upon a strip of paper, and tied to the eye; two or three dozen bone rings, of more or less elaborate workmanship, disposed upon the branches of a little tree carved of pine; a large collection of crosses, hearts, clasped hands, dogs'-heads, and other trinkets, in bone, some white, and some stained black; a careful drawing of a crooked and grotesque old negro, in a frame of carved wood; and, finally, a suit of clothes hung against the wall in the position of a human figure, consisting of a jaunty scarlet cap, with a little flag of the United States fastened to the front by an army-badge; a basque, skirt, and trousers of blue cloth, with a worn and clumsy pair of boots below. From a belt fastened across the waist hung a little barrel, a flask, and by a wide ribbon of red, white and blue, a boat-swain's silver whistle.

Singular ornaments, we have said, for a young girl's sleeping-room, and yet, in this case, touchingly appropriate and harmonious: for they were the keepsakes given to the daughter of the regiment by the six hund-red brave men, who each loved her as his own; they were the mementoes of a year in Dora Darling's life, of such vivid experiences that it threatened to make all the years that should come after pale and vapid in comparison.

Just now, however, all the girl's strong sympathies were aroused and glowing; and as she tenderly cared for the child so strangely placed within her hands, and finally laid her to sleep in the clover-scented sheets of the fair white bed, she felt happier than she had for months before.

A light tap at the door, and Kitty entered.

"I'll stay with her while you go and eat supper. Charles said he'd come; but I'd like well enough to sit down a little while. My! - she's pretty-looking; isn't she?"

"The prettiest child I ever saw," replied Dora, with her usual decision; and then the two girls stood for a moment looking down at the delicate little face, where, since the food and broth Dora had administered, a bright color showed itself upon the cheeks and lips; while the short, thick curls, carefully brushed, clustered around the white forehead, defining its classic shape, and contrasting with its pearly tints.

"Who can she be?" asked Kitty in a whisper.

"Some sort of foreigner, - French maybe, or perhaps Italian. She has talked considerably since I gave her the broth; but I can't make out a word she says. She spoke English when I first met her; but I don't believe she knows much of it," said Dora thoughtfully.

"There is something sewed up in a little bag, and hung round her neck," added she, "just such as some of our foreign volunteers had, - a sort of charm, you know, to keep them from being struck by the evil eye. That shows that her friends must have been foreigners."

"Yes; and Catholics too, likely enough," said Kitty rather contemptuously; adding, after a pause, -

"Well, you go down, and I'll sit by her a while. If she sleeps as sound as this, I don't suppose I need stay a great while. There's the supper-dishes to do."

"I'll wash them, of course; but, if you want to come down, you might leave the door open at the head of the back stairs, and I should hear if she called or cried. And, now I think of it, I have a letter to show Karl and you. I got it at the post-office."

"From Mr. Brown?" asked Kitty quickly.

"No, from a Mr. Burroughs; a man I never heard of in my life till to-day. But come down in a few minutes, and I will read it to you."

"Well, don't read it till I come."

"No: I won't." And Dora quietly went out of the room, leaving Kitty to swing backward and forward in the white-cushioned rocking-chair, her dark eyes wandering half contemptuously, half enviously, over Dora's collection of treasures, with an occasional glance at the sleeping child.

CHAPTER XX.

A LETTER AND AN OFFER.

IN the kitchen, Dora found Karl waiting for her; and, while she eat her supper with the healthy relish of a young and vigorous creature, she gave her cousin an account of all the circumstances attending her meeting with the little girl, whom she described again as a foreigner, and probably French.

"And what's to be done with her, Dora?" asked the young man rather gravely, when she had finished.

"Why, when she is well enough to tell who she is, and where she came from, - that is, if she can talk English at all, - we can return her to her friends; or, if they are not to be discovered, I will keep her myself. That is,"- and the young girl paused suddenly, the blood rushing to her face, as she added, - " that is, if you and Kitty are willing. It is your house, not mine; though I'm afraid I am apt to forget."

Karl looked at her reproachfully.

"When I brought you here, Dora Darling, I brought you home; and when my mother died, not yet a year ago, did she not bid us live together as brother and sisters, in love and harmony?"

"Yes; but" -

"But what, Dora?"

"I am afraid sometimes I behave too much as if it were my own house," faltered Dora.

"And so it is your own house, just as it is my own and Kitty's own. Have either of us ever made you feel that there was any difference, or that you had less right here than we?"

Dora made no reply; and, while Karl still waited for one the staircase-door opened softly, and Kitty appeared.

"The child is fast asleep," said she: "so I thought I would come down and hear the letter."

"What letter?" asked Karl a little impatiently.

"Oh! I haven't told you. Here it is."

And Dora drew from her pocket, and held toward him, a large white envelope, boldly directed to "Miss DORA DARLING, care of Capt. Charles Windsor"

"That's nonsense. I have beaten my sword into a ploughshare now, and am only plain mister," said Capt. Karl, glancing at the direction.

"Well, read the letter, do; I'm dying to hear it," said Kitty impatiently; and her brother, with an affectation of extreme haste, unfolded the thick, large sheet of note-paper and read aloud: -

"Having been requested to communicate with Miss Darling upon a matter of importance, Mr. Thomas

Burroughs will do himself the honor of calling upon her, probably in the afternoon of Thursday, Aug. 25. "CINCINNATI, Aug. 20."

"Thursday, 25th! Why, that is to-morrow!" exclaimed Karl, as he finished reading.

"Dated Cincinnati, you see! It is some message from Mr. Brown. He lives about twenty miles from Cincinnati," said Kitty eagerly.

"I don't think so. Why should Mr. Brown send a message when he writes to me so often?" replied Dora with simplicity.

"I should think he did. I suppose you expected a letter this afternoon, and that was what made you so bent upon driving to town in all the heat."

"It wasn't very hot, and you know we needed these things from the shop."

"From the grocery-store, do you mean?" asked Kitty sharply.

"Yes."

"Why can't you talk as we do, then? You have been here long enough now, I should think."

"Because she knows how to talk better, Miss Kit," said Karl good-humoredly. "Calling a shop a store is an Americanism, like calling a station-house a d‚p"t, or trousers pants."

"Well, I thought we were Americans, Dora and all,"

retorted Kitty.

"Mercy, child! don't let us plunge from philology into ethnology. I prefer to speculate upon Mr. Thomas Burroughs. Who is he? and what does he want of our Dora?"

"To marry her, I suppose, or to ask her to marry Mr. Brown," snapped Kitty.

"Perhaps he wants to ask my good word toward marrying you," suggested Dora, coloring deeply.

"No such good luck as that, eh, Kitty?" said Karl with a laugh.

"Good luck! I'm sure I'm in no hurry to be married; and, though I haven't had Dora's chances of seeing all sorts of men, I dare say I shall get as good a husband in the end," replied Kitty loftily.

"But, contemplating for one moment the idea that it may not be an offer of marriage that Mr. Thomas Burroughs means by a 'matter of importance,' let us consider what else it can be," said Karl with a quizzical smile.

"Perhaps he wants your ideas upon the campaign in Western Virginia, and a report of the general's real motives and intentions," suggested Dora gayly.

"Perhaps he wants to engage his winter's butter; though I don't believe Dora is the one to ask about that," said Kitty.

"Now, Kitty! I'm sure I made up the last, and you said

it was as nice as you could do yourself."

"Yes; but you turned all the buttermilk into the pig's pail instead of saving it for biscuits."

"So I did. Well, as dear old Picter used to say, 'What's the use ob libin' if you've got trew larnin'?'"

"O Dora! how can you, how can you!-you cruel, cruel girl, how can you speak of him!" cried Kitty in a passion of anger and grief; and, pushing back her chair so violently as to upset it, she rushed out of the room.

"Oh, I am so sorry!" exclaimed Dora in great distress; and would have followed her, had not Karl held her back.

"Don't go, dear; it will be of no use: she will not let you into her room. Poor Kitty! she loved her mother so passionately, and her nature is so intense! We must make great excuses, Dora, for our sister's little inequalities of temper: I think her great loss is at the bottom of all."

Dora looked thoughtful, and presently said slowly, "I know it, Karl; but it does seem to me rather unjust that she should hate poor Pic's memory so bitterly even now. He did not know any more than I that he had small-pox when he came back that time from New York; and when Kitty told him that Aunt Lucy had taken it from him, and was very sick, he felt so badly, that I think it prevented his getting well."

"O Dora, don't say that! Kitty could not have blamed him openly."

"I don't know what she said; but, from that day, he grew worse, and died without being able to bid me good-by, - Pic, who brought me away from those cruel people, and cared for me as if I had been his child. O dear, dear old Pic!"

She did not cry; she very seldom did: but she clasped her hands tightly together, and looked so white and wild, that Karl came to her, and, taking her in his arms, would have soothed and caressed her like a little child, had not she repulsed him.

"Please not, dear Karl! I must bear my griefs alone for I am alone in all the world."

It was the bitterest sentence Dora had ever spoken, and her cousin looked at her in dismay.

"If Picter could have given the disease to me instead of to aunt, and he and I could have journeyed on together into another world as we had through this, and left your mother to Kitty and you!" continued Dora; while in her eyes, and about her white lips, quivered a passion of grief far beyond any tears, - far beyond, thank God! any grief that eyes and lips so young are often called to express. And as it rose and swelled in her girl heart, and shook her strong young soul, Dora uttered in one word all the bitterness of her orphaned life.

"Mother!" cried she, and clinched her hands above the sharp pain that seemed to suffocate her, the pain we call heart-ache, and might sometimes more justly call heart-break.

Karl looked at her, and his gay young face grew

strong, and full of meaning. He folded her again in his arms, and said, -

"Dora, I had not meant to speak yet; but I cannot see you so, or hear you say such words. Do not you know, cousin, that there is nothing in all the world I love like you; and that, while I live, you can never be alone; and, while I have a home, you can never want one, or be other than its head and centre? Dora, marry me, and I will make you forget all other loves in the excess of mine." Dora allowed her head to droop upon his shoulder, and a sudden sense of peace and rest fell temptingly upon her spirit.

"Dora, Dora Darling always, even when you are all my Dora!" whispered Karl; but Dora released herself from his arms, and stood upright. Her face was strong again now, although very white; and she said, -

"Thank you, cousin. You are good and kind, as you always have been, and I am glad you love me as I love you; but what else you have said we will forget. I am too young to think of such things, and you will not feel so to-morrow or next day. Be my brother, as you have been, and let me be sister to you and Kitty, as aunt told us. I wish I could make Kitty love me."

The young man would have persisted; but Dora, gravely shaking her head, said, -

"Karl dear, you only distress me, and I want to be quiet. Do not speak of this again for at least another year, and then, perhaps, you will not want to."

"But in a year I may, if I do want to?" asked Karl eagerly.

"I don't want to say that; for I don't know that I should want you to then," said Dora, with such exquisite simplicity, that the young man laughed outright, and said, -

"But you don't know that you sha'n't, do you, darling Dorelle?"

"I didn't say so."

"No; but - Well, I won't insist; only I shall put down the date. Let me see: Aug. 24, isn't it?"

He took out his note-book, wrote a few words, and, glancing at Dora with a suppressed smile, put it away again. Then, more seriously, he took her hand, saying,-

"Only remember one thing, Dora; and that is, whatever may come in the future, this house is your home as long as it is ours; and, while I live, there is always some one who loves you best of all God's creatures."

CHAPTER XXI.

GIOVANNI'S ROOM.

"OCHONE! an' it's weary work climbin' thim stairs," groaned Mrs. Ginniss, pausing upon the landing outside the organ-grinder's door.

"An' mabbe she's wid him still. Anyway, I'll see, and save the coomin' down agin."

With these words, Mrs. Ginniss gave a modest rap upon the door, and, as it remained unanswered, a somewhat louder one, calling at the same time, -

"Misther Jovarny! Misther Jovarny, I say! Is it out yees still are?"

The question remaining unanswered, the good woman waited no longer, but, climbing the remaining flight of stairs took the key of her room from the shelf in Teddy's closet where it had been left, and unlocked the door.

"Cherry, darlint, be ye widin?" asked she, throwing it open; and then, recollecting herself, added, -

"An' sure how could she, be, widout she kim in trew the kayhole? But, blissid Vargin! where would they be all the day long?"

So saying, Mrs. Ginniss threw up the window, and

looked anxiously down the street in the direction where Giovanni and Cherry had that morning disappeared.

Nothing was to be seen of them; but, just turning the corner, came Teddy, his straw-hat pushed back upon his forehead, and his steps slow and undecided. He was thinking wearily, as he often thought of late, that the time had come when he could no longer withhold his little sister from the friends to whom she really belonged; and it was not alone the heat of the August night that brought the great drops of perspiration to the boy's forehead, or drew the white line around his mouth.

"It's quicker nor that you'll stip, my b'y, whin you hear the little sisther's not in yit, an' it's wid Jovarny she is," muttered Mrs. Ginniss; and, half dreading the entrance of her son, she applied herself so diligently to making a fire in preparation for supper, that she did not appear to notice him.

"Good-evening, mother. Where's Cherry?" asked Teddy, throwing himself wearily into a chair just inside the door.

"An' is it yersilf, gossoon? An' it's the big hate is in it intirely."

"Yes: it's hot enough. Where's Cherry?"

"Takin' a little walk, honey. You wouldn't be shuttin' the poor child into the house this wedder, sure?"

"Taking a walk! - what, alone!" exclaimed Teddy, sitting upright very suddenly.

"Of coorse not. Misther Jovarny was perlite enough to ax her; an' she wor that wild to go, I couldn't say her no."

"I wish you had said no, mother. I hate to let her be with that fellow, anyway. I'd have taken her to walk myself, if I was twice as tired. How long have they been gone?"

And Teddy, in his turn, looked anxiously out at the window, but saw nothing more than the squalid street weltering in the last rays of the August sun; a knot of children fighting in the gutter over the body of a dead cat; an old-clothes man sauntering wearily along the pavement, and a dog, with lolling tongue and blood-shot eyes, following close at his heels.

"How long have they been out? asked Teddy again, as he drew in his head, and looked full at his mother, whose confusion struck him with a sudden dismay.

"O mother!" cried he, "what is it? There's more than you're telling me amiss. How long is she gone?"

"Sure an' I didn't mind the clock whin they wint," said Mrs. Ginniss, still struggling to avoid the shock she felt approaching.

"No, no; but you can tell! O mother! do speak out, for the love of God! I can see how scared you are, though you won't say it. Tell me right out all there is to tell."

"An' it's no great there is to till, Teddy darlint; on'y this mornin', whin I was sint for to Ann Dolan (an' she that bad it's dead we thought she wor one spell, but for Docther Wintworth), Jovarny kim up, an' axed might the child go for a walk to the Gardens wid him; an' I jist puttin' on me shawl to go out, an' not wantin' to take the little crather in wid a sick woman, nor yet to lock the door on her, an' lave her to fret. So I says she might go wid him; and, whin she coom home, I tould Jovarny to open the door wid the kay an' let her in, an' showed her the dinner on the shelf by: an' if it's harm that's coom to her, it's harder on me than on yersilf it'll fall; an' my heart is bruck, is bruck intirely."

Throwing her apron over her head, Mrs. Ginniss fell into at chair, and gave way to the agitation and alarm she had so long suppressed; but Teddy, ordinarily so kind, and tender of his mother, stared at her blankly, and repeated, -

"This morning! How early this morning?"

"I wor jist afther washin' the bit breakfast-dishes," sobbed Mrs. Ginniss.

"Twelve hours or near!" exclaimed Teddy in dismay. "And is it to the Gardens he said he'd take her?"

"Shure an' did he!"

"To the Public Gardens, the City Gardens, just by the Commons?" persisted Teddy.

"Jist the Gardens wor all he said; an' towld me the shwans that wor in it, an' the bit posies."

"Yes: there's swans there, and posies enough," muttered Teddy, and, snatching the hat he had thrown upon a chair as he entered, rushed out of the room and down the stairs at headlong speed.

But, before he could possibly have reached the Garden, the sun had set, all visitors were excluded, and the gatekeeper had gone home. Nothing daunted, Teddy scaled the high iron fence; ran rapidly through all the paths, arbors, nooks, and corners of the place; and finally returned over the fence, just in time, to be collared by a policeman, who had been watching him: but so sincere was the boy's tone and manner, as he assured the official that he was after no harm but was looking for his little sister, who had been taken away from home, and, as he feared, lost, that the guardian of the public peace not only released him, but inquired with some interest into the particulars of the case; saying that he had been likely to notice any one remaining in the Garden longer than usual.

Teddy, with anxious minuteness, described the appearance both of the lost child and the "organ-fellow," as he called Giovanni; and gave the particulars of their leaving home as his mother had given them to him. The policeman listened attentively, but shook his head at the end.

"Haven't seen any sich," said he. "Them I-talian fellers is a bad lot; and I shouldn't wonder if he'd took off the child to learn her to play a tambourine, and go round picking up croppers for him. You'd better wait till morning; and, if they don't turn up, her mother can go and tell the chief about it."

"Chief of police?" asked Teddy.

"Yes; but it ain't always he can do any thing. There was that little gal, a year ago pretty nigh, belonged to a man by the name of Legrange. She was lost, and they offered a reward of ten thousand dollars finally; but she warn't never heard from. You see, there's sich a many children all about: and come to change their clothes, and crop their hair, it's hard to tell t'other from which," said the policeman meditatively; and then, suddenly resuming his official dignity, added, "You mustn't never get over that fence again, though: mind that, young man."

"Thank you, sir," said Teddy, turning away to hide the guilty confusion of his face; and, as he hurried home, he anxiously revolved the idea of applying to the police for aid, should Cherry remain absent after the next morning. But Teddy knew something of the law, and had too often seen better hidden secrets than his own ferreted out and brought to the light by its searching finger, to wish to trust himself within its grasp; at any rate, just yet.

"If I find her, I'll give her up, and tell all, and never touch the reward; but how can I go and say she's lost again?" thought Teddy, with a sick heart. And when, running up the stairs, his quick eyes caught sight of his mother's face, his own turned so ghastly white, that she ran toward him, crying, -

"An' is it dead you've found her, Teddy?"

"Worse; for she's lost; and all that comes to her is on my shoulders," said Teddy hoarsely, as he stood just within the door, looking hungrily about the room, as if he hoped, in some forgotten corner, to light upon his lost treasure.

"Did Jovarny take his organ and the monkey?" asked he suddenly.

"Sure, and he didn't; for I mind luckin' afther him going down the street."

"Then he'll be back!" exclaimed the boy eagerly; but the next moment the new hope died out of his face, and he muttered, -

"He might have taken them before. Anyway, I'll soon see;" and, running down the stairs, Teddy applied his sturdy shoulder and knee to the rickety door of the Italian's room. Neither door nor lock was fitted to withstand much force, and, with a sharp sound of rending wood and breaking iron, they flew apart; and Teddy, stepping over the threshold, glanced eagerly around. The room was stripped of everything except the poor furniture, which Teddy knew the Italian had hired with it, and the wooden box where he had kept his clothes. Of this the key remained in the lock; and, the boy, lifting the lid, soon discovered that a few worthless rags were all that remained.

"He's gone, and she with him!" groaned Teddy, dropping the box-cover, and standing upright to look again through the deserted room. His mother stood in the doorway.

"Och, Teddy! an' it's desaved us intirely he has, - the black-hearted crather; an' may the cuss O' Crom'ell stick to him day an' night, an' turn his sleep to wakin', an' his mate to pizen, till all I wish him is wished out!"

"It's no good cursing or wishing, mother," said Teddy bitterly. "If there was, I'd curse myself the first; for it's on me it had ought to fall."

"Sorra a bit of that, thin, Teddy mavourneen; for iver

an' always it was yersilf that wor tinder an' careful uv her that's gone; an' yersilf it wor that saved the life of her, the night she first come home to us; an' it's none but good that iver yees did her in all the days of yer life; an', if there's any blame to be had betwixt us, it's on yer poor owld mother it should be laid, - her that loved the purty darlint as if she'd been her own, an', if she's lost, will carry a brucken heart to her grave wid mournin' afther her. O wurra, wurra, acushla machree! Och the heavy day an' the black night that's in it! Holy Jasus, have mercy on us! Spake the good word for us, blissid Vargin! Saint Bridget (that's me own names ake), stip up an' intersade for us now, if iver; for black is the nade we have uv help."

Falling upon her knees, and pulling a rosary of wooden beads from her bosom, the Irish woman pursued her petitions, mingling them with tears and exclamations more or less pathetic and grotesque; while Teddy, seated upon the Italian's empty box, his head between his hands, his elbows upon his knees, his eyes fixed steadily upon the floor, gave up his young heart a prey to such remorse as might fitly punish even a heavier crime than that of which his conscience accused him.

CHAPTER XXII.

THE CONFESSION.

THE morning came, but brought no comfort. Mrs. Ginniss had crept up stairs, and, throwing herself upon the bed, had fallen asleep with the tears still trickling down her honest face; but to Teddy's haggard eyes no sleep had come, and he had only changed his position by stretching himself upon the floor beside the box, his head upon his arm, his aching eyeballs still shaping in the darkness the form and features of the little sister whom he had sullenly resolved was lost to him forever as punishment for his fault in concealing her.

"If I'd brought her back," thought he again and again, "they'd have let me get seeing her once in a while; they couldn't have refused me so much; and maybe some day I'd have been a gentleman, and could have talked with her free and equal. But now she's lost to them and to me; and, when I tell the master, he'll call me a mean thief and a liar, and a rascal every way, and he'll never look at me again; and mother" -

Then he would wander away into dreary speculation upon what his another would say when the truth was made known to her, and she found the boy on whom she had lavished her love and pride dishonored and discarded by the master to whom he owed so much, and whose patronage she had taken such pains to secure for him; and then, like the weary burden of a never-ending song, would come again the thought, -

"But if I'd brought her back at the first!"

The bitter growth of the night, however, had borne fruit in a resolution firm as it was painful; and, when Teddy came up stairs to make himself fit to go to the office, he was able to say some words of comfort to his mother, assuring her that no blame to her could come of what had happened, and that it was possible the child might yet be found, as he should warn those of her loss who could use surer means to search for her than any at their command.

"An' is it the perlice ye're manin'?" asked Mrs. Ginniss. "Sure it's little they'd heed the loss o' poor folks like us, or look for one little child that's missin', whin there's more nor enough uv 'em to the fore in ivery poor man's house. But niver a one like ours, Teddy b'y, - niver another purty darlint like her that's gone."

Teddy made no reply to this, but, hastily swallowing some food, took his hat, and left the room.

Upon the stairs he met the landlord, who, followed by a furniture-broker, entered the room of the organ-grinder. Going in after them, Teddy learned, in answer to his eager questions, that the broker had, early in the morning of the previous day, received a visit from the Italian, who, announcing that he had no further use for the furniture, paid what was owing for the rent of it, and made a bargain for a box he was about to leave behind him; but, as to his subsequent movements, the man had no information to give, nor could even judge whether he intended leaving the city, or only the house.

Thanking him or the information, Teddy went drearily on his way, more hopelessly convinced than ever that

Giovanni had deliberately stolen the child, and absconded with her.

"Well," muttered he, "all I've got to do now is to tell the master, and take what I'll get. If he finds the little-no: she's none of that, nor ever was-if he finds her, and takes her home to them that lost her, I'll be content, if it's to prison, or to sweeping the streets, or to be a slave in the South, he sends me."

Arrived at the office, Teddy faithfully performed his morning duties, and then seated himself to wait for Mr. Barlow, who was again occupying Mr. Burroughs's office during that gentleman's absence in the West. While arranging upon his table some papers he was to copy, Teddy suddenly remembered that other morning, now nearly a year ago, when Mr. Burroughs had laid upon his very table the picture and advertisement of the lost child; and all the months of guilty hesitation and concealment that since had passed seemed to roll back upon the boy's heart, crushing it into the very dust. He threw down the pen he had just taken up, and laid his head upon his folded arms, groaning aloud, -

"Oh! if I had told him then! if I had just told him that morning!"

The door of the office opened quickly; and Mr. Barlow, a grave and reserved young man, who had never taken much notice of Teddy, entered, and, as he passed to the inner room, glanced with some curiosity at the boy, whose emotion was not to be quite concealed.

"If you please, sir" -

"Well, Teddy?"

"I should like to send a letter to Mr. Burroughs."

"Do you mean a letter from yourself?"

"Yes, sir."

A slight smile crossed Mr. Barlow's face, as he replied a little sneeringly, -

"I am afraid your business will have to wait till Mr. Burroughs's return, my boy."

"Don't you be sending him letters, sir?"

"I have; but, when I heard from him yesterday, he was about leaving Cincinnati, and gave me no further address. He will be at home in a day or two."

Mr. Barlow passed on, and Teddy stooped over his work, but to so little purpose, that, on submitting it for inspection, he received a sharp reproof for his negligence, and an order to do the whole afresh.

"What a Quixotism of Burroughs's to try to educate this stupid fellow!" muttered Mr. Barlow to a friend who lounged beside his table; and Teddy, hearing the criticism upon his patron, felt an added weight fall upon his own conscience.

"They laugh at him because I'm stupid, and I'm stupid because I'm thinking of what I've done. It's good that they'll soon be shut of me altogether. Maybe I can sweep the crossings, or clean the gutters," thought poor miserable Teddy, bending afresh to his task.

Mr. Burroughs did not come so soon as expected; and

Mr. Barlow became quite impatient of the constant inquiry addressed to him by Teddy as to the probable movements of his master. At last, about noon of Friday, he walked into the office, looking more cheerful and like his old self than he had been since the heavy sorrow had fallen upon the household so near to his heart.

Mr. Barlow greeted him heartily, and, calling him into the inner office, closed the door; while Teddy remain-ned without, his heart beating with a sick hard throb, a tingling pain creeping from his brain to the ends of his icy fingers, and his whole frame trembling with agitation.

It was no light task that he had set himself; and so he well knew. To stand before the man he loved and reverenced before all men and say to him that he had been for months deliberately deceiving and injuring him and his; to confess that he had not once, but persistently, refused the only chance ever offered him of repaying, in some measure, the kindness and gener-osity of his patron; to acknowledge grateful, - oh! it was no light task that the boy had set himself; and yet his resolution never faltered.

Great acts are only great in the light of the actor's previous history and training; and perhaps the atonem-ent Teddy now contemplated was for him as heroic as that of the martyred bishop who held the hand that had signed the recantation steadily in the flame until it was consumed.

The door of the office opened, and the two gentlemen were passing out together, when Teddy started up, - "If you please, sir, might I speak with you by yourself?"

"Oh, yes! Teddy has been very anxious for an interview with you all the week. I will go on, and expect you down there presently," said Mr. Barlow.

"Yes, in two minutes. Come in here, Teddy, and let us hear what you have to say."

Mr. Burroughs threw himself into the chair he had just quitted, and stirred the fire, saying good-humoredly, -

"Out with it, my boy! What's amiss?"

Teddy, standing beside the table, one clammy hand grasping the edge of it, seemed to feel the floor heave beneath his feet, and the whole room to reel and swim before his eyes. His tongue seemed paralyzed, his lips quivered, his voice came to his own ears strange and hollow; but still he struggled on, resolute to reach the worst.

"It's about the little girl that was lost, sir, your little cousin Antoinette."

"'Toinette Legrange, cried Mr. Burroughs, his face suddenly growing earnest as he turned it upon the boy, and asked, -

"What is it? Have you heard of her?"

"Yes, sir. I found her in the street the night she was lost. She was dressed in poor clothes, and her hair was cut off. I didn't know who she was; and I took her home to my mother, and asked her to keep her for my little sister, because I never got one, and always wanted her. Then she was sick; and one day you told me she was lost, and showed me the picture and the piece in the paper; and I knew it was her. Then I thought she was going to die, and I waited to know; and, when she got better, I waited a while longer; and at last she was well, and I couldn't bear to part with her" -

"But she is safe now?" interrupted Mr. Burroughs, his look of stern reproach mingling with a sudden hope.

"No, sir: she's lost!"

"What!"

Teddy's white lips tried again and again before they could form the words, -

"She's lost again, sir! She went out walking with Jovarny, that's an organ-grinder, last Monday morning; and he has taken her off."

"You miserable fellow! You had better have killed as well as stolen her!" exclaimed Mr. Burroughs.

Teddy clung to the table, and reeled as if a physical blow had fallen upon him. It was the first time in the four years they had spent together that his master had spoken to him in anger, and now, -

"Five days ago! And what have you done in that time towards looking for her?" asked Mr. Burroughs sternly.

"Nothing, sir. I wanted to write to you, but couldn't get any direction."

"And why didn't you tell Mr. Barlow, and let him set the police at work? If you had warned him as soon as you discovered the loss, this organgrinder might have been caught. Now he is perhaps in New Orleans, perhaps halfway to Europe. Why didn't you tell Barlow, I say?"

"Please, sir, I couldn't bear telling any one but you that I done it," said Teddy in a low voice.

"Well, sir, and, now you have told me, you will please walk out of this office, and never enter it again. I did not imagine, that, in all these months, you were preparing such a pleasant surprise for me. One question, however: did your mother know who the child was?"

"No, sir: never."

"Then you may thank her that I let you off so easily; but I never desire to see either of you again after to-day. Wait here for one hour, while I go with a detective to hear your mother's story and to get a description of this organ-grinder. At two o'clock, leave the office; and take with you whatever belongs to yourself, and nothing more."

Mechanically obeying his master's gesture, Teddy staggered out of the room. Mr. Burroughs followed him, and, locking the door of the inner office, put the key in his pocket, and went out.

"He thinks I'm a thief!" was the bitter thought that darted through Teddy's mind; and then, "And how could I steal more than when I stole her? He's right to lock up from me."

CHAPTER XXIII.

TEDDY LOSES AND FINDS HIS HOME.

AN hour later, Teddy, leaving behind him the books, papers, pictures, every thing that Mr. Burroughs had given him, and taking only the few articles of his clothing which happened to be at the office, crept out of the door and down the stairs with the look of a veritable thief.

Choosing the least-frequented streets, and avoiding the recognition of such of his acquaintance as chanced to meet him, he slunk homeward, feeling a little less wretched, but infinitely more degraded, than he had done before his confession.

Burroughs knew, his mother knew, the police-officials knew, - how could he tell who did not know? - of his shame and guilt. Every pair of eyes seemed to accuse him; every step seemed to pursue him; every distant voice seemed to summon him to receive the punishment of his misdoing; and it was as to a refuge that he at last hurried in at the door and up the stairs of the tenement-house.

At the upper landing, however, he paused. His mother! - oh the sorrow and the shame that he had brought upon her in payment for all her love and effort, and the constant sacrifices she had made, ever since he could remember, to enable him to rise above his natural station, and to appear as well as his future associates! It came back to him now, - not a new thought, but one intensified by the more immediate suffering of the last two hours. He leaned for a moment against the wall, and wiped his clammy brow, feeling that any sudden death, any strange chance that could befall him, would be welcome, so that it swallowed up the coming moment, and spared him the sight of the misery he had wrought.

Only a moment. Then the desperate courage that had carried him through his confession to his master gave him strength to open the door and enter.

The ironing-table was spread, and upon a half-finished shirt lay alittle pile of money. Teddy knew that it was the wages owing him since the last payment, and turned away his eyes with loathing.

Mrs. Ginniss was lying upon the bed, her face buried in the pillow, sobbing heavily and wearily, as if exhausted by excessive emotion.

Teddy closed the door softly, and stood looking at her, uncertain whether she had heard him enter. In the room below, the little child of the new tenants sung, at her play, an air that Cherry had often sung.

Teddy listened, and, when the little song was done, cried out, -

"O mother! haven't you a word for me? I believe I'll go mad next."

"Don't be spakin' to me, you bowld, bad b'y! It's niver a word I have for yees, or wants from yees!" sobbed Mrs. Ginniss.

Teddy looked at her drearily for a moment; then softly seated himself, his hands folded listlessly in his lap, his eyes wandering idly about the familiar room, and his mind journeying on and on in the weary, mechanical manner of a mind over-wrought and stunned by long-continued or excessive suffering.

From the street below rose the hum and bustle of city life; from the room that had been Giovanni's, the voice of the child, still singing at her play. In at the open window streamed the thick yellow sunshine of the August afternoon, and a great droning blue fly buzzed upon the pane.

Teddy noted every sound; watched the motes dancing in the sunshine, the fly bouncing up and down the little window, the movements of the cat, who, rising from her nap, stretched every limb separately, yawned, lazily lapped at her saucer of milk, and then, seating herself in the patch of lurid sunshine, with her tail curled round her fore-paws, blinked drowsily for a few minutes, and then dozed off again.

But, whether he listened or whether he looked, it was but ear and eye that noted these familiar and homely sounds or sights. The mind still journeyed on and on in that weary journey without beginning or end; that dull, heavy tramp through black night, with no hope of ever reaching morning; that vain flight from a pain not for one moment to be forgotten or left behind; that numb consciousness of an evil, that, wait as we will, must sooner or later be met and recognized.

A long hour passed, and Mrs. Ginniss suddenly arose and confronted her son.

"If iver I larnt ye any thin', ye black-hearted b'y, what wor it?"

Teddy raised his heavy eyes to his mother's face, but made no answer.

"Worn't it to search iver an' always for the chance to do a good turn to him as has done all for 'yees that yer own father could, an' more? Worn't that the lesson I've struv to larn ye this four year back, Teddy Ginniss?"

"Yes, mother," said the boy in a low voice.

"An' haven't I towld ye, that, so as ye did it, my blessin' was wid yees, an' so as ye turned yer back on it my cuss 'ud folly yees, an' the cuss uv God an' all his saints and angels?"

"Yes, mother."

"An it's yersilf that's tuck heed uv me words, an' done yer best to kape 'em; isn't it, me fine lad?" pursued the mother with bitter irony.

"I did always, mother, till" - began Teddy humbly; but his mother angrily interrupted him.

"Alluz till ye got the chance to do contrairy, an' plaze yersilf at his expense. Sure, an' it wor mighty perlite uv yees to wait that long, an' it's greatly obleeged to yees he shud be."

She waited a moment, standing before the boy, who, still seated droopingly in the chair where he had first fallen, his heavy eyes looking straight before him, offered neither reply nor remonstrance; while his mother, setting her hands upon her hips, looked scornfully at him a moment longer, and then exclaimed, -

"An' have ye niver a word to say for yersilf, ye white-livered coward? Is there niver anudder lie on yer tongue like thim ye found so handy this twelvemonth back? Git out uv me sight, ye spalpeen, and out uv me doors! Go find them as'll kape yees to stale rich folks' children, an' thin lie to the mother as bore yees, and the kind masther as tried to make a gintleman out uv a thafe. Begone, I say, Teddy Ginniss, and quit pizenin' the air of an honest woman's room wid yer prisince!"

Teddy rose, and was leaving the room without a word, but at the door turned back; looked long and wistfully at his mother, who had turned away, and affected not to see him; then slowly said, -

"Good-by, mother! It's worse nor you can I'm feeling. Good-by! If ever I come to any good, I'll let you know; and, if I don't, you're shut of me for always."

The mother made no answer; and Teddy, lingering one moment on the threshold to turn his sad eyes for the last time upon the familiar objects that had surrounded him since childhood, went out, and down the stairs.

In the street he paused a moment, looking up and down, wondering where he should first go, and how food and shelter for the coming night were to be obtained. The question yet unsolved, he was walking slowly on; when a voice far overhead called, -

"Teddy! - Teddy Ginniss! Come here, I say!"

It was his mother's voice; and, as he looked up, it was

his mother's face and hand summoning him.

In the same forlorn, stunned way that he had come down, Teddy climbed the stairs again, feeling as if his feet were shod with lead, or the terrible weight at his heart was too heavy to be carried a step farther.

He pushed open the door of his mother's room, but never looked up or spoke, although he knew she stood close behind it. But, indeed, there could have been no time, had the boy wished to speak; for already his mother's arms were around his neck, and her head upon his stout shoulder, while the passionate tears fell like rain upon his hands.

"Ochone, ochone! An' it's me own an' only b'y yees are, an' must be, Teddy darlint; an' it's mesilf that 'ud be worse nor a haythin to turn yees inter the strate, so long as it's a roof an' a bit I have left for yees. An' sure, if ye've gone astray, it's the heart uv yees that's bruck wid frettin' afther it; an' there's a many as has done wuss, and niver a hape it harmed 'em here nor hereafter. An', if Michael wor here the day, it's himself 'ud say to pass it by; an' it wor little I should be plazin' his blissid sowl to turn yees off for one fault. Kiss yer owld mother, honey, an' be her own b'y again!"

"Thank you, mother," said Teddy, still in the strange, low voice he had used before; and, putting his arms round her neck, he met and returned her hearty kiss, and then, without another word, went and shut himself into the little loft he called his own, and was seen no more that night.

CHAPTER XXIV.

MR. BURROUGHS'S BUSINESS.

It was the afternoon of Thursday, Aug. 25: and Dora, sitting beside the bed where her little charge lay sleeping heavily, heard the rattle of wheels, and, peeping from the window, saw Karl jumping from the wagon, followed more slowly by a tall, handsome young gentleman, whom she concluded to be Mr. Burroughs; her cousin having gone to meet him at the railwaystation, seven miles away.

"He's good-looking enough for a colonel," thought Dora, and then started back, coloring a little; for Mr. Burroughs, in entering the house, had glanced up, and caught her eye. The next minute, Kitty darted into the room from her own chamber.

"They've come! Did you see him? Isn't he a real beauty? I do love a tall man! - He's as tall as Mr. Brown, and his whiskers are ever so much prettier; but, then, Mr. Brown's a minister. My! How nice you look, Dora! Go right down, and I'll stay with little Molly."

Dora glanced involuntarily at the mirror, and caught the reflection of a bright face, surrounded by heavy chestnut curls, and lighted with clear hazel eyes, and flashing teeth, a head of queenly shape and poise, and a firm, graceful figure, well set off by its white dress, black bodice, and scarlet ribbons, - a charming picture, with the quaintly decorated chamber for background, and the heavy black frame of the old mirror for setting: and a brighter color washed into the young girl's cheek as she recognized the fact; but she only said, -

"Why do you call her Molly, Kitty?"

"Oh! just a fancy name. We must call her something, and can't find out her right name."

"She called it Sunshine," said Dora, bending to kiss the pale little face upon the pillow as she passed.

"Moonshine, more like," replied Kitty. "She didn't mean it for a name, of course. You didn't understand. But come: your beau is waiting."

"Don't, Kitty, please!"

"I might as well begin. Every man is a beau that comes near you. I never saw such luck!"

Dora opened her lips, closed them tightly, and left the room. The next moment she stood in the low doorway of the parlor, bowing gravely, but not shyly, to the stately gentleman, whose head grazed the great white beam in the ceiling as he came forward to meet her.

"Miss Darling, I presume," said he.

"Yes, sir; I am Dora Darling: and you are Mr. Burroughs; are you not?"

"At your service," said the gentleman, bowing again; and, handing Dora a chair, he took another for himself.

"Won't you have some water, or a glass of milk, after

your drive, Mr. Burroughs?" asked Dora with anxious hospitality; and, as the gentleman confessed to an inclination for some water, she tripped away, and presently returned with a tumbler, which Mr. Burroughs very willingly took from her slender fingers instead of a salver.

"You know I was a vivandiŠre, sir," said Dora, smiling frankly; "and I always think of people being thirsty and tired when they come in so."

Mr. Burroughs smiled, too, as he handed back the empty glass.

"I wish we had all turned our army experiences to as good account," said he.

"Were you in the army?" asked Dora with sudden animation.

"Yes: I was lieutenant in the Massachusetts Sixth, and went through Baltimore with them," said Burroughs, tightening himself a little as the associations of military drill came back upon him.

"Oh! were you there? Wasn't it glorious to be the very first?" exclaimed Dora; and, with no further preamble, the two plunged into a series of army reminiscences and gossip, that kept them busy until Karl entered the room, saying, -

"Well, Dora, what do you think of Mr. Burroughs's news?"

"She has not heard it yet," said Mr. Burroughs, laughing a little. "We have been so busy talking over our army experiences, that we have not come to business."

"I am glad you have not; for I want to see how Dora will take it: but you will be grieved, as well as pleased, little girl."

"Yes," pursued Mr. Burroughs. "I am sorry to inform Miss Dora, that your friend Col. Blank is dead."

"Oh, Col. Blank dead!" exclaimed Dora, while a sudden shadow fell upon her bright face.

"I am very, very sorry," continued she. "Mr. Brown went to see him two months ago, and he was quite well then."

"Yes: this was rather a sudden illness; a fever, I believe. They tell me, that, since his wife died, he has never been very well, and at last was only ill three weeks."

"I am so sorry!" said Dora again. "He was very kind to me always."

"And no doubt died with feelings of affection and confidence for you, Miss, Dora; since he has made you his heir."

"Me!" exclaimed the young girl in a tone more of fright than of pleasure.

"Yes; and, although the property is not of any great available value at present, I think, if properly managed, it may, in the future, become something very handsome," said the lawyer.

"But I am so sorry Col. Blank is dead! Why, on Cheat Mountain, he seemed so strong and well! He was never tired on the marches, and hardly ever rode, but walked at the head of the column so straight and soldierly!"

The two men glanced at each other, then at her, and gravely smiled. The regret was so unaffected, so unselfish, and so unworldly, that each, after his own fashion, admired and marvelled at it. Mr. Burroughs was the first to speak; and, drawing a packet of papers from his pocket, he spread before Dora's sorrowful eyes a copy of Col. Blank's will, a plan of the estate bequeathed by it to her, and an official letter from Mr. Ferrars, the principal executor. This Mr. Ferrars, the lawyer informed his young client, was a personal friend of his own, and had placed the matter in his hands, thinking that the news might be more satisfactorily arranged by an interview than by correspondence.

"And, as I was coming East at the time, I could very conveniently call to see you on my way home," concluded Mr. Burroughs.

"Thank you, sir," said Dora meekly; and then, rather sadly, but very patiently, listened while the lawyer described the property she had inherited, and indicated the best course to pursue with regard to it.

"You will perceive, Miss Dora, that the bulk of the estate consists of this large tract of territory in Iowa, containing a great deal of valuable timber, a hundred or so common-sized farms of superb soil, and prairie-land enough to graze all the herds of the West.

"Col. Blank had just invested all his property, except

the estate in Cincinnati, in the purchase of this tract, and was about to remove thither, when Mrs. Blank died; and, as I said, he never seemed quite himself after that event, and took no further steps toward emigration. The house in Cincinnati might sell, Mr. Ferrars thought, for three or four thousand dollars; enough, you see, to make a beginning at 'Outpost,' as the colonel called it."

"Did he name the Iowa farm Outpost?" asked Dora rather eagerly.

"Yes: you see the name is written on this map of the estate."

"Then we will call it so; won't we, Karl?"

"But you don't advise my cousin to emigrate to the backwoods, do you, Mr. Burroughs?" asked Karl disapprovingly.

"It is the only method of reaping any immediate benefit from her inheritance," said the lawyer. "The territory is valuable, very; but would not sell to-day for anything like the price paid by Col. Blank, who fancied its situation, and intended to live there. The only way to get back the money is to hold the land until better times, or until emigration reaches the Des Moines more freely than it has yet done."

"I shall certainly go there and live," said Dora with quiet positiveness.

"You have decided?" asked Mr. Burroughs, looking into her face, and smiling.

"Quite," said Dora.

Karl looked too, saw the firm line of the young girl's rosy lips, and slightly raised his eyebrows.

"It is settled," said he with comic resignation.

Dora returned his gaze wistfully. She could not, in presence of a stranger, say what was in her heart: but she longed to let him know that this prospect of independence, of making a home of her own, of assuming duties and pursuits of her own, was such a prospect as no friend could wish her to forego; was the full and only cure for the bitterness of heart she had been unable to conceal from him upon the previous evening, - a bitterness so foreign to the sweet and noble nature of the young girl, that it had affected her cousin's mind with a sort of terror.

Something of all she meant must have stood visibly in the clear eyes Dora now fixed upon Karl; for, in meeting that gaze, the young man changed color, and said hastily, -

"But if you will be happier, Dora; if you are not contented here - It is a humdrum sort of life, I know."

"Oh, no! not that; but I want to be doing something. I mean something almost more than I can do, not ever so much less. I like to feel as if I must use every bit of strength and courage I have, and then I always find more than I thought I had."

Mr. Burroughs looked sharply at the young girl who made this ungirlish avowal. Was this utter simplicity? or was it an ingenious affectation? Was Dora Darling one of the noblest, or one of the most crafty, of womankind?

Tom Burroughs was a man of the world and of society, and flattered himself that neither man nor woman had art deeper than his penetration; but as he rapidly scanned the broad brow, clear, level-glancing eyes, firm, sweet mouth, queenly head, and mien of innocent self-confidence, he asked himself again, -

"Is it the perfection of art, or can it be the perfection of nature?"

But Karl was saying rather gloomily, -

"And what is to become of us, Dora?"

"Kitty and you?" asked Dora, open-eyed. "Why, of course, you are to come too! Did you suppose I wanted to leave you? Of course, it is your home and mine, just as this house has been: we are all one family, you know."

"To be sure. Well, I fancy there will be something for me to do on your Outpost farm. You must make me overseer."

"No: you shall be confidential adviser; but I am going to oversee every thing myself, and you must go on with your medical studies."

"You are going to become practical farmer, then?" asked Mr. Burroughs, raising his eyebrows never so slightly.

"Yes, sir; not to really work with my own hands out of

doors, you know, but to see to every thing. At first, I shan't understand much about it, I suppose; but I shall learn, and I shall be so happy!"

"And how soon will you be ready to go?" asked Mr. Burroughs.

Dora considered for a moment, "To-day is Thursday. I think we might start Monday morning; couldn't we, Karl?"

"And meantime sell this place and furniture?" asked Mr. Windsor, smiling.

"Not sell, but let the place. There is Jacob Minot would be glad to hire it, and a good tenant too. As for the furniture, we had better carry it with us. Shall we have to build a house when we get there, Mr. Burroughs?"

"Yes. Col. Blank had selected a site, and made some little beginning: I believe nothing more than having the land cleared and a cellar dug, however. You will begin with a log-cabin; shall you not?"

"Yes: I suppose so. Well, Karl, mightn't we start on Monday?"

"Not in heavy marching order, I am afraid; but very soon, if you are quite determined."

"Yes, quite; but what will Kitty think?" asked Dora suddenly.

"Oh! I think she will like it. Here she comes, and we can ask her."

The crisp rustle of muslin skirts swept down the stairs; and Mr. Burroughs, turning his head, saw standing in the doorway a tall, handsome brunette, with masses of black hair rolled away from a low forehead, glancing black eyes, and ripe lips, showing just now the sparkle of white teeth between, as the young lady half waited for an introduction before entering.

"Mr. Burroughs, Kitty; my sister, sir," said Karl, rising, and handing a chair to Kitty, who, with rather too wide a sweep of her bright muslin skirts, seated herself, and said, half laughing, -

"I suppose you are through with your secrets by this time?"

"We were just wanting to tell you the new plan, and see how you will like it," said Dora quickly; for she felt an involuntary dread lest Kitty should, in presence of this courteous stranger, say something to do herself discredit.

CHAPTER XXV.

MAN VERSUS DOG.

Mr. Burroughs staid to tea, and, while it was being prepared, strolled with Karl about the little farm; looked at the Alderney cow, the Suffolk pigs, the span of Morgan horses named Pope and Pagan; quietly sounded the depths of Capt. Karl's open and joyous nature, and made him talk of his cousin Dora, and reveal his love and his hopes regarding her.

"They will marry out there, and she will manage him, and make him very happy," thought Mr. Burroughs, returning toward the farmhouse, and admiring the long slope of the mossy roof, and the clinging masses of woodbine creeping to the ridge-pole.

"You won't make so picturesque a thing of your new home for several years to come, if ever, Mr. Windsor," added he aloud.

"No, I suppose not; but the genius of our people is more for beginning than ending, and this old place was built by my grandfather," said the young man.

"An excellent and most American reason for deserting it," said Mr. Burroughs gravely; "and, if you are thinking of selling, I should like the opportunity of becoming purchaser. This sort of thing is going out of the market, and I should like to secure a specimen before it is too late. It is same as a picture, except that it is stationary, and one must come to it instead of carrying it away in triumph."

"I think we may like to sell; but I must consult my sister and cousin first," said Karl rather gravely: for, after all, he did not just like the tone assumed by this fine city gentleman in speaking of the place that had been a home to Karl and his ancestors for more than a century. The quick tact of the lawyer perceived the slight wound he had given, and repaired it by carelessly saying, -

"And, besides the beauty of the place, I should be proud possessing any thing that had belonged to a grandfather. My family has been so migratory, that I can hardly say I had a grandfather or not: certainly I have not the remotest idea where he lived."

Capt. Karl laughed.

"Our family has been settled here since the days of the Pilgrims" said he; "and Kitty could show you a family chart, as large as a table-cloth, of which she is mightily proud, although I never could see any particular benefit it has been to us."

"And Miss Dora - is she fond of recalling her ancestors and their fame? or is she satisfied with her own?" asked Mr. Burroughs.

"I don't believe it ever occurred to her that either she or they deserved any," said Karl, laughing. "You never knew a creature so entirely simple and self-forgetful in your life, and yet of so wide and noble a nature. She is never so happy as in doing good to other people."

"But likes to do it in her own way?" suggested the lawyer pleasantly.

"Likes to do it in the best way, and her own way is sure to be that," replied Karl somewhat decidedly; and Mr. Burroughs smiled and bowed.

In the, doorway, under the swinging branch of the tall sweetbrier, suddenly appeared Kitty, her brown face becoming flushed, and the buttons of her under-sleeves not yet adjusted.

"Tea is ready; will you please to walk in, Mr. Burroughs?" said she: and the guest followed, well pleased, to the wide, cool kitchen, with its white, scoured floor, its vine-shaded windows and open door giving a view of broad meadow-lands, with a brook curling crisply through them, and a dark pine-wood beyond. In the centre stood the neat tea-table, with its country dainties of rich cream, yellow butter, custards, ripe peaches sliced and served with sugar, buttermilk-biscuit, and the fresh sponge-cake, on which Kitty justly prided herself.

"You see we are plain country-folks, and eat in the kitchen, Mr. Burroughs," said she, with a little laugh, as they seated themselves.

"Is this room called a kitchen? You amuse yourself by jesting with my ignorance," said Mr. Burroughs, looking about him with affected simplicity. "If ever I should live here, I would call this the refreshing-room; for I can imagine nothing more soothing to eyes weary of a summer sun than these vine-covered windows, and the cool greens of that meadow and the pine-forest beyond."

Kitty smiled a little vaguely, half inclined to insist upon the kitchen-side of the question; when Karl asked, in a disappointed tone, -

"Where is Dora? Isn't she coming?"

"Not yet. Molly waked up, and Dora is giving her some supper. She said she would come as soon as she had done. You didn't know, Mr. Burroughs, that Dora has an adopted child, did you?"

"No, indeed. She is young to undertake such responsibility," said Mr. Burroughs a little curiously.

"This is a little foreigner too, that Dora picked up in the road. No one knows who she may be, or what dreadful people may come after her any day. Dora is so queer!"

"Will you have a biscuit, Kitty? Mr. Burroughs, let me give you some of this peach? We shall be sorry to leave our peach-orchard behind in going to the West. I suppose, however, one can soon be started there."

And Karl, determined not to allow Kitty the chance of making any of her spiteful little speeches about Dora in presence of the visitor, kept the conversation upon purely impersonal topics, until they rose from table, and the two gentlemen strolled out upon the porch at the western door; while Kitty ran up to call Dora, whom she found sitting beside the bed, with Sunshine's head lying upon her arm.

"Isn't she asleep?" whispered Kitty.

The child half opened her eyes, and murmured drowsily, -

"I want to ride on the elephant. It's my little wife."

"What did she say, Dora?"

"Hush! She is out of her head, I think. She has been saying I was her little wife," whispered Dora.

"Well, that's English, anyway," replied Kitty, staring at the child. "What do you suppose she is?"

"I don't know. There, pet, there! Hus-h!" As she spoke, Dora carefully withdrew her arm from under the little head, where, in the August night, the hair clung in moist golden spirals, and a soft dew stood upon the white forehead.

"I'll stay and fan her for a while longer, she looks so warm," whispered Dora.

"No, no! come down and eat your supper, and help clear away. Charley asked Mr. Burroughs to stay all night, and I guess he will. Isn't he real splendid? Come down, and talk about him."

Sunshine slept soundly; and Dora, half reluctantly, suffered herself to be led away by her cousin, closing the door softly behind her, and leaving the little child to dreams of a home so far away, and yet so near; of a vanished past, that, even in this moment, stretched a detaining hand from out the darkness, groping for her own; of human love immortal as heaven, and yet, for the moment, less trustworthy than the instinct of the brutes: for if Mr. Thomas Burroughs, instead of being a highly cultivated and intellectual man, had been a dog of only average intelligence, 'Toinette Legrange would already have been discovered and, before another sunset, the slow agony devouring her mother's heart would have been relieved.

But to each of us our gifts; and Mr. Burroughs, never suspecting how deficient were his own, strolled with his host beneath the trees, until the appearance of the young ladies upon the porch; when he joined them, and resumed his conversation with Dora. From army matters, the talk soon wandered to the new prospects of Col. Blank's heiress; and Mr. Burroughs found himself first amused, then animated and interested, quite beyond his wont, in the young girl's plans and expectations.

It was late when the party separated; and as the guest closed the door of the rosy-room, and cast an admiring glance over its neat appointments, he muttered to himself, -

"What a bright, fresh little room! and what a brighter, fresher little girl!-as different from thy city friends, Tom Burroughs, as the cream she pours is from the chalky composition of the hotels. Thou dost half persuade me to turn Hoosier, and help thee convert the wilderness to a blooming garden, O darlingest of Darlings!"

And as the young man, with a half-smile upon his lips, set sail for the vague and beautiful shores of Dreamland, a bright, sweet face lighted by two earnest eyes, seemed to herald him the way, and join itself to all his fairest fancies.

CHAPTER XXVI.

MRS. GINNISS HAS A VISITOR.

HEAVILY went the days in the lowly home of Mrs. Ginniss and her son. Teddy sought early and late for employment, disdaining nothing, however humble, whereby he might earn a few cents, and working as diligently at street-sweeping, dust-gathering, errand-running, or horse-holding, as he had ever done in the way of gaining an education under the kind tuition of his late master.

Every night he brought home some small sum, and silently placed it in his mother's hand; nor, though she urged it, would he retain a penny for himself, or indulge in any of the small luxuries he had in former days enjoyed so much.

"Go buy a wather-million, honey, or get an ice-crame; sure it's nothin' at all ye're atin'," the fond mother would say: but Teddy always shook his head, or, if the matter were urged, took his cap and went out, always with the weary step that had become habitual to him, and returned no more until bedtime.

"It's frettin' himsilf to his grave the crather is," said poor Mrs. Ginniss, and tried in many a motherly way to make home pleasant to her boy, and to re-awaken the ambition that seemed quite dead in his heart. No more reading aloud now, of which he had been so fond; no more recitals of interesting or humorous scenes in office or street; no more wise opinions upon public events: all the boy's boyish conceit and self-esteem, germs in a strong character of worthy self - respect, seemed crushed out of him. Patient, humble, silent, one could hardly recognize in this Teddy Ginniss that other Teddy, whose cheery voice, frequent laugh, positive opinions and wishes, and good-humored self-satisfaction, had been the leading features of his modest home.

Poor Mrs. Ginniss longed to be contradicted or instructed or laughed at once more, and fought against her son's submissive respect as another mother might have done against disobedience or insolence.

"Can't ye be mad nor yet be merry at nothin', Teddy?" asked she impatiently one day.

"I'm thinking I'll never be merry again, mother," said Teddy sadly, as he left the room.

It was in the afternoon of the same day, that Mrs. Ginniss, sitting at her sewing in melancholy mood enough, heard a little tap at her door, and, opening it, found upon the threshold a lady, elegant in her simple dress of gray, who asked, -

"Are you Mrs. Ginniss?"

"Yes, ma'am; I'm that same," said the laundress, staring strangely at the lovely face framed in a shower of feathery golden ringlets, and lighted by large violet eyes as sad as they were sweet.

"Will ye be plazed to walk in, ma'am?" continued she. "It's but a poor place for the likes uv yees."

The lady made no reply, but, gliding into the room, stood for a moment looking about it, and then turning to the Irish woman, who still regarded her in the same awestruck manner, said piteously, -

"I am her mother!"

"Sure an' I knowed it the minute I sot eyes on ye; for it's the same swate face, an' eyes that's worse nor cryin, ye've got; an' the same way of a born lady, so quite an' so grand. Och! it wor a purty darlint, it wor; an' it's me own heart that's sore for her the day, forbye your'n that's her borned mother; and, if it wor my own life that 'ud fetch her back to yees" -

But here the long breath on which Mrs. Ginniss had started came to an end, and with it the impulse of cons- olation and self-defence that had so far sustained her; and with a wild cry of "Wurra, wurra! Och the black day that's in it!" she sank upon a chair, and buried her head in her apron, sobbing loudly.

The visitor, hardly regarding her, still stood in the centre of the little room, her sad eyes wandering over its humble furniture and adornments as if each one were a relic.

"Are there some little things of hers, clothes or playthings or books, - any thing she touched or loved?" asked she presently in a hushed voice.

Mrs. Ginniss, still crying, rose, and opened a drawer in the pine bureau, which, with a looking-glass and some vases of blue china upon it, stood as the ornamental piece of furniture of the place.

"Here they bees, ivery one uv 'em, and poor enough for her, an' yit the bist we could git," said she.

More as a bird, long restrained and suddenly set free, would dart toward the tree where nest and young awaited it, than in the ordinary mode of human movement, the mother, so long hungering for smallest tidings of her child, darted upon this sudden mine of wealth, and, bending low, seemed to caress each object with her eyes before touching it. Then tearing off her gloves, she laid her white fingers softly upon the coarse garments, the broken toys, the few worn books, and bits of paper covered with pencil-marks, the strip of gay patchwork with the needle still sticking in it, and the little brass thimble upon it.

At one end of the drawer stood a little pair of slippers, with some slightly soiled white stockings rolled up and laid within them. At sight of these, a low cry-it might have been of pain, it might have been of joy-crept from between the pale lips of the mother; and, reverently lifting the little shoes, she kissed them again and again, in an eager, longing fashion, as one might kiss the lips of a dying child whom human love may yet recall to human life.

"Thim's the little shlippers that Teddy saved his bit uv spinding-money till he could buy for her, bekase he said the fut uv her wor too purty to put in sich sthrong shoe's as I'd got; and thin it was mesilf that saved the white little shtockings out uv me tay an' sugar; an' it's like a little fairy (save me for spakin' the word) that she lucked in 'em."

Pressing the little shoes close to her bosom with both hands, the mother turned those mournful eyes upon the speaker, listening to every word, and, at the end, said eagerly, -

"Tell me some more! Tell me every thing she said and did! Oh! Was she happy?"

The word had grown so strange upon her lips and in her heart, that, as she said it, all the tense chords, so long attuned to grief, thrilled with a sharp discord; and, turning yet paler than before, she sank upon a chair, and, leaning her forehead on the edge of the open drawer, wept such tears as, pray God, happy mothers, you and I may never weep.

"O my baby, my baby! O my little child!" moaned she again and again, until the tender heart of the Irish woman could endure no longer; and, coming to the side of her guest, she knelt beside her, and put her arms about the slender figure that shook with every sob, and drew the bright head to rest upon her own shoulder.

"O ye poor darlint! ye poor, young crather, that's got the black sorrer atin' inter yer heart, all the same as if ye wor owld an' mane an' oogly, like mesilf!-it's none but Him aboov as kin comfort yees. Blissid Vargin, as was a moother yersilf, an' knowed a moother's pains an' a moother's love, an' all the ins an' outs uv a moother's heart, luck down on this young moother an' help her, an' spake to thim as can help her bether nor yees, an' give back her child; bekase ye mind the time yer own Howly Child wor lost, an' ye sought him sorrerin'; an' ye mind the joy an' the comfort that wor in it whin he was foun'. Och Mother of Jasus! hear us this day, if niver again."

As the passionate prayer ended, the lady raised her

head, and kissed the tear-stained cheek of the petitioner.

"Thank you," said she. "I know that you were good to her, and that she loved you; but, oh! did she forget me so soon?"

Alas poor human heart whose purest impulses are tinged with selfishness! You who have lost your nearest and dearest, can you say from your inmost soul that you would be content to know yourself and all of earth forgotten, or that it is sorrow to you to fancy that a lingering memory, a faint regret for the love you so lavished, stains the perfection of heavenly bliss?

Tact is not a matter of breeding; and Chesterfield or Machiavelli could have found no better answer than that of Mrs. Ginniss: -

"Sure, honey, it wor alluz she remembered yees, an' longed for yees; though the little crather wor that yoong, an' the faver had so poot her about, that she didn' know what it wor she wanted nor missed; but it wor 'mother' as wor writ in the blue eyes uv her as plain as prentin'."

"And was she very, very sick?" asked the sad voice again.

"The sickest crather that iver coom back from hivin's gate," replied the other; and then, seating herself beside her visitor, she began at the beginning, and gave a long detail of the circumstances attending Cherry's first appearance in the garret, and her subsequent illness and convalescence. Then came the story of her acquaintance with Giovanni; her passion for dancing and singing with him; and finally their flight, and the consternation and sorrow of her adopted mother.

Mrs. Legrange listened to every thing with the most profound attention, asking now and then a question, or uttering an exclamation; even smiling faintly at mention of the child's graceful dancing and sweet voice in singing.

"Yes, she had an extraordinary ear for music," murmured she; "and to think of her remembering being called Cerito!"

Nor did the mother fail to notice how the whole coarse fabric of the Irish woman's story was embroidered with a golden thread of love and admiration, and even reverence, for the exquisite little creature she had cherished and cared for so tenderly.

"Yes, you loved her; and I love you for it, and will always be your friend. But Teddy?" asked she at last; for Mrs. Ginniss, through the whole story, had carefully avoided all mention of her son, except in the most casual and general fashion. Now, however, she boldly answered, -

"An' its mesilf loved the purty crather well; but my love kim no nearer the love the b'y had for her than the light of a taller candle does to the sun in hiven. He loved her that sthrong, that it med him do a mane thing in kapin' her whin he knowed who she wor; but sure it's betther ter sin fer love than ter sin fer sin's sake."

Mrs. Legrange smiled sadly. To her it had seemed, from the first, small matter of surprise, however great of regret, that Teddy should have found 'Toinette's attractions irresistible; or that, having once appropriated her as his little sister, he should have found it almost impossible to relinquish her.

She had not, therefore, shared at all in the indignation of her cousin and husband toward the boy, and had even solicited the former to retain him in his employ. But Mr. Burroughs, kind, generous, and forbearing as he was, cherished implacable ideas of integrity and honor, and never forgave an offence against either, whether in friend or servant; so that his cousin had finally withdrawn her request, asking, instead, that he should conduct her to Mrs. Ginniss's dwelling, and leave the rest to her. This the young man had consented to do; and, as Mrs. Legrange would not allow him to wait for her, he had privately instructed James to do so, and had not left the outer door until he saw that faithful servitor upon guard.

Just what were her own intentions with regard to Teddy, or his mother, Mrs. Legrange did not herself know; and, once arrived in the room where 'Toinette had lived out the weary months since her loss, all other ideas had faded and disappeared before the memories there confronting her. Now, however, the sweet and generous nature of the woman re-asserted itself, and she kindly said, -

"Yes: I see how great Teddy's temptation was, and I cannot wonder that he yielded to it. Any one would have found it hard to part with 'Toinette; and he, poor boy! could not know how I was suffering. It would have been different if you had known who she was."

"Indade an' it would. One moother can fale fer another; but these childhren hasn't the sinse till they gits the sorrer. Small fear that Teddy'll iver go asthray agin from light-heartedness."

"Does he feel very sorry, then?" asked Mrs. Legrange timidly.

"Sorry isn't the word, ma'am. It's his own heart as he consumes day an' night," said Mrs. Ginniss gloomily.

"Because she is lost, or because he kept her in the first place?" asked the lady.

"It's hard tellin', an' he niver spakin' whin he can help it; but I belave it's all together. He wor sich a bowld b'y, an' so sthrong for risin' in the world; an' wor alluz sayin' as he'd be a gintleman afore he died, an' readin' his bit books and writins, an' tillin' me about the way the counthry wor goin'; an', right or wrong, it's he wor ready to guide the whole of 'em. An', sure, it wor wondherful to see the sinse that wor in him when he get spakin' of thim things; an' one day, whin I said to him, -

"'Sure, Teddy, an', if it's one or tither of 'em is Prisident, what differ'll it make to us?' An' he says, says he, 'Whist, moother! Fer one day, mabbe, it's I'll be the Prisident mesilf; an' what way 'ud that be fer me moot-her to be talkin'?'

"But now it's no sich talk ye'll git out uv him, an' niver a laugh nor a joke, nor the bit bowld ways he used to have wid him. An' och, honey! if ye've lost yer purty darlint, it's I've lost me b'y that wor as mooch to me; an' it's I'm the heavy-hearted woman, this' day an' alluz."

CHAPTER XXVII.

TEDDY FINDS A NEW PATRON.

TEDDY, dragging his heavy feet up the stairs in the stifling September twilight, paused suddenly to listen to a murmur of voices in his mother's room.

Some one was speaking; and the pure, clear tone sent a thrill through his veins like the shock of an electric battery. No voice but one had ever sounded like that to him; and, springing up the remaining stairs, Teddy threw open the door of the chamber, and looked eagerly about it.

The one for whom he looked was not there; but, instead, a lady, whose fragile loveliness reminded him so strangely of the little sister as she had looked in her long days of convalescence, that he stood still, staring dumbly.

"An' where's yer manners, Teddy Ginniss? Couldn' ye see the lady forenenst ye, widout starin' like a stuck pig? - It's dazed he is, ma'am, wid seein' the likes uv yees in this poor place."

"Come here, Teddy; I am waiting to see you," said the lady. And again the pure, silvery tones tingled along Teddy's nerves with a sharp, sweet thrill.

"O ma'am! are you her mother?" cried he breathlessly.

"Yes, I am her mother, and have come to see you, who loved her so well, and your good mother, who cared for her when she was motherless" -

The sweet voice faltered, and Teddy broke in, -

"And you needn't be afraid to say the worst that can be said, ma'am. I've said it all before; and you can't hate me worse than I hate myself."

"Hate you, my poor boy? I only pity you; for I have heard, and can see, how much you suffer. I cannot wonder that you should love her so well; and, when you knew who she was, I dare say you were meaning to restore her, so soon as you could bring yourself to it."

"Indeed I was, ma'am. I can take God to witness that I was," said Teddy solemnly, his eyes brimming, and his face working with the strong emotion he tried so hard to subdue.

"I am sure of it; and I love you more for the love you bore her than I blame you for the fault that love led you into." She paused a moment; and then the insatiate mother pride and love burst out, demanding sympathy.

"She was a lovely child, wasn't she, Teddy?" asked she with a tremulous smile.

The boy's rough face lighted, as if by reflection from her own, as he replied, -

"O ma'am! it's so good of you to let me talk about her! There was never another like her in all the world, I believe. I used to take her walking Sundays, and look at all the children we met (some of them rich folks' children, and dressed all out in their best); but there was never one could hold a candle to my little sister. Oh! And I hope you'll forgive me that word, ma'am; for I know it's no business I had ever to call her so, or think of her so; but I was so proud of her!"

"I don't need to forgive you, Teddy. It shows how much you loved her; and that is what I like to think best."

"But if you please, ma'am, will you tell me what is doing about looking for her?" asked Teddy eagerly.

"Very little now," answered the lady sadly. "The police traced Giovanni, the Italian organ-grinder, to the station, where he took the cars for the West. At Springfield, a man answering to his description, with a little girl, staid all night; and next day the child danced-in the streets."

The mother's face grew deadly pale as she said the last words, and she paused a moment. Teddy turned away his head, and Mrs. Ginniss groaned aloud. Mrs. Legrange went on hurriedly: -

"Where they went afterwards is not yet discovered; but they are looking everywhere. It seems so strange" -

She fell into a momentary revery, thinking, as she thought so many, many times in every day, how hard and strange it seemed that no clew could be found to her lost darling beyond the terrible day that saw her dancing in the public streets, - an ignominy, that, to the lady's sensitive mind, seemed almost equivalent to death.

Perhaps it would have been kinder had her husband and cousin told her the worst they knew or suspected, and allowed her to mourn her child as dead. The acute detective in whose hands the new clew had been placed had not only traced the fugitives to Springfield, as Mrs. Legrange had said, but had ascertained at what hour they left the hotel for the railway-station. It was impossible, however, to discover for what point the Italian had purchased tickets, as the station-master had no recollection of him, and the baggage-master was sure he had seen "no sich lot" as was described to him.

And, from Springfield, a man may take passage to almost any point in the Union. One startling fact remainned, and upon this fact the whole report of the detective turned.

The train leaving Springfield for Albany upon the night when Giovanni left that town, encountered, at a certain point, another train, which, by some incomprehensible stupidity, was supposed to have passed that point half an hour before.

Consequences as usual, - frightful loss of life; a game of give and take in the newspapers, as to who should bear the blame, finally resulting in a service of plate to one party, and a donation in money to the other; several lawsuits brought by enterprising widowers who demand consolation for the loss of their wives; by other men, who, having skulked the draft, now found themselves minus both legs and glory; by spinsters whose bandboxes had been crushed, and by young ladies whose beauty had suffered damage from broken noses and scattered teeth.

But, among all these sufferers, not one remembered

seeing an Italian organ-grinder with a little girl until, at the very last, a small boy was found, who averred, that, on the morning after the disaster, he had seen a sort of box, with a little creature chained to the top of it, floating down the river; and that the little creature had seemed very much scared, and kept laughing, and showing all his teeth; and that they had gone on and out of sight. And that was all he knew about it.

The river!-what use to question those dark and swollen waters? What use to demand of them the bright form, that, it might be, slept beneath them? - it might be, had been washed piecemeal to the ocean?

At the brink of that river, mournful and terrible as Styx, river of the dead, ended, that night, the story of many a life; and why not that of the child so strangely lost, so nearly recovered, and now, perhaps, lost again forever?

"We have found her, I am afraid, Tom," said Mr. Legrange to his cousin, as the detective closed his report, and his two hearers looked at each other. "But," added the father, "keep on; keep every engine at work; search everywhere; spend any amount of money that is needful; leave no chance untried. Remember, the reward is always ready." And, when they were alone, he added, -

"But, Tom, don't tell her. She can't bear it as we can. Poor little Sunshine!" And, to show how well he bore it, the father hid his face, and sobbed like a woman.

"No, I won't say any thing," said Tom Burroughs in a strange, choked voice. And so we come back to Mrs. Legrange wistfully saying, "It seems so strange" -

And then, with the patience of a woman, she put aside her own great grief, and added, -

"But, Teddy, I am going to do something for you; and what shall it be? You wish to be educated; do you not?"

"O ma'am! but I've give it up now."

Mrs. Legrange smiled at the sudden enthusiasm and the sudden blank upon the boy's face, and answered, almost gayly, -

"But I have not given it up for you, Teddy. - By the way, Mrs. Ginniss, is that your son's real name? - his whole name, I mean?"

"It's short for Taodoor, I'm thinkin', ma'am; but joost Teddy we alluz calls it."

"Ah, yes! Theodore. That is a very nice name, and will sound better, when he comes to be a lawyer or doctor or minister, than Teddy. Don't you think so?"

"Ye're right, ma'am: it's a dale the dacenter name uv the two; an' Taodoor I'll call him iver an' always," said Mrs. Ginniss complacently.

"I was thinking more of what other people would call him," said Mrs. Legrange, smiling a little. "Some friends of mine are interested in a school and college at the West, - somewhere in Ohio, I believe. It is a very fine school and the West is the place for a young man who means to rise. So, Theodore, if you would like to go, I shall be very happy to see to all your expenses until you graduate, and to help you about settling in a profession, or in trade, as you like."

Teddy's healthy face turned deadly white; and, although his lips trembled violently, not a word came from between them. But Mrs. Ginniss, raising hands and eyes to heaven, called down such a shower of blessings from so many and varied sources, in such an inimitable brogue, that the pen refuses to transcribe her rhapsody, as Mrs. Legrange failed to comprehend more than the half of it.

"I am glad you are pleased; and it pleases me as much as it can you," said she, half frightened at the Celtic vehemence of the other's manner and language.

"I can't say what I want to, ma'am," spoke a low voice beside her; "but if you'll believe I'm grateful, and wait till some time when I can show it better than I can now-that time will come, if we both live. And when I'm a man, if she isn't found first, I'll go the world round but I'll find her, and Jovarny too: I'll promise that."

A wan smile played over the lovely face, as Mrs. Legrange, laying her hand upon the boy's, said kindly,-

"If she is not found before then, Teddy, I shall not be here to know it."

Then going to the drawer, still standing open, she said,

"May I have some of these little things, Mrs. Ginniss; not all, - for I know that you love them too, - but some of them?"

So Mrs. Ginniss made a package of the relics; and

Teddy asked and obtained the privilege of carrying it home for his new friend, while James stalked discontentedly behind.

Upon the way, Mrs. Legrange said quietly, "I left a little money in the drawer, Theodore. It is to buy you some new clothes, and whatever else you and your mother need most. And I have just thought of something else. How would your mother like living in the country?"

"Very much, ma'am, I think. Her father had a farm in Ireland, and she is mighty fond of telling about it."

"Well, Mr. Legrange has recently made me a present of a nice old farmhouse somewhere in the western part of the State, thinking I might like to go there for a few weeks in the summer. It is a lovely place, they say; and, if your mother would like it, she might go there and keep the house for me. A man is going to take care of the farm, and he could board with her."

"That would be first-rate, ma'am," said Teddy enthusiastically. "But you're doing too much for us entirely."

"You were kind to her, Teddy; and I cannot do too much for you," said Mrs. Legrange, lowering her veil.

CHAPTER XXVIII.

WELCOME HOME.

"TIME they was here, ain't it, miss?" asked Mehitable Ross, wiping the flour from her bare arms, and coming out upon the step of the door.

"Yes," said Dora: "I expect them every moment. Is tea all ready?"

"All but the short-cakes. I hain't put them down to bake yet, because they're best when they're first done. But the cold meat is sliced, and the strawberries dished, and the johnny-cake a-baking."

"Well, keep them all as nice as you can; and I will walk out a little, and meet the wagon."

"Take Argus along, you'd better, case you should meet one of them tiger-cats Silas told on."

Dora smiled, but called, "Argus!" and at the word a great hound came leaping from one of the out-buildings, and fawned upon his young mistress; then, with stately step and uplifted head, followed her along the faint track worn by the wheels of the ox-cart in the short, sweet grass of the prairie.

The young girl walked slowly, and, at the distance of some rods from the house, stopped, and, leaning against the stem of a great chestnut-tree, stood looking earnestly down the path as it wound into the forest, and out of sight. Then her eyes turned slowly back, and lingered with a strange and solemn joy upon the scene she had just left; while from her full heart came one whispered word that told the whole story of her emotion, -

"Home!"

For this was Outpost, Dora's inheritance from her friend and father, Col. Blank; and she felt to-night, as she waited to welcome home the family whose head she had become, that her duties and responsibilities were indeed solemn and onerous. Not too much so, however, for the courage and strength the young girl felt within her soul, - the energy and will so long without an adequate field of action.

"Plenty to do, and, thank God, plenty of health and strength to do it. Experience will come of itself," thought Dora; and from her throbbing heart went up a "song without words," of joy and praise and high resolve.

It was June now; but the house at Outpost had only been ready for occupancy a week or so. The family had left Massachusetts about the first of October in the previous autumn, and had spent the winter in Cincinnati; Dora having been reluctantly convinced of the folly of proceeding to Iowa at that season. With the opening of spring, however, she had made a journey thither, escorted by Charles Windsor, and accompanied by Seth and Mehitable Ross, - a sturdy New-England couple, who were very glad, in emigrating to the West, to avail themselves of the offers made by Dora, who engaged the man as principal workman upon the new farm, and his wife as assistant in the labors of the house.

The site selected by Col. Blank proved a very satisfactory one. But Dora rejected his plans of a house, submitted to her by Mr. Ferrars, as too expensive, and too elaborate for the style of living she proposed; and chose, instead, a simple log-cabin, divided into four rooms, with another at a little distance for the accommodation of Ross and his wife, who were also to keep whatever additional workmen should be required upon the place.

These buildings, neatly and substantially formed of logs from the neighboring wood, were placed at the top of a natural lawn half enclosed by primeval forest; while at its foot nearly a quarter of a mile away, wound the blue waters of the Des Moines; and beyond it, swept to the horizon, mile after mile of prairie, limitless, apparently, as ocean, and, like ocean, solemnly beautiful in its loneliness and calm.

The house faced south; and eastward from its door, across the lawn and into the rustling wood, wound the faint wheel-track, leading back to civilization, ease, and safety: but Dora, standing beneath the chestnut-tree, fixed her dreamy eyes upon the setting sun, and, half smiling at her own fancy, thought, -

"I wonder if God doesn't make the western sky so beautiful just to draw us toward it. There is so much to do here, and so few to do it!"

A distant noise in the forest attracted her attention; and Argus, who had been dreaming at the feet of his mistress, started up with a short bark.

"Hush, Argus! It's the wagon; don't you know?" explained Dora, as she hastened down the path, and, at the distance of a few hundred rods, caught sight of the black heads of Pope and Pagan, and, the next moment, of the wagon and its occupants.

These were Karl, Kitty, and Sunshine, the two last of whom had remained all the spring in Cincinnati, while Karl and Dora had vibrated between that city and Outpost; for Dora, while choosing to superintend the building of her house and opening of the farm operations in person, had not wished to expose her cousin or the delicate child to such discomforts as she cheerfully and even gaily bore for herself.

Kitty, moreover, had found the change from her native seclusion to a gay city very pleasant; and had made so many acquaintances in Cincinnati, that she declared it was a great deal worse than leaving home to abandon them all.

"Oho! here's the general come to meet us! Whoa, Pope! don't you see your mistress? Now, then!" shouted Karl; while Kitty cried, -

"O Dora! I'm so glad to see you alive!" And little Sunshine, jumping up and down in the front of the wagon, exclaimed, -

"Dora's come! Dora's come! Karlo said we'd come to Dora by and by!"

"O you little darling! if Dora isn't glad to see you again! Kitty, how do you do? I'm so glad to see you!"

She had jumped into the wagon as she spoke; and, after

giving Kitty a hearty kiss and hug, she took Sunshine in her arms, and buried her face in the child's sunny curls.

"Am I your own little girl, Dora? and do you love me same as you always did?" asked Sunshine anxiously. "Kitty said you'd so much to think about now, that maybe you wouldn't care for us."

"Oh! Kitty never meant that, dear," said Dora quickly; and Kitty, with rather a forced laugh, added, -

"Of course I didn't. It was only a joke, Molly. You talked so much about Dora, I wanted to plague you a little."

The child looked earnestly at her for a moment; and then, putting her arms about Dora's neck, hid her face upon her bosom, murmuring, -

"I'm glad I've got Dora again!"

"Well, now everybody else is attended to, hasn't the general a word for his humble orderly?" asked Karl, turning to smile over his shoulder at the group behind.

"Why, you jealous old Karl! you know you've only been away two weeks, and the girls I have not seen for almost as many months: besides, I told you not to call me general, and yourself orderly."

"Oh! that reminds me of a new name for pet. You know she persists in calling me Karlo; so I have given her the title of Dolce: and the two of us together are going some day to paint pictures far fairer than those of our great original."

"Carlo Dolce? Yes: Mr. Brown told me about him once, and said his name only meant sweet Charley," said Dora simply.

"I wonder, then, that you should have left it for Sunshine to discover how appropriate the name is to me," said Karl with mock gravity.

"I'll call you sweet Charley if you like; only it must be at all times, and before all persons," said Dora roguishly.

"No, I thank you," replied her cousin, laughing. "Fancy Parson Brown's face if he should hear such a title, or Seth's astonishment if you told him to call sweet Charley to dinner! But isn't Dolce a pretty name? Let us really adopt it for her."

"Well, if she likes; but I shall call her Sunshine still sometimes."

"What say, pet? will you have Dolce for a name?" asked Karl, turning to pinch the little ear peeping from Sunshine's curls.

"I don't know; would you, Dora?" asked the child, gravely deliberating.

"Yes: I think it is pretty."

"And Kitty sha'n't call me Molly any more; shall she?"

"Don't you like Molly?"

"No: because that man in Cincinnati asked me if my last name was Coddle; and it ain't."

"Oh, dear! what an odd little thing she is!" exclaimed Kitty. "It was Mr. Thomson, Dora; and he is so witty, you know! And one day he asked the child if her name wasn't Miss Molly Coddle, just for a joke, you see; and we all laughed: but she ran away; and, when I went to my room, there she was crying, and wouldn't come down again for ever so long. She's a regular little fuss-bunch about such things."

"Very strange, when you and I are so fond of being ridiculed and laughed at!" remarked Karl gravely; and Sunshine whispered, -

"Am I a fuss-bunch, Dora?"

Dora did not answer, except by a little pat upon the child's rosy cheek, as she exclaimed, -

"Here we are! Look, Kitty! that is home; and we must bid each other welcome, since there is no one to do it for us both except Mehitable, and I don't believe she will think of it."

"Well, I must say, Dora, you've got things to going a great deal better than I should expect," said Kitty graciously, as she looked about her. "Why, that sweetbrier beside the door, and the white rose the other side, are just like ours at home; and the woodbine growing up the corner too!"

"They came from the old home, every one of them," said Dora, smiling happily. "I wrote in the spring, and asked Mr. Burroughs to be so kind as to ask whoever lives in the house to take up a little root of each of the roses, and send them to me by express. You know he said, when we left, that we should have any thing we liked from the place, then or afterwards. So he wrote such a pleasant note, and said he had sold the house to a cousin of his, a Mr. Legrange, who had made a present of it to his wife; but I could have the slips all the same: and next day, to be sure, they came, all nicely packed in matting, and some other plants with them. Karl brought them out and set them in April; and they are growing beautifully, you see. Wasn't Mr. Burroughs good?"

Kitty did not answer. She was bending low over the sweetbrier, and inhaling the fragrance of its leaves. Karl and Sunshine had driven to the barn, and the girls remained alone. Dora glanced sharply at her cousin once, and then was turning away, when Kitty detained her, and said in a low voice, -

"My mother planted that sweetbrier, and used to call it her Marnie-bush, after me."

"I know it," said Dora softly.

"And that was the reason you brought it here. And I have been cross to you so much! But I did love her so, Dora! oh, you don't know how much I loved my mother! That is the reason I never will let any one call me Marnie now. It was the name she always called me, though Kitty belongs to me too; but she said it so softly! And to think you should bring the Marnie-bush all the way from Massachusetts!"

"I thought you would like it, dear," said Dora absently; while her eyes grew dim and vague, and around her mouth settled the white, hard line, that, in her reticent nature, showed an emotion no less intense because it was suppressed.

Then her arm stole round Kitty's waist, and she whispered in her ear, -

"We two motherless girls ought to feel for each other, and love each other better than those who never knew what it is; shouldn't we, Kitty?"

"We should that, Dora," returned her cousin with emphasis; "and I don't believe I shall forget again right away. Let us begin from now, and see how good we can be to each other."

Dora's kisses, except for Sunshine, were almost as rare as her tears; but she gave one now to Kitty, who accepted it as sufficient answer to her proposition.

At this moment, Mehitable, who had, at the appearance of the wagon, rushed home to give a finishing touch to her toilet, was seen crossing the little interval between the two houses with an elaborate air of unconsciousness of observation, and carrying a large white handkerchief by its exact centre.

"My!-how fine we look!" whispered Kitty.

"This is my cousin, Miss Windsor, Mehitable," said Dora simply. "I believe you didn't see her in Cincinnati?"

"No: she was away when we was there. - Happy to make your acquaintance, Miss Windsor. How do you like out here?"

"Well, I don't know yet. I never tried keeping house in a log-cabin. You'll have to show me how, I expect," said Kitty rather loftily.

"Lor! I guess you know as much as I do about it. I never see a log-cabin in my life till we come out here. My father had a fust-rate house, cla'borded and shingled, and all, down in Maine; and we alluz had a plenty to do with of every sort: so I hain't no experience at all in this sort of way."

"But you have a way of getting on without it that is almost as good. I don't know what I should have done without Mehitable, Kitty; and I dare say she will help you very much by telling all the ingenious ways she has contrived to make our rude accommodations answer. You know, as we are all beginning together, each must help on the other; and we must all keep up our courage, and try to be contented."

"Well, I must say I never see one that kep' up her own courage, and everybody else's, like her, since I was born into the world," said Mehitable, turning confidentially to Kitty. "Talk of my helping her! Lor! if it hadn't been for her, I never would have stopped here over night, in the world. Why, the first night, I didn't do nothing but roar the whole night long. Mr. Ross he said I'd raise the river if I didn't stop: but in the morning down come Miss Dora, looking so bright and sunshiny, that I couldn't somehow open my head to say I wouldn't stop; and then she begun to talk" -

"Mehitable, the short-cake is done. Will you speak to Mr. Windsor?" called Dora from within; and Kitty entered, saying, -

"How nice the tea-table looks! - just like home, Dora; the old India china and all."

"It is home, Kit-cat. Here is Karl, and here is little

Sunshine. Come, friends, and let us sit down to our first meal in the new house," said Dora: and Kitty, subduing a little feeling of fallen dignity, seated herself at the side of the table; leaving the head for Dora, who colored a little, but took it quietly.

CHAPTER XXIX.

LIFE AT OUTPOST.

AND now began for each member of the family at Outpost a new and active life.

Kitty, who, young as she was, had already achieved reputation as a notable housekeeper, found quite enough to attend to in domestic matters, and, with Mehitable's help and counsel, soon had all the interests and nearly all the comforts of New-England farm-life established in her Western home. Even the marigolds her mother had always raised as a flavoring to broths; and the catnip, motherwort, peppermint, and tansy, grown and dried as sovereign remedies in case of illness; and the parsley, sage, and marjoram, to be used in various branches of cookery, - flourished in their garden-bed under Kitty's fostering care; while poor Silas Ross was fairly worried, in spite of himself, into digging and roofing an ice-cellar in the intervals of his more important duties.

"Now we'll see, another summer, if we can't have some butter that's like butter, and not like soft-soap," remarked Kitty complacently, when the unhappy Silas announced his task complete.

"And now I hope I can sleep in my bed o' nights without hearing 'Ice-house, ice-house!' till I'm sick o' the sound of ice," muttered Silas, walking away.

It is not to be averred, however, that all this thrift was established without much commotion or many stormy scenes; and, not unfrequently, Mehitable Ross announced to her husband that "she wouldn't stan' it nohow, to be nosed round this way by a gal not so old as herself!" And Kitty "declared to gracious" that she "never saw such a topping piece as that Hitty Ross since she was born;" and, if "folks undertook to work for other folks, they ought to be willing to do the way they were told;" and she'd "rather do the whole alone than keep round after that contrary creature, seeing that she didn't get the upper-hands as soon as her back was turned!"

But Dora, without appearing to listen or to look, heard all and saw all. Dora, cheerful, energetic, and calm, knew how to heal, without appearing to notice the wound; had a faculty, all her own, of leading the mind, vexed with a thousand trifles, to the contemplation of some aim so grand, some thought so high, some love or beauty so serene, that it turned back to daily life calm and refreshed, and strengthened to do or to endure, with new courage.

"Somehow I felt ashamed of jawing so about that wash, when Dora came in, and put her hands into the tub, and, while she was rubbing away, began to tell what a crop of corn we're going to have; and how the folks down South, the freedmen and all, might have plenty to eat, if every one did as well as we're doing," said Mehitable to her husband.

"Yes," replied Seth: "she stood by me there in the sun as much as an hour, and told the cutest story you ever heard about the Injins believing that corn is a live creter, and appeared once, in the shape of a young man named Odahmin, to one of the Injin chiefs called

Hiawatha; and they had a wrastle. Hiawatha beat, and killed the other feller, and buried him up in the ground; but he hadn't more 'n got him under 'fore up he come agin, or ruther some Injin-corn come up: but they called the green leaves his clothes; and the tossel atop, his plume; and the sprouts was his hands, each holding an ear of corn, that he give to Hiawatha, just as a feller that's whipped gives another his hat, you know."

"Do the Injins believe all that now?" asked Mehitable contemptuously.

"They do so. But, I tell you, I never knew how those two rows got hoed while she was talking: they seemed to slip right along somehow; and, after she was gone, the time seemed dreadful short till sundown, I was thinking so busy of what she said."

"Guess you'd been cross 'cause that cultivator didn't come; hadn't you?" asked Mehitable slyly.

"Yes: I felt real mad all the morning about it, and was pretty grumpy to Windsor; for I thought he might as well have sent a week ago. But, by George! I'd like to see the feller that 'ud be grumpy to her."

"Well, Dora," Kitty was saying at the same moment, "I'm glad you've got home; for the first thing isn't ready for supper, and I've just done ironing. That Hit went off home an hour ago; said her head ached, and she'd got to get the men's supper. I do declare, I'd like to shake that woman till her teeth rattled; and I believe I'll do it some day!"

"How beautifully the clothes look, Kitty! I think they bleach even whiter here than they used to in the old drying yard. But I am sorry you ironed that white waist of mine: I was going to do it myself. Now, Sunshine, come and tell Aunt Kitty about the woodchuck and her baby that we saw; and how we caught little chucky, as you called him; and all the rest."

"Dear me! I can't stop. Well, come and sit in my lap, Dolly, and tell if you want to. Dora, do sit and rest a minute: you look all tired out."

"Oh, no! but Karl is, I am afraid. He walked away out behind the wheat-lot this afternoon to see to setting some traps for the poor little things that come to eat it. I never saw such a boy when there is any thing to be done. He goes right at it, no matter what lies between."

"You're right there, Dora; and he always was so from a child. Well, Dolly, what's the story?"

"Don't call me Dolly, please," said the little girl coaxingly.

"Well, Dolce, then," said Kitty, smiling with renewed good-nature. And while Sunshine, all unconsciously, completed by her prattle the cure that Dora had begun, the latter quietly and rapidly finished the preparations for tea.

As for Sunshine, never did a child so well deserve her name. In the house or on the prairie, running with Argus, walking demurely beside Karl, or riding behind Dora upon the stout little pony reserved for the use of the young mistress of the place, it was always as a gleam of veritable sunshine that she came; and no heart so dark, or temper so gloomy, as to resist her sweet influence. Constant exercise and fresh air, proper food, and the rigid sanitary laws established by Dora, had brought to the child's cheek a richer bloom than it had ever known before; while her blue eyes seemed two sparkling fountains of joy, and a vivid life danced and glittered even among her sunny curls. Lithe and straight, and strong of limb too, grew our slender little Cerito; and, although every motion was still one of grace, it was now the assured grace of strength, instead of that of fragility. She danced too, but it was with the west wind, who, rough companion that he was, whirled her round and round in his strong arms, or tossed her hair in a bright cloud across her face; while he snatched her hat, and sent it spinning into the prairie; or kissed the laugh from her lips, and carried it away to the wild woods to mock at the singing-birds. Argus too-what friends he and the child, who at first had been afraid of him, became before the summer was through! What talks they held! How merrily they laughed together! and how serenely Argus listened while Sunshine told him long histories of imaginary wanderings among the clouds, in enchanted forests, or "away beyond the blue up in the sky"! Confidences these; for, as the narrator whispered, -

"Dora doesn't like dream-stories, and Kitty says, 'Oh, nonsense!' and Karlo laughs: so you mustn't tell a word, old Argus." And Argus, wagging his tail, and blinking his bright brown eyes, promised never to tell, and faithfully kept the promise.

Perhaps it was a vague sense of loneliness in these fancies; perhaps it was the lingering longing for something she had lost even from her memory, and yet not wholly from her heart, where, as we all know, linger loves for which we no longer have a name or a thought; perhaps it was only the dim reflex of that agony consuming her mother's heart, and the earnestness with which it longed for her: but something there was, that, at intervals, cast a sudden shadow over Sunshine's heart; something that made her pale and still, and deepened the dimples at the corners of her mouth, until each might have held a tear. At these times, she would always steal away by herself if possible; sometimes, and especially if the stars were out, to sit with folded hands, gazing at the sky; sometimes to lie upon her little bed, her eyes fixed on vacancy, until the bright tears gathered, and rolled slowly down her cheeks: but, oftenest of all, she would call Argus, and, with one hand upon his glossy head, wander away to the dim forest, and seated at the foot of one of those patriarchal trees, the hound lying close beside her, would talk to him as she never talked to human ears.

Once, Karl, returning from an expedition to a distant part of the farm, saw her thus, and half in fun, half in curiosity, crept up behind the great oak at whose foot she sat, and listened.

"And up there in heaven, Argus," she was saying, "it's all so beautiful! and no one ever speaks loud or cross; and every one has shining white clothes, and flowers on their heads; and some one is there-I don't know - I guess it's an angel; but she's got soft hands, and such pretty shiny hair, and eyes all full of loving me. I dream about her sometimes; but I don't know who she is: and you mustn't tell, Argus. Sometimes I want to die, so as to go to heaven and look for her. Argus, do you want to go to heaven?"

The brown eyes said that Argus wished whatever she did; and Sunshine continued: -

"Well, some day we'll go. I don't know just how; I don't believe we'd find the way if we went now: but some day I shall know, and then I'll tell you. Sometimes I feel so lonesome, Argus! oh, so dreadful homesick! but I don't now. You're a real little comforter, Argus. That's what Dora called me the other night when Kitty was cross: and Dora cried a little when she came to bed, and didn't know I was awake; and I kissed her just so, Argus, and so."

In the game of romps and kisses that ensued, Karl stole away, and, after repeating the child's prattle to Dora, said thoughtfully, -

"There's something strange about her, Dora; something different from any of us. She seems so finely and delicately made, and as if one rude jar might destroy the whole tone of her life. If ever a creature was formed of peculiar, instead of common clay, it is Sunshine."

"Yes, and she must be shielded accordingly," said Dora. But, as she walked on beside Karl, she vaguely wondered if there were not natures as finely strung and as sensitive to suffering as Sunshine's, but united with so reticent an exterior, and such outward strength, as never to gain the sympathy or appreciation so freely bestowed upon the exquisite child.

Such introspection, however, was no part of Dora's healthy temperament; and the next moment she had plunged into a talk upon farm-matters with her cousin, and displayed such shrewdness and clear-sighted wisdom upon the subject, that Capt. Karl laughingly exclaimed, as they entered the house, -

"O general! why weren't you born a man?"

CHAPTER XXX.

KITTY IN THE WOODS.

LEFT to his own guidance, Capt. Karl would have asked no better life than to follow Dora about the farm, or fulfil for her such duties as she could not conveniently perform for herself. Nor was he ever troubled, as a man of less sweet and genial temper might have been, by fears, lest, in thus attending upon his cousin's pleasure, he sacrificed somewhat of manly dignity and the awful supremacy of the sterner sex. "Dora knows" had become to Karl a sufficient explanation of every thing, either in the character or the administration of the girl-farmer, however mysterious it might seem to others; and to defer to Dora's judgment and wishes was perhaps pleasanter and safer in the eyes of the young man than to attempt to consult his own.

But, pleasant though this life might be to both, it came by no means within the scope of Dora's plans; and, so soon as the family were thoroughly settled at Outpost, Karl found himself urged by irresistible pressure to the pursuance of his medical studies.

Five miles from Outpost, in the youthful town of Greenfield, was already established a respectable physician of the old school, who, troubled with certain qualms and doubts as to the ability of the system he had practised so many years to bear the scrutiny of the new lights thrown upon it by the progress of science, was very glad to secure the services, and even advice, of a young man educated in the best medical schools of the Eastern States; and not only consented to take Karl into his office as student until the nominal term of his studies should have expired, but offered him a partnership in his practice so soon as he should receive his diploma.

The arrangement was accordingly made; and every morning after breakfast, Karl, often with a rueful face, often with an audible protest, mounted his horse, and rode to Greenfield, leaving the household at Outpost to a long day of various occupations until his return at night.

Sometimes Dora, upon Max, her little Indian pony, would accompany him a few miles, or as far as his road led toward the scene of her own labors; but no Spartan dame or Roman matron could more sternly have resisted the young man's frequent entreaties to be allowed to accompany her farther than the point at which their roads diverged.

"No, sir! You to your work, and I to mine. Suppose I were to neglect the farm, and come to sit in Dr. Gershom's office all day," argued the fair young moralist, but found herself rather disconcerted by her pupil's gleeful laugh, as he replied, -

"Good, good! Try it once, do; and let me see if it would be so very bad. I think I could forgive you."

"Suppose, then, instead of arguing any more with you, I jump Max over this brook, and leave you where you are?" said Dora, a little vexed; and, suiting the action to the word, she was off before her cousin could remonstrate.

In the evening of the day when this little scene occurred, Karl, upon his return home, found Dora seated with Sunshine upon the grass under the great chestnut-tree.

"A letter for you, you horrid tyrant!" said he, taking one from his pocket, and tossing it into her lap.

"She isn't; and you are a naughty old Karlo to say such names!" cried Sunshine, flashing her blue eyes indignantly upon the laughing face of the young man.

"Such names as what, Dolce?" asked he, jumping from his horse, and trying to catch the child, who evaded his grasp, and replied with dignity, -

"It isn't any consequence, Karlo. She isn't it, and you know she isn't."

"But it is of consequence; for I don't know what it is she isn't. Please tell me, mousey; won't you?"

"She isn't a tireout, you know she isn't, then. You sha'n't laugh! Dora, shall Karlo laugh at me? shall he?"

"No, dear, he won't; but you mustn't be a cross little girl if he does. Now run to the house, and tell Aunt Kitty that Karlo has come home, and see if tea is ready."

The child put up her lips for a kiss, bestowed a glance of dignified severity upon the offender, and walked towards the house with measured steps for a little distance; then, with the frolicsome caprice of a kitten, made a little caper in the air, and danced on, singing, in her clear, sweet voice, - "Dear, dear, what can the matter be? Karlo can't stay from here!"

"Funny child!" exclaimed the object of the stave. "A true little woman, with her loves and spites. Who is the letter from, Dolo?"

"Mr. Brown," said Dora, slowly folding it, and rising from her seat under the tree to return to the house.

"Aha! Seems to me the parson is not so attentive as he used to be. Have you and he fallen out?"

"No, indeed! we are the best of friends; and, in proof of it, this letter is to say he is coming to make a little visit at Outpost, if convenient to us."

"And is it convenient?" asked Karl somewhat curtly.

"Certainly; or, at least, we can make it so. Either you can take him into your room, or Kitty can give him hers, and come into mine."

Karl said nothing; but, as they walked toward the house, his face remained unusually serious, and he seemed to be thinking deeply. Dora glanced at him once or twice, and at last asked abruptly, -

"Don't you want Mr. Brown to come, Karl?"

"Certainly, certainly, if you do. It is your own house, and you have a right to your own guests," replied the young man coldly.

Dora colored indignantly.

"For shame, Karl! Did I ever say a thing like that to you in the old house? and would you have been pleased if I had?"

"No, Dolo; and no again. But you never were a selfish fool, like me. Yes, I am glad Mr. Brown is coming; and I think I will stay at Greenfield while he is here. Then he can have my room."

"No, no: that won't do at all. He comes to see us all; and, of course, we can manage a room without turning you out. Kitty can come into mine" -

"Dora, what is the day of the month?"

"The 17th, I believe."

"Yes, the 17th of August; and seven days more will bring the 24th of August, Dora."

"Of course. Do you suppose he will be here by that time?" asked Dora unconsciously.

Karl looked at her in a sort of comic despair.

"Dora, if you were not the most utterly truthful of girls, you would be the most cruel of coquettes."

Dora's eyes rose swiftly to his face, read it for a moment, and then fell; while a sudden color dyed her own.

"You remember the date now?" asked Karl, almost mockingly. "See here!" and, taking from his pocket the memorandum-book of a year before, he opened it to a page bearing only the words, -

"Dora. Wednesday, Aug. 24."

"O Karl! I thought" -

"Stop, general! It is I who must be officer of the day on this occasion; and I forbid one word. I only wished to let you see that I have not forgotten. And so Mr. Brown is coming to see us?"

Again Dora glanced in perplexity at her cousin's face, but, this time, said not a word. Indeed, if she had wished, there was hardly time; for Kitty, appearing at the door, called, -

"Come, folks, come! Supper is ready and cooling."

"Coming, Kit-kat; and so is somebody else!" cried Karl.

"Somebody? Christmas is coming, I suppose; but not just yet. Did you hear that over at Greenfield?" replied Kitty, resting her hands on her brother's shoulders, and graciously receiving his kiss of greeting.

"It's not Christmas, but Parson Brown, who is coming; and I brought the news from Greenfield, although I did not know it until I arrived here," said Karl.

"Oh, a letter to Dora!" exclaimed Kitty quickly; and over her face, a moment before so bright, fell a scowling cloud, as she turned away, and busied herself with putting tea upon the table.

The meal was rather a silent one. Kitty was decidedly sulky, Dora thoughtful, and Karl a little bitter in his forced gayety; so that Sunshine, sensitive as a mimosa, ate but little, and, creeping close to Dora's side as they rose from the table, whispered, -

"What's the reason it isn't happier, Dora?"

"Aren't you happy, pet? Come and help me wash the teacups, and tell me how the kitties do to-day. Have you given them their milk?"

"I suppose you can do up these dishes without me. I got tea all alone; and I'd like to take my turn at a walk, or something pleasant, now," said Kitty crossly.

"Yes, do, Kitty. Dolce and I will do all that is to be done. It isn't much, because you always clear up as you go along," said Dora.

"There's no need of leaving every thing round, the way some folks do. Dolly, I do wish you'd set up your chair when you've done with it; and here's a mess of stuff" -

"Oh, don't throw it away, Kitty! It's my moss; and I'm going to make the pussies a house of stones, and have it grow all over moss. Dora said I might - Oh, oh! you're real naughty and ugly now, Kitty Windsor; and I sha'n't love you, and Argus shall bite you" -

But Kitty, with a contemptuous laugh, was already walking away, taking especial pains to tread upon the bits of bright moss as they lay scattered along the path.

"Dora, see! I do hate-no, I dislike-Kitty, just as hard as I can; and I can't get any more pretty moss" -

The child was crying passionately; and Dora left every thing to take her in her arms, and soothe and quiet her.

"Aunt Kitty is very neat and nice, little Sunshine; and the moss has earth clinging to it that might drop on the floor; and, besides, it takes up room, and we have so little, - hardly more than a mouse has in its nest. Oh! I never told you how I found a whole nest of mice in one of my slippers once, - six little tiny fellows, no bigger than your thumb; and every one with two little black, beady eyes, and a funny little tail."

"When was it? When you was a little teenty girl, like me? And was you afraid of the big mouse? What did you do with them?"

"Come, wipe the teaspoons, and I will tell you," said Dora, going back to her work; and, the April cloud having passed, the Sunshine was as bright as ever.

Karl, behind his newspaper, heard, saw, and understood the whole; and his mental comment might have seemed to some hearers but little connected with the scene that called it forth. It was simply, -

"Confound old Brown!"

Kitty, meantime, had walked rapidly towards the wood; but though the sunset-clouds were gorgeous, the lights and shadows of the forest rare and shifting, and the birds jubilant in their evening song, she saw nothing, heard nothing, knew nothing, except the tumult in her own heart.

For, in the recesses of the wood, she paused, and throwing herself upon the ground, her face hidden upon her arms, gave way to a paroxysm of tears. Then, rising to her feet as suddenly, she paced up and down, her hands clinched before her, her black brows knit, and her mouth hard and sullen.

"I can't help it," muttered she: "it's the way I was made, and the way I shall die, I expect. I know I'm mean and hateful, and not half as good as she; but - Oh! it's too bad, too bad! - it's cruel, and I can't bear it! Mother loved me, - yes, she loved me best of every thing; and that hateful Pic killed her: whose fault was that but Dora's? Then Charlie-what does he care for me beside her? and, and - Well, perhaps Mr. Brown never would have noticed me at any rate; but, while she's round, he has no eyes for any one else. Even the child, and the cats, and the dog, and the horses, every living thing, loves her better than me; and now he's coming to court her right before my eyes! I wish I was dead! I wish I'd never been born! I'm not fit to live!"

She then threw herself again upon the ground, pressing her burning forehead against the cool moss, and grasping handfuls of the leaves rustling about her, while she wailed again and again, -

"I'm not fit to live, - not fit to live! Oh, I wish I was dead this minute! O God! if you love me any better than the rest, let me die, let me die this minute; for I am not fit to live."

"Then you cannot be fit to die, my child," said a voice above her; and, starting up, Kitty found herself confronted by a tall, fine-looking man, of about thirty years of age; his handsome face just now wearing an expression of sorrowful sternness as he fixed his eyes upon Kitty's, which fell before them.

"Mr. Brown!" stammered she.

"Yes, Kitty: my journey has been more rapid than I could have expected; and I arrived at Greenfield about an hour ago. Finding you so near, I took a horse, and came out here to-night. You did not hear me approach; and, when I saw you through the trees, I dismounted, and came to ask you what was the matter. I heard only your last words, and perhaps I should not have noticed them; yet, as a friend of you and yours, I will say again, Kitty, he who is not fit to live should feel himself most unfit to die, which is but to live with all the passions that made life unendurable made ours forever."

"Do you think so? If I should die now, should I feel just as badly when I came to in the other world?" asked Kitty with at startled look.

Mr. Brown smiled, as he answered, -

"I cannot think, Kitty, that your remorse or your sorrows can be as deep as you fancy. Perhaps they are only trifling vexations connected with outside matters, not rising from real wrong within. But you won't want to hear a sermon before I even reach the house: so come and show me the way there, and tell me how you all are."

"Dora is very well," said Kitty, so crisply, that Mr. Brown glanced at her sharply, and walked on in silence. Presently he said, -

"You must not think, Kitty, that I mean to treat your troubles lightly, whatever they may be. Think about them a little longer by yourself; and in a day or two, if they still seem as unendurable, perhaps it will relieve you to talk to me as plainly as you choose. I shall be very glad to help you if I can, Kitty; very glad and willing. You must look upon me as another brother."

"Or a cousin, maybe, sir?" suggested Kitty, turning away her head.

CHAPTER XXXI.

THE FOX UNDER THE ROBE.

DORA sitting upon the doorstep, with Sunshine nestled close beside her, was quite astonished to see Mr. Brown appearing from the forest with Kitty, as his letter had named no day for his arrival; and she had not expected him so soon.

She went to meet him, however, with a greeting of unaffected cordiality; and as, while holding out her hand, she raised to his her clear and steadfast eyes, the young man's somewhat serious face lighted with a sudden, happy glow, making it so handsome, that Kitty, eagerly watching the meeting, turned white to the very lips, and hastily passed on toward the house.

"Come, Dolce," said she, "I will put you to bed. Dora's lover has come to see her, and she won't have a look for either of us to-night."

"I love you, Kitty; and I don't mind if you did throw away my moss. I won't bring any more into the house."

But Sunshine, well disposed as, through Dora's careful suggestions, she had become toward Kitty, was rather alarmed than pleased at the sudden embrace in which she found herself wrapped, and the eager kisses, among which Kitty whispered, -

"O Dolce! Do you, do you love poor Kitty a little?

You're an angel, and I'm real sorry about the moss; but you can get some more, can't you? I'll help you hunt for it to-morrow while they're gone to walk or ride. They'll be off all day; but we won't mind. Do you love me, Dolly?"

"Yes, I do, Kitty; and I know a place where the moss is so thick, you can't step unless you put your foot on it. But I didn't, 'cause" -

"'Cause what, you darling?"

"'Cause the little creatures that live in the woods come and dance there nights, and they wouldn't like it if it was dirty."

"What creatures? The woodchucks?"

"Why, no, Aunt Kitty! the little girls and boys, or something. They whisper way off among the trees, and dance too, just when the sun sets. Didn't you ever see them skipping in and out among the trees just as far off as you could look?"

"Those are shadows, Dolly; and the whispering in the trees is the wind. You mustn't have so many fancies, child, or by and by you'll get cracked."

"Then you can boil me in milk, just as you did the teacup," murmured Sunshine, half asleep.

Kitty made no answer, but, smoothing the sheet over the little girl, went to seat herself at the open window.

Far off upon the prairie she heard the night-winds come and go, - now moaning like some vast spirit wandering disquieted, now falling soft and low as the breath of the sleeping earth; and the vague voice and the cool touch seemed to quiet the fever of the young girl's heart, although she knew not how or why.

Above, in the purple skies, stood all the host of heaven, looking down with solemn benediction upon the earth, lying peaceful and loving beneath their gaze; and even Kitty-poor, lonely, heartsick Kitty-lifted her hot, tearful face toward them, and felt the holy calm descend upon her aching heart.

Falling upon her knees, she raised her arms yearningly toward heaven; and her whole soul struggled upward in the cry, -

"Oh I wish I could, I wish I could, be good! O God! make me good enough to die and go to where my mother is!"

A light step upon the stair, a gentle hand upon the latch, and strange Kitty, perverse even among her best impulses, started up, and stood cold and silent in the darkness.

"Kitty!" said Dora's voice softly.

"Well. I'm here."

"Won't you come down now? Sunshine is asleep; isn't she?"

"Yes."

"Well, won't you come?"

"By and by: I've got to see to the beds. Where is Mr. Brown going to sleep?"

"I thought you might give him your room, and come in here."

"Indeed I sha'n't!" replied Kitty in a strange voice. "He is no company of mine; and I don't want him even to look into my room. I'd never sleep there again if he did once!"

"Well, then, we can make a bed for Karl on the floor, and Mr. Brown can have his bed," said Dora quietly, seeing nothing deeper in Kitty's refusal than a little impulse of perversity.

Kitty made no reply; and Dora, groping her way toward where she stood, put an arm about her waist, saying, -

"Come, Kitty, come down with me. You're tired, I know; and it is too bad you have so much to do. To-morrow I will stay at home and help you. Karl can take a holiday, and show Mr. Brown over the farm."

"What nonsense! I don't do any thing to hurt; and it would be pretty well for you to send Mr. Brown off with Karl, when he came here on purpose to see you."

"Oh, no, he didn't! He came to see us all; and he asked where you were just now, when we came in."

"And that was why you came to look for me; wasn't it?" asked Kitty suspiciously.

"Not wholly. I had been thinking of it for some minutes."

"But couldn't bear to leave long enough," suggested Kitty; adding, however, "Well, I'll come. I suppose it is no more than polite, as long as he's company."

"Of course it isn't; and you know Mr. Brown is very ceremonious," said Dora, so archly, that Kitty paused in smoothing her hair to say, -

"Now, if you're going to make fun of me, Dora" -

"Oh, I'm not!-not a bit of it. There, now, you're nice enough for any thing."

In the kitchen, besides Mr. Brown and Karl, the girls found Mr. And Mrs. Ross; Mehitable demurely seated in a corner, and knitting a long woollen stocking; while Seth, under the skilful management of Mr. Brown, was giving quite an interesting description of life in a Maine logging-camp.

"Do you ever have any trouble from wild beasts in that region?" asked the chaplain.

"Waal, some. There's lots of b'ar about by spells; and once't in a while a painter or a wild-cat-wolverines, some calls 'em out here."

"Did you ever meet one yourself?"

"Which on 'em?"

"Either. Bears, for instance."

"Yes, sir. I've took b'ar ever since I wor old enough to set a trap."

"Did you ever have any trouble with one?"

"Waal, I don' know as I did. They was mostly pooty 'commodatin'," said Seth, drawing the back of his brown hand across his mouth to hide a self-complacent grin at the recollection of his own exploits.

"Tell Mr. Brown 'bout the painter and Uncle 'Siah's Harnah," suggested Mehitable in a low voice; and as Seth only stirred in his chair, and looked rather reprovingly at his wife, the guest added, -

"Yes, Mr. Ross, tell us that, by all means."

"Ho! 'twa'n't much of a story; only the woman thinks consid'able about it, 'cause it wor a cousin of ourn that wor took off."

"Indeed! and what were the circumstances?" politely insisted Mr. Brown. So Seth, tilting his chair upon its hind-legs, and crossing his own, stuck his chin into the air; fixed his eyes upon the ceiling, and began, in the inimitable nasal whining voice of a Down-East Yankee, the story narrated in the following chapter.

CHAPTER XXXII.

THE PAINTER AND UNCLE 'SIAH'S HARNAH.

"WHEN father settled up nigh the head-waters of the Penobscot, folks said we'd have to be mighty car'ful, or some o' the young ones would tumble over the jumping-off-place, we'd got so nigh. But Uncle 'Siah went right along, and took up land furder on, whar there wa'n't nothing but hemlock-trees and chipmunks for company, and no passing to keep the women-folks running to the winders. Thar was a good road cut through the woods, and there was the river run within a stone's-throw of both houses: so, one way and another, we got back'ards and for'ards consid'able often, 'specially when the young folks begun to grow up.

"Harnah wor Uncle 'Siah's second gal, and just as pooty as a picter. She looked suthin' like Dolcy, Dora's little adopted darter, you know: but she wor alluz a-larfin', and gitting off her jokes; and had a sort of a wicked look by spells, enough to make a feller's flesh creep on his bones."

"Lor', that's enough o' Harnah! She wa'n't so dreffal different from other folks. Git along to the story part on't," interrupted Mehitable, clicking her knitting-needles energetically.

Seth looked at her a little indignantly for a moment, and then burst into a loud laugh, -

"Lor'! I'd clear forgot how it used ter spite Hit to hear me praise up Harnah. You see, sir, Mehitabul wor a sort o' cousin o' my mother's, and so come to live long of us when her father died: but she never cottoned to Harnah very strong when she see how well I liked her; though, now she's got me for her own man, I'd think" -

"But the panther, Mr. Ross," interposed Dora, who saw, with womanly sympathy, the flush of mortification upon Mehitable's face: "do tell us about the panther."

"Yes: I b'lieve my idees was kind o' wandering from the pint; but that's nothing strange, if you knowed what an out-an-outer that gal was. Well, well, 'tain't no use a-crying over spilt milk, and by-gones may as well be stay-gones.

"Sam Hedge, he was my uncle's hired man, and a plaguy smart feller too; good-looking, merry as a grig, a live Yankee for faculty, and pretty forehanded too, though he hadn't set up for himself then. I more than suspicioned he'd ruther live with Uncle 'Siah, and see Harnah from morning to night, than go off and take up land for himself; or maybe he didn't feel as if he'd the peth to take right hold of new land all alone. Anyway, there he wor, and there he stuck, right squar in my way, do as much as I might to git him out on't.

"Of course, you onderstand about being in my way means all along o' Harnah. We was both sweet on her, and no mistake; though nary one on us, nor, I believe, the gal herself, could ha' told which one she favored.

"Waal, to skip over all the rest (though there's the stuff for half a dozen stories in it), I'll come to one night when I'd been up to Uncle 'Siah's, and Harnah and Sam had come down to the crick to see me off; for I'd come in my boat. I felt kind o' savage; for Harnah had been mighty pooty with me all that evening; and I knew Sam had come down to the boat a purpose to go back to the house with her, and, 'fore they was half-way, she'd come right round, and be just as clever to him as she'd been before to me."

"If you knew your cousin to be such a terrible little flirt as that, I shouldn't think you would have cared so much about her, Seth," suggested Karl, laughing.

"No more shouldn't I, cap'n," replied Seth ruefully. "But somehow I couldn't help it. I'd think it over nights, and say to myself, 'You darned fool! don't you see the gal's a-playing one of you off agin t'other, and maybe don't care a pin for neither? Get shet of her once for all, and be a man; can't ye?' And then I'd find I couldn't; and so it went till we come to that night, and stood there on the edge of the crick, - two on us ready to clinch and fight till one cried enough, and t'other a-laughing at us both.

"So, all to once, Harnah says, says she, -

"'I do believe them harebells are blowed out by this time. Ain't they, boys?'

"'You and I'll go to-morrow and see, anyway,' says Sam, speaking up quick, 'fore I got the chance.

"'I'm a-going to see; and, if Harnah'll come too, all the better,' says I, as pleasant as a bear with a sore head.

"'Two's company, and three's a crowd; so you'd better

stop to home, Seth,' says Sam.

"'Two's company, that's Harnah and me; and three's a crowd, that's you: so, ef you don't like crowding nor being crowded, you'd better stop to home yourself,' says I.

"'I believe I spoke first, Seth Ross,' says Sam, pretty savage at last.

"'That don't make no difference, as I know on. Harnah was my cousin long afore you was her father's hired man; and that puts me in mind you hain't asked leave yet. Maybe the old man won't let you go. What you going to do then?' asked I, dreadful kind of sneering; for I felt mad.

"Sam he didn't say nothing; but he drew back, and doubled up his fists. I caught the glint of his eye in the moonlight, and my darnder riz.

"'Come on,' says I; 'I'm ready for you; and we'll fight it out like men. The feller that's licked shall give up once for all.'

"But 'fore Sam could speak, or I could hit out as I wanted ter, Harnah come right in between us. I swow ef that gal didn't look harnsome! Her eyes was wide open, and shining just like blue steel in the moonlight. Her cheeks and lips was white; and seemed to me the very curls of her hair shot out sparks, she was so mad.

"'You'd better stop while there's time,' says she, still and cold. 'If you strike one another, or if you ever fight, and I the cause, I swear to God I never will speak a civil word to either one of you again as long as I live.

So now you know.

"'As for the harebells, you sha'n't neither one of you go for 'em. Ef I want harebells, there's them that can get 'em for me, and not make so much fuss about it neither.'

"She turned, and stepped off toward the house as if she'd got steel springs in the soles of her feet.

"Sam and I eyed each other. It seemed as if Harnah felt that look; for she turned all of a sudden, and come back.

"'Sam,' says she, p'inting up to the house, 'go home; and don't you speak to me again to-night. Seth, get into your boat, and push her off. You needn't come up to-morrow night.'

"We sort o' looked at one another and at her, and then meeched off the way she told us, for all the world like two dogs that's got a licking, and been sent home 'fore the hunt was done.

"I didn't sleep a great deal that night. Fact is, I was turning over in my own mind what Harnah had said about them as would git harebells for her, and not make so much fuss about it neither.

"'I swow,' says I, 'I'd like to clinch that feller, whoever he may be, and not have Harnah nigh enough to interfere.' Then I rec'lected a Cap'n Harris, a British officer, that come down from Canady the summer before, hunting and fishing, and had stopped a week or more at Uncle 'Siah's, mostly for the sake of seeing Harnah, as I thought then, and do now. Ever since, when Harnah didn't know how else to plague Sam and me, she'd set up to talk about 'real gentlemen,' and 'folks that knowed manners,' and all sech stuff. Then she'd pretend she'd got a letter from Cap'n Harris, and that he was coming agin, and all that. So now I got it in my head that Cap'n Harris was coming, and that she meant he'd get the harebells.

"'But I'll bet he won't, without a fight, anyway,' says I, clinching up my fist; and then I went to sleep quite comf'table.

"Now, there wa'n't but one place, as I knew of, where harebells was to be found; and Harnah had showed me that place herself the summer afore, and I had picked the flowers for her. So I made up my mind to go next day and see if they was in blow; and, if they was, to get a bunch anyway, and take the resk of giving 'em to Harnah arterwards.

"I couldn't git away in the morning nohow; for Hitty seemed to know it was something about Harnah that was calling me, and contrived all sorts of business to keep me to hum: but, after dinner, I jist took my hat, and cleared out afore she knowed it, and, by the time she missed me, was half a mile up the river.

"'Twas a pooty day as ever you see; and as I rowed along, listening to the water running by the boat, and the wind rustling in the trees, I began to feel real sort of good, and didn't care half so much about Sam or the British cap'n as I did when I started. When I come to the landing at Uncle 'Siah's, I never stopped, though I looked with all my eyes for any signs of Harnah; but couldn't see no one but Sam going out to the cornfield, with a hoe on his shoulder.

"'Good for you, Sam,' says I to myself. 'Hard work's dreadful wholesome for love-sickness.' So I rowed along as merry as a cricket, and pretty soon tied up my boat, and struck off into the woods. It was consid'able of a walk; and I strolled along easy till I came to the place whar the harebells growed, 'bout a mile and a half from the river. This was a high clift, covered with brush and trees on one side, and on the other falling sheer down to a little deep valley, with another clift rising opposite. These clifts joined each other at the two ends of the valley: so there was no getting into it anyway but down the faces of 'em, and that was as much as a man's neck was worth; but, fur's I know, no man had ever wanted to, nor ever tried to, till that day.

"The harebells growed on the very edge of the fust clift, and a little way down the face of it, and looked mighty pooty a-floating in the wind. Harnah, who was kind of romantic, said they was the plume in the old clift's hat; and she called the place the Lovers' Rock, 'case, she said, the two clifts seemed taking hold of hands, and jist going to kiss."

"That sounds like Harnah, anyway," muttered Mehitable contemptuously.

"Yes, it's more uv an idee than you'd 'a been likely to git off, ain't it, Hit?" asked Seth with a malicious grin, and winking at the company.

But Mehitable preserving a prudent silence, and only showing her feelings by an accelerated movement of her knitting-needles, her husband elevated his eyes again to the ceiling, recrossed his legs, and continued: -

"I scrambled up the back of the clift easy enough; and,

sure enough, there was the posies, all in blow, and tossing their heads at me as if they knowed how pooty they was, and dared me not to say so. Somehow they made me think of Harnah; and I spoke right out, -

"'Yes, I know you be; and I hain't never said you ain't as pooty a cretur as walks the airth: but I wish you wan't so awful changeable.'

"Then I laffed right out, to think I was talking to a lot of flowers same as if they was a gal; and, when I done laffin', I went down on my knees, and begun to pick 'em. But I hadn't more than got the first fist-ful when I heerd a groan, a sort uv a faint holler groan, that sounded as if it come right out uv the ground underneath me. I dropped the flowers, and riz right up on eend. My ha'r riz too; for I was scaart, I tell you. 'But,' thinks I, "twon't do to run away the fust lick:' so I held on, and pooty soon it come agin. This time I listened sharp, and had my wits about me; so that, when it wor thro-ugh, I clim' right up to the top uv the ledge, and looked down into the valley, hollerin' -

"'Who be you? Is any one thar?'

"A voice answered, faint and weak; but what it said, or whar it was, I couldn't for the life of me tell.

"So I hollered agin, -

"'Whar be you, stranger ? Holler as loud as you kin!'

"The voice answered back; and I heerd my own name, and, as I thought, in a voice that turned me as sick and weak as a gal.

"It was Harnah's voice; and my first idee was that she wor dead, and wor ha'nting me.

"'Harnah!' says I, soft and low, 'is it you?'

"There wa'n't no answer, but another groan, and along of it a curious kind of noise, like a lot of cats all growling together. I knowed that noise; and, afore it eended, I knowed whar it come from. And, all to once, the hull story come to me: Harnah was down thar in a painter's den; and the kittens was a-growling round her. The old ones must be away, or one of 'em would 'a been out to see to me afore this.

"I hadn't the fust thing in the way of a we'pon with me; but there was plenty of stones down in the hollow, and I cut a good oak-sapling with my jack-knife. Then I sot myself to scramble down the face of the clift; and, I tell you, I sweat before I got to the bottom. Ef it hadn't been for Harnah, I couldn't 'a done it; but, somehow or 'nother, I reached the bottom, and looked about me. Sure enough, close to my feet was the mouth of a cave, running right in under the ledge, though not more than three foot high. I knelt down and peeked in, calling, -

"'Harnah, be you thar?'

"'Seth, is it you?' asked a voice very faint.

"'Yes, my dear, it is,' says I, 'and bound to get you out uv this scrape about the quickest. What's a-keeping you in there?'

"'My leg is broke, and the horrid creature is lying on my feet!' says Harnah.

"I didn't wait for no more questions, but crawled inter the hole. A dozen feet from the mouth, I come to a snarl of fur, and glary eyes, and snapping teeth, and savage growls, that I finally made out to be a couple of painter-kittens, not more'n a few days old, but savage enough for a hundred. They was snuggled close up to something: what it was I couldn't at fust make out in the darkness; but putty soon I see that it was a full-grown painter, lying stretched out at length. I started back, with all the blood in me pricking at my fingers' ends with the scare I'd got; but Harnah's voice from beyond says, -

"Don't be frightened at the old panther. She's dead. They fought, and one ran away; and this one is dead.'

"And is she a-lying on your feet, did you say? It's so dark in here, I can't see the fust thing,' says I, feeling round for the critter's head, and gitting my paws tore by the young ones, who, I must say for 'em, was mighty handy with their claws for their age. So says I,-

"'Well, fust thing, I'll get red o' these little devils; and then I'll drag out the karkiss, and see to you, my poor gal.'

"So I clinched the fust one by the throat, and, when he hung like a rag, pitched him out, and grappled t'other; but he was a case, I tell you. Fight! - you'd ought ter have seen him! - and scratch and bite, and spit and yowl, till the whole woods rung with his uproar. I mastered him finally; but he'd done his work, and come nigh beating me even arter he was dead, as ye shall hear.

"When the kittens was out of the way, I clinched the

karkiss uv the old painter, and dragged it to'rst the mouth uv the cave. It wor hard work; and, when I'd got part way, I left it lying, and squeezed by (for it most filled up the passage), and went to see how bad Harnah might be hurt; for, when I spoke to her last, she hadn't made no reply. Leaning over her, I felt round for her face, and had jist touched her cold cheek, and called to her to know if she was alive, when I heerd jist over my head the awfulest roar that ever come out uv a creter's throat; and so loud, that it echoed through and through the cave enough to deaf you. The minute I heerd it, I knew what was tew pay, and give up for lost. It wor the man o' the house come home in a hurry to see what them squalls uv the dying kittens meant; and that's how I said they come nigh beating me even arter they was dead.

"Now, mister, what would you say a man had ought to have done in such a fix as that? - run, or stay? Mind ye, I hadn't the fust thing in shape uv a we'pon, nor couldn't get hold even uv my stick, nor the stones outside; and what could a feller do with his naked fists, shet up in a hole with a wild-cat?"

"It was a trying situation; but I don't believe you ran away," said Mr. Brown good-humoredly.

"Yer bet your life on that, stranger," replied Seth with emphasis. "I hadn't no idee on't; though the only other chance seemed to be to jump down the critter's throat, and choke him, so's ter spile his stomach for Harnah.

"I looked to the mouth uv the cave, and thought, 'He won't get by that karkiss very easy;' and then, all of a sudden, the strangest idee you ever heerd come acrost me, and I jumped as though I'd been shot. It wor to play off one of the critters agin the other, and keep the old painter out uv his den with the karkiss of his mate.

"It wor a curus idee, now, worn't it; but they say a drownding man'll clinch to a straw, and this wor worth the trying to a feller in as tight a place as I. So I tumbled the old lady over as well as I could, and got her wedged inter the narrerest part uv the road, with her back rounded out, and her paws in, so's't I should have a better chance for hanging on than the old feller outside 'ud have for pulling. Then, with my jack-knife, I cut a slit in one of the fore-legs and one of the hind, to put my hands inter; and then I held on.

"'Twa'n't but a minute arter I got fixed 'fore he wor down upon me, yelling and squalling enough ter make a man's blood run cold. They call 'em Injin Devils down our way; and I guess there ain't no kind uv devils make a wuss-soundin' noise. I jist shut my eyes, and lay low; for when I knowed that furce, wild creter wor within two foot uv me, and nothing ter keep him off but a karkiss that he'd claw ter pieces in ten minutes, I kinder wondered how I'd been sich a plaguy fool as to think uv the plan, and ter feel so pleased with it.

"And didn't yer never mind, sir, when you've been laying out for some great pull, you feel as if you'd got fixed fustrate, and was sure ter win, till the minute comes; and then, all ter once, your gitting-ready seems no account somehow, and you feel downright shamed uv what, a minute before, made you so chirk?"

"Yes, that is human nature, Seth; but it is well to remember that cool precaution is worth more than excitement, after all," said Mr. Brown.

"Yes, sir, I suppose so now; but I didn't then. It only seemed to me as ef I was a darned fool, though I couldn't hev said what I'd ought to hev done different ef I'd been ever so wise. Well, the critter come, and he stuck his head in, snuffing and smelling for a minute; and then reached in one paw, jest as softly as you've seed a pussy-cat feeling uv a ball uv yarn on the floor. Then he growled; for either he'd smelt or he'd seed me a-peekin' over the old woman's corpse at him. Hokey! didn't I wish I'd a good gun handy jis' then, with sech a splendid chance to sight it! But I hadn't; and thar was the critter, growling and tearing away at the karkiss like mad: fer he'd pooty much made up his mind by this time what sort o' game lay behind it, and he was bound to be at it. Any one would 'a thought his nateral feelings would 'a stood in the way some, seein' as 'twor his own wife he wor clapper-clawin' at sich a rate; but they didn't seem to a bit: and, I tell you, he made the fur fly 'thout con-sideration. The blood streamed down inter my face, and the smell of that and the flesh choked me. My arms wor straightened clean out with holding on; and sometimes I could jest see the green eyes o' the painter, an' feel his hot breath, as he opened his jaws to hiss and spit at me jis' like a big cat. I felt the eend uv all things wor at hand; an', shettin' my eyes, I tried hard ter say a prayer, or somethin' good an' fittin'. I couldn't think o' none, hows'ever: so I jis' turned raound, and sez, 'Harnah! good-by, Harnah!' an' felt most as if I'd prayed; though she, poor gal! wor clean swownded away, and never heerd a word on't.

"Jes' then, when my thoughts wor so took up that I'd act'ally most forgot where I wor, and jes' held on to the critter kind o' mechanical-like, I heerd a shot, and then another. The painter heerd 'em too, an' more than heerd 'em, I reckon; for, with a growl an' a roar that made me scringe, he let go the karkiss, an' backed hisself out o' the hole 'thout never sayin good-by to me nor to the old lady.

"Next minute I heerd another shot, and then another; and then sech horrid groans and screams, mixed up with growls and hisses from the painter, that I knew he wor hit hard, an' like to die; and, ef I should say I wor sorry, it 'ud be a lie. Then I heerd feet climbing and scrambling down the rocks; and next I heerd a v'ice calling, kind o' frightened-like, -

"'Be you raound here, Harnah, or Seth?'

"'Yes, we be,' says I, waking up all uv a sudden; for I'd lay sort o' stupid till then: but now I wor wide enough awake, and soon made Sam understand where we was, and what was to be done. He didn't say much, but worked away like a good feller, till he got out, fust the mauled karkiss o' the painter, with the flesh all hanging from it in strips; then me, covered with blood, and looking wuss than a dead man, I expect; and finally Harnah, jes' coming to after her dead faint.

"We must git her out o' this horrid den 'fore she knows whar she is, or it'll skeer her to death,' says I, as soon as I could speak. 'But how'll we do it?'

"'You look as if you b'longed here; so I reckon you'd better stop behind, and I'll git Harnah out by myself,' says Sam, laffin' in a kind o' hard way.

"I didn't say nothing; but I thought I wouldn't 'a took that time to laff at a feller, nor yet to show a spite agin him, if I'd been Sam, and he me.

It's more nor I could do to justly tell you how we ever got that gal up them rocks. I expect it wor more the hand o' God, so to speak, than us that did it. Fust place, we tied our handkerchers raound her waist, fer a hold; and then Sam went ahead, pulling her after him, and I sort o' helped behind, and clim' along as well's I could; and bimby we got up, and laid Harnah down to rest among the harebells. When she got a little smarter, she told us how she thought she'd come and git 'em fer herself, and then pertend some one had given 'em to her, jest so's to plague us, and see what we'd say. Then, whilst she was a-picking of 'em, she heerd a painter cry right clost to her, and was so scared, she sot out to run, and, fust she knew, was over the edge of the clift, and rolling down the face on't. When she got to the bottom, her leg was broke, and she couldn't stir; and up to the top o' the rocks she see the painter's head, with his green eyeballs a-glaring down at her, and his ears laid back, ready for a spring. What with the pain, and what with the scare, I expect the poor gal fainted. Anyways, the next thing she knowed was finding herself in the cave with the two painter-kittens playing round her, and the old one lying close to, moving his tail from side to side, and yawning till she could see all his white teeth and great red throat. Ef she wor scart afore, she didn't feel no better now, you'd better believe. But Harnah was a stout-hearted gal, with all her delicate ways; and she never stirred, no made a sound, only lay still, and fixed her eyes as stiddy as she could on those uv the great brute beside her. Pooty soon she see that he wor a-looking at her; and pooty soon he began to make a purring sort of noise, like 'bout forty big tomc-ats tied up in one bag. Then Harnah spoke to him, like as she'd have coaxed a dog, and, arter a while, began to play with the cubs a little. One way and another, they'd got to be 'mazin' good friends all raound, when a cry was heerd outside; and the old man and the little ones pricked up their ears, and yowled in answer. It wor the old woman coming home, sure enough; and the minute she poked her snout inter the den, and see what company her man had got while she wor gone, the trouble begun. Harnah, naterally, wor too much skeered to see justly what went on: but there were a big fight somehow; and she got a notion that the she-painter wanted to fall afoul uv her, and that he wouldn't let her; and, like other married folks, from words they come to blows; and the upshot uv the hull was, that the old lady got the wust on't, and lay dead on the field uv action.

"Whether the husband felt bad, or whether he wanted sunthin' to eat, or whether he had an engagement with another lady, I couldn't say; but, the minute he'd given the finishing blow to his wife, he cleared out, and didn't come back till the cubs called him to see to me.

"Well, we got Harnah home somehow; and next day we come again, and skun the old tiger and the cubs; and I got a hull heap o' harebells. I was bound, that, after all the fuss, Harnah shouldn't lose her harebells; and she didn't."

Seth was silent; and, tilting his chair a little farther back, crossed his hands above his chest, and began to whistle softly. The company looked at him inquiringly; and, after a pause, Karl asked, -

"Well, what next, Seth?"

"Nothing, cap'n: that's all; except I didn't tell how Sam see me going up the river, and suspicioned I wor a going to meet Harnah, and so dropped all, and followed on. What he brought his gun fer, I didn't never ask him."

"But Hannah-what became of her?"

"Oh! she was kind o' peeked a while, with her broken leg; but, arter that, she was as well as ever."

"Yes; but how did her love-affairs terminate?" persisted Karl.

"Waal, she married Sam Hedge the next fall; and I guess their love-affairs turned out like other folkses a good deal, - lots o' 'lasses at fust, and, arter a while, lots o' vinegar: that's the way o' married life."

In delivering this sentiment, Seth bestowed a sidelong glance upon Mehitable, far more merry than sincere in its expression; but she, tranquilly pursuing her knitting, let fall her retort, as if she had not perceived the sarcasm.

"Oh, waal!" said she, "I don't know as I've any call to find fault with married life. Seth's made as good a husband as a gal has a right to expect that takes a feller out o' pity 'cause he's been mittened by another gal."

The laugh remained upon the feminine side of the argument, and the party merrily separated for the night.

CHAPTER XXXIII.

A GLEAM OF DAWN.

ONCE more a summer sunset at the old farm-house among the Berkshire Hills, where, for a hundred years, successive generations of Windsors had been born and bred; once more we see the level rays glance from the diamond-paned, dairy casement, left ajar to admit the fresh evening air; once more the airy banners of eglantine and maiden's-bower float against the clear blue sky; once more we tread in fancy the green velvet of the turf, creeping over the very edge of the irregular door-stone, worn smooth by feet that long since have travelled beyond earthly limits, and now tread celestial fields and sunny slopes of Paradise. Far across the meadow lies the shadow of the old house, - a strange, fantastic suggestion of a dwellings vague and enticing as the gray turrets of the Castle of St. John, which, as the legend says, are to be shaped at twilight from the crags and ravines of the lonely mountains, but vanish in the daylight. And beside it, not vague, but clear and sharp, lay the shadow of the old well-sweep, like a giant finger, pointing, always pointing, now to the east, whence cometh light and hope, and the promise of another day; and anon due west, as showing to the sad eyes that watched it the road to joy and comfort.

Within the house, much was changed. The floors were covered with matting, the walls with delicate paper-hangings; the old furniture replaced with Indian couches and arm-chairs, whose shape and material suggested luxurious ease and coolness. In the chamber that had been Dora's, was wrought, perhaps, the greatest change of all; for to the rugged simplicity, and, so to speak, severity, of the young girl's surroundings, had succeeded the luxury, the exquisite refinement, essential to the comfort of a woman born and bred in the innermost sanctuary of modern civilization. The martial relics of Dora's camp-life had disappeared from the walls, no longer simply whitewashed, but covered with a pearl-gray paper, over which trailed in graceful curves a mimic ivy-vine, colored like nature. Upon this hung a few choice pictures, - proof-engravings of Correggio's Cherubs; a Christ blessing Little Children; a Madonna, with sad, soft eyes resting upon the Holy Child, whose fixed gaze seemed to read his own sublime destiny; and a Babes in the Wood.

Over the fireplace, the rude sketch of the deformed negro was replaced by an exquisite painting, representing a little girl, - her sweet face framed in a shower of golden ringlets, her blue eyes fixed with a sort of wistful tenderness upon the beholder; this expression repeating itself in the lines of the curving mouth. The dress was carefully copied from that worn by 'Toinette Legrange upon the day she was lost; and the picture had been painted, soon after her disappearance, by an artist friend of the family, who had so often admired the beautiful child, that he found it easy to reproduce her face upon canvas; although his own knowledge of the circumstances, and perhaps the haunting presence of the sad eyes of the mother, as she asked, "Oh! can you give me even a picture of her?" had tinged the whole composition with a pathos not intended by the artist, but indescribably touching to the spectator.

Between the windows, in place of Dora's simple pine

table, with its white drapery, its few plain books, and little work-box, stood a toilet-table, covered with the luxurious necessities of an elegant woman's wardrobe. The dressing-case, the jewel-box, the perfume-bottles; the velvet-lined and delicately-scented mouchoir and glove boxes; the varied trifles, so idle in detail, so essential to the whole, - all were there, and all evidently in constant use.

Nor let us too harshly judge the mode of life, differ though it may from our own, which regards these superfluities as essential, and can hardly less dispense with them than with its daily bread. The violet, the anemone, the May-flower, a hundred sweet and hardy blossoms, thrive amid the chills and storms of early spring in the most exposed situations. But are not the exquisite tea-rose, the fragile garden-lily, or the cereus, that dies after one sweet night of perfumed beauty, as true to their nature and to God's law? Did not the same hand form the sparrow, who scatters the late snow from his wings, and gayly pecks the crumbs from our doorstep, and the humming-bird, who waits for gorgeous summer noons to come and sip the honey from our jessamine?

So let us, if we will, love Dora in the Spartan simplicity of her soldierly adornments, and none the less love and cherish the woman who now lies upon the very spot, where, but a year ago, lay little Sunshine, wavering between this life and a better. For some reason unknown to herself, Mrs. Legrange had, from the first, felt a strong affection for this chamber, haunted, though she knew it not, by the presence of the beloved child; and she had taken much pleasure in its adornment; though, now that all was done, she rarely noticed the beautiful articles collected about her, liking best of all to lie in dreamy revery, recalling, day after day, with the minute fondness of a woman's memory, the looks, the gestures, the careless words, the pretty, graceful ways, the artless fascinations, of her whom now she rarely named, holding her memory as something too sacred for common speech, too far withdrawn into her own heart to be lightly brought to the surface.

Thus lying in the twilight of this evening, dreamily watching the long white curtains as they filled with the night-air and floated out into the room like the shadowy sails of a bark anchored in some Dreamland bay, and never guessing whose eyes had watched their waving but one short year before, when 'Toinette was first laid in Dora's little bed, Mrs. Legrange heard her husband coming up the stairs, and rose to receive him, with a strange fluttering at her heart, - a sort of nervous hope and terror all in one, as if she had known him the bearer of great news, but could not yet determine its tenor.

Mr. Legrange entered, holding a letter in his hand, and glanced tenderly, but with some surprise, at his wife, who stood with one hand pressing the white folds of her muslin wrapper convulsively to her bosom, the other outstretched toward him, a sudden hectic burning in her cheeks, and her eyes bright with feverish light.

"Fanny! what is it?" exclaimed the husband, pausing upon the threshold.

"That letter-you have some news! O Paul, you have news of" -

Her voice died in a breathless flutter; and Mr. Legrange, coming hastily to her side, drew her to a seat, saying tenderly, -

"No, darling, no news of her, - not yet, at least. What made you fancy it? This is only a letter from your prot,g, at Antioch College: at least, I suppose so from the postmark. Do you care to read it now?"

Mrs. Legrange hid her face upon her husband's breast, trembling nervously.

"O Paul! when I heard you coming up the stairs, such a feeling came over me! I seemed to feel some great revelation approaching. I was sure it was news of her. Paul, Paul, I cannot bear it; I cannot live! My heart is broken; but it will not die, and let me rest. O my God! how long?"

"Hush, dearest, hush! Your wild words are to me worse than the grief we both suffer so keenly. But, my wife, have we not each other? And would you kill me by your own despair? Will God be pleased, that, because he has taken away our Sunshine, we refuse all other blessings, and disdain all other ties and obligations? Fanny, dearest, is it not an earnest duty with you to strive for strength?"

But the mother only moaned impatiently, -

"O Paul! do not try, do not talk: it is useless. When you let fall that crystal vinaigrette this morning, did you tell it that its duty was to be whole, and filled with perfume again? Do you tell those flowers that it is their duty to be fresh and sweet as they were yesterday? or, if you did, would they heed you?"

"No, darling; for they have neither mind nor soul,"

suggested the husband significantly.

"And mine are swallowed up in the sorrow that has swallowed all else. O Paul! forgive me, and ask God to forgive me; but I cannot, I never can, become resigned. I cannot live; I cannot wish or try to live. A little while, and I shall see her."

She spoke the last words softly, as to her own heart; and over her face passed such a look of solemn joy, such yearning tenderness, mingled with an infinite pathos, that the stronger and less sensitive male organization stood awed and subdued before it.

"Her love and grief are deeper than any words of mine can reach," thought the husband, and, so, tenderly soothed her head upon his breast, and said no more for several minutes, until, to his surprise, it was lifted, and the pale face looked into his with the pensive calmness under which it habitually hid its more intimate expressions.

"From whom did you say the letter came, Paul?" asked Mrs. Legrange.

"From Theodore Ginniss, I believe. Will you read it now?" asked her husband, in some surprise at the sudden transition: for no man ever thoroughly comprehends a woman, no woman a man; and so is the distinctive temperament of the sexes preserved.

"Yes: I told him to write to me once in every month, and he is very punctual."

She opened the letter, and read aloud: - "DEAR MRS. LEGRANGE, -

"Since writing to you last month, I have been going on with my studies under the Rev. Mr. Brown, as I then mentioned. I do not find that it hurts me to study in the hot weather at all; and I have enjoyed my vacation better this way than if I had been idle.

"Part of the month, however, Mr. Brown has been away on a visit to some friends in Iowa; and he says so much about the prairies, and the great rivers, and the wild life out there, that I think I should like to take the two remaining weeks of the vacation, and go and see them, if you have no objection. I have a great plenty of money from my last quarter's allowance, as I have only needed to spend a dollar and forty-five cents. Mr. Brown thinks I should come back fresher to my studies for a little rest; though I do not feel the need of it, and am glad of every day's new chance of learning.

"I hope you will excuse me, Mrs. Legrange, if it is too bold for me to say, but I do wish you could talk with Mr. Brown a little; he is so high in all his ideas, and seems to feel so strong about all the troubles of this world, and puts what a man ought to live for so much above the way he has to live!

"I took the liberty of talking with him about you, and about the great trouble I had helped to bring upon you; and what he said was first-rate, though I cannot tell it again. I felt ever so much better about my own doing wrong, and I could not help wishing you could hear what he said about you.

"This place is a great resort for invalids, and people who like to be retired. The iron-springs, that give the name to the town, are said to be very strengthening; and the Neff House, near them, is a beautiful hotel in very romantic scenery, and quite still. It seems to me that the ladies I see riding out from it on horseback get healthier-looking every day.

"I enclose a letter for mother, and will ask of you the favor to read it to her. I cannot tell you, Mrs. Legrange, how grateful I feel to you for making her so comfortable, as well as for what you are doing for me. And it is not only you I thank and remember every morning and every night; but, with yours, I say the name of the angel that we both love so dear.

"Yours respectfully,
"THEODORE GINNISS."

Mrs. Legrange slowly folded the letter, and looked at her husband, saying dreamily, -

"I should like to see this Mr. Brown. Perhaps he has some comfort for me; and that was what I felt approachhing in that letter."

Mr. Legrange smiled a little compassionately, and more than a little tenderly.

"I am afraid, love, you would be disappointed. A man might seem a marvel of eloquence and wisdom to poor Theodore, while you would find him a very commonplace, perhaps obtrusive individual."

Mrs. Legrange slowly shook her head.

"I feel just as if that man could give me comfort. I must see him."

"Very well, dear: if it will give you the slightest

pleasure, you shall certainly do so. Shall I send and invite him here? or do you think the journey to Ohio would be a pleasant variety for you? Perhaps it might; and Teddy's elaborately artless recommendation of the Neff House and the iron-springs is worthy of some attention."

"Yes: I will go there. I think I should like the journey, and I don't object to trying the springs; and I should like to see Theodore, and hear him talk about her. And I am sure I shall not find Mr. Brown commonplace or obtrusive."

"Very well, dear: it shall be as you say. When shall we go? It will be very hot travelling now, I am afraid."

"Oh, no! I don't mind. But I don't want to interfere with the Western excursion Theodore so modestly suggests; nor do I wish to go while he is away. We will go in the middle of September, I think."

"Yes, that will do, and will give you something to be thinking of meantime," said Mr. Legrange, looking with satisfaction at the healthy animation of his wife's face, as she re-read the portion of Teddy's letter relating to Yellow Springs and the Neff House.

"And now," said she, "go and send Mrs. Ginniss up to me to hear her letter too, that is, if you please; for, you humor me so much, I know I am growing tyrannical in speech as well as in act."

Mr. Legrange stooped to kiss his wife's cheek; and, to his eyes, the faint smile with which she repaid the caress was the fair dawn of a brighter day.

CHAPTER XXXIV.

THE FIRST CHANCE.

MR. BROWN had been a week at Outpost, and, at breakfast one morning, announced his departure for the succeeding day.

"And if you feel able to ride so far, Dora," continued he, "perhaps you will show me the way to the curious mounds we heard of from Dr. Gershom."

"They are full ten miles from here, he said," remarked Kitty disapprovingly.

"To-day is the 24th, isn't it, Dora? the 24th of August?" inquired Karl; and Dora, if no other of his auditors, saw the connection between this remark and the proposed long ride with Mr. Brown.

"Yes, Karl; it is the 24th: and I think we can make a party for the mounds, Mr. Brown. Kitty, wouldn't you like to go? and, Karl, can't you take a holiday? Sunshine might stay with Mehitable for once; mightn't she?"

"No; because she speaks too loud, and through her nose: but I'll stay with Argus and the woods," said Sunshine quietly.

"But have we horses enough?" asked Kitty with animation.

"That is easily settled," interposed Karl eagerly. "I will fix Sunshine's pillion upon Major, and Dora can ride behind me. Then Kitty can take Max, and Mr. Brown will ride his own horse."

"Oh! there is no need of Major's carrying double," said Dora hastily. "Seth can spare Sally as well as not, and Kitty can ride her better than she can Max."

At this decision, Kitty looked a little vexed, and Karl a little discomfited; while Mr. Brown bent over his plate to hide a sudden gleam of humor in his dark eyes. As they all rose from table, Karl passed close to his cousin, and whispered, -

"I want to speak to you before we go."

Dora made no answer; nor, in the busy hour before they started, could her cousin find opportunity for a single private word. Nor was he more successful in the bold push made by him, so soon as they had started, for the place beside Dora; for she, thinking just then of some important communication for Kitty's ear, reined her pony close to that younger lady's, and good-humoredly desired him to ride on out of earshot. Karl obeyed the mandate with something less than his usual amiability, and was riding on in advance of the whole party, when he found himself detained by Mr. Brown, who asked some trifling, question about the road, and then attempted a conversation upon the crops and other ordinary topics for a few moments; until, unable to contend with the indifference, if not impatience, Karl was at no trouble to conceal, he remained silent for a moment, and then said abruptly, -

"Windsor, this is not soldierly or manly."

Karl looked at him, but made no reply.

"We both know what is in the other's mind," continued Mr. Brown, and we know that we cannot both succeed; but that is no reason for ill feeling toward each other. If we were Don Quixotes, we might fight; if we were gamesters, we might throw for the first chance: but as we are, I trust, Christian gentlemen, we owe each other every kindly feeling short of a wish for success."

"Yes: you can hardly expect that of me; and I'm sure I don't of you," said Karl, half laughing.

"No: that were inconsistent with a true earnestness of purpose," said Mr. Brown. "And, after all, the girl we both love is no such weakling as to accept a man simply because he asks her. She will decide between us fairly and justly."

"Then let me have the first chance, since you think it no advantage," said Karl impetuously.

Mr. Brown smiled grimly.

"Is there not some proverb about age before merit?" asked he. "Besides, you have had more than four years to ask your question in, and can very well wait a few hours longer. I came to Iowa on purpose to ask mine, and shall go away to-morrow."

"I don't see, sir, but you saints are just as obstinate in getting what you want as we sinners," said the younger man petulantly.

The chaplain laughed outright.

"A man at thirty has seldom subdued his worldly passions and intentions to the degree of sainthood," said he. "And I will not deny that my heart is very much engaged in this matter. However, I will be generous, and you may take your chance first."

He reined in his steed as he spoke, and, waiting beside the road until the young ladies came up, made some remark to Kitty relating to a question she had asked him concerning Virginian roads as compared with those of the West, and, by turning into the track beside her, rather obliged Dora to ride forward to the turn of the road, where Karl awaited her. But Kitty's satisfaction in the decided intention Mr. Brown had shown of speaking to her was rather dampened by perceiving how frequently his attention wandered from what she was saying, and how earnestly his eyes were fixed upon the two figures riding briskly in advance.

"If he can only look at Dora, why don't he go and ride with her?" muttered Kitty; and, as her companion turned his eyes inquiringly upon her, she asked aloud, -

"Are you pretty quick at hearing, Mr. Brown?"

"Not especially. Why?"

"Oh! I thought you looked as if you would like to hear what Charlie s saying to Dora."

"And you thought it was very rude of me to be so inattentive to ou," added Mr. Brown, bending his dark eyes upon her with a smile.

Kitty colored guiltily, and answered hastily, -

"Oh dear, no! I'm used to finding myself of no account beside Dora."

Mr. Brown looked again at her, and then, with a sudden association of ideas, asked, -

"Kitty, are you going to tell me, before I go away, what made you feel so badly the day I came and found you in the wood?"

Again Kitty's face glowed beneath his gaze, and her bright black eyes drooped in rare confusion. She was about to answer hastily and coldly, but found herself checked by a softer impulse. Why should she not tell him somewhat of the trouble at her heart, and so win at least sympathy and pity, if nothing more? So she said in a low voice, -

"No one cares much for me, I think."

"No one? - not your brother?"

Kitty raised her eyes to the far vista point where Karl and Dora vanished into the forest, their horses moving close to each other's side, and then brought them back to the face of her companion. The look was eloquent, and he said, -

"Yes; but by and by, perhaps, he will not be so engrossed."

The young girl raised her head with a superb gesture.

"To wait for by and by, when some one else has done with him, is not my idea of love."

Mr. Brown looked at her more attentively, and smiled.

"I think the day will come when some man will love you first and best of all," said he, in a tone, not of flattery, but of honest admiration, which fell like sunlight upon the waste places of poor Kitty's heart.

"Oh! I'm not good enough, or smart enough, or good-looking enough. He never will," replied she hastily, and then colored crimson again at the meaning beneath her words.

Again Mr. Brown keenly eyed her, and asked, -

"He? Do you mean some one in particular? No: forgive me. I have no right to ask such a question. I am only your friend, not a father confessor."

Kitty, dumb with confusion and a sudden terror, made no effort to reply; and, after a moment, Mr. Brown led the way to a quiet conversation upon the young girl's previous life, her early pursuits and affections, and finally to the passionate love and regret for her dead mother, in which he found the key to all she was and all she might be. So employed, the psychological student even forgot his own affairs, and for half an hour hardly remembered Dora riding on beside Karl, who, like the cowardly bather, dallying first with one foot and then the other in the water's edge, and losing all his courage before the final plunge, had talked with her of almost every thing beneath the sun, and worn out his own patience and hers, before she said, turning her clear eyes full upon him, -

"Karl, be honest and straightforward. It is kinder to us both."

The young man heaved a sigh of relief.

"That's it, Dora. There isn't another such girl in the world. Don't you know, in camp I used to say I relied upon you for protection, and for making a man of me instead of an idle boy? O Dora! there's nothing you couldn't do with me."

He spoke the last words in an imploring voice, and fixed his eyes upon her averted face. Then, as she did not speak, he went on: -

"It isn't any thing I can offer you, Dora, except the chance of doing good: I know that well enough. What I am, you know; but what I might become to please you none of us can know. And I do love you so, Dora! I know it sounds bald and silly to say just those few words; but they mean so much to me! and I've meant it so long and so heartily! No; don't speak just yet: I want to make you feel first, if I can, how dreadfully in earnest I am. When I first saw you there at your old home, and you took care of me so tenderly, and looked at me, so pityingly out of your great brown eyes, my heart warmed to you; and then in camp, you know-O Dora Darling! you cannot say but you knew how dearly I grew to love you even then: and when I found you were my own kin; and when you came to my own home, and my mother took you to her heart, and than-ked God for having given her another daughter, and such a daughter; and when I saw your daily life among us, and saw how noble, and how unselfish, and how true, and brave, you were through all the sorrow, and the trials, and the loneliness, and the petty spite and insults, you had to endure; and then here, where you are like a wise and gracious queen among her subjects, - O Dora! what is there in you that does not call forth my highest love, my truest reverence? and what better could life do for me than to grant me the privilege of worshipping and following you all my days, and making myself into just what sort of man would suit you best?"

And the true-hearted young fellow felt his words strike home to his own soul so earnestly that he could add to them nothing of the flood of tenderness and homage swelling there, but only looked at his cousin piteously; while she, with drooping head and averted eyes, rode on for a few moments in silence, and then said softly, -

"I hoped, dear Karl, you would never speak of it again. We have been so happy the last year!" -

"O Dora!" interposed the young man in a voice of agony, "never say you are going to refuse me! Happy! yes, I have been happy, because I have looked forward to this day, and thought it might be the beginning of a life to which this has been but the gray dawn before the sunrise. You have been so kind to me, so frank and affectionate! and all the time you knew - oh! you must have known-what was in my heart. Yes; and, if it had not been for this meddling parson's visit" -

"Hush, Karl!" interrupted Dora decisively. "I will not have you unjust or ungenerous to a man far nobler and purer and wiser than either you or I. Mr. Brown's visit has nothing to do with what I say to-day; nor did I know, as you think I did, that you would again ask me the question you asked a year ago. I only remembered it, when, last week, you reminded me of the date; and I only let you speak to-day, because it is better for us both to say out all that is in our hearts, and then to let the matter rest."

She, paused a moment, and recommenced in a lower and more tender voice: -

"I am so sorry, Karl, to give you pain! If the only trouble was that I don't want to marry you, I wouldn't mind saying no; for I love you very much: only I don't believe it is the way girls commonly love the men they marry. But it wouldn't be right."

"Not right! Oh! why not right, Dora?"

"Because it would spoil both of us. You ask me to make any thing of you I like; but that is not the way. It is you yourself that must make a man of yourself. If I should try to do it, I should only make a puppet of you, and a conceited, tyrannical woman of myself. It would not be good for me to rule as you want me to do; and surely no man would deliberately say it would be good for him to be ruled, and that by his wife."

There was a touch of scorn in the tone of the last words; and Karl's check flushed hotly, as he said, -

"It's hard that you should despise me for loving you so well that I am ready to forget pride and manly dignity, and every thing else, for the sake of it."

"No; but, Karl, don't you see yourself what an injury such a love must be to you? Forget pride and manly dignity and self-respect do you say? A true love, a good love, would make you cherish them as you never did before; would make you claim and hold every inch of manhood that is in you, so that you might feel yourself worthy of that love. O, Karl! never again offer to put yourself under the foot of any woman, but wait till you meet one whom you can hold by the hand, and lead along, keeping equal step with yourself, and both pressing forward to a common goal."

She turned her face upon him, all aglow with a noble enthusiasm far above the maiden bashfulness that but now had held it averted, and extended her hand, saying, -

"Come, dear Karl, forget this idle dream. Be once more my brother and my helper. Trust me, no one cares more for you so than I; not Kitty herself."

He took the hand, put it to his lips, then rode on silently.

Dora's kind eyes sought his again and again, but vainly. His face, pale and somewhat stern gave no clew to the feelings within: the mouth, more firmly set than its wont, seemed sealed to love forever.

For the first time in all the interview, Dora found herself troubled and perplexed. Here was nothing to soothe, nothing to combat, nothing to answer or to silence; and her womanly sympathies fluttered about this manly reticence like a humming-bird around a flower frozen into the heart of an iceberg.

At last, she spoke; and her voice had grown almost caressing in its softness: -

"You're not angry with me, Karl?"

He glanced at her, then away.

"Certainly not, Dora. On the contrary, I am much obliged to you."

"Obliged to me!" exclaimed Dora; her feminine pique just touched a trifle. "What, for saying no?"

"For showing me that I am a fool. It was time I knew it, and I had rather hear it from you than any one. Why should you care for me? I am not a man to respect, like Mr. Brown, or one to admire, like Mr. Burroughs, - I suppose it will be one of them; but I only hope either one may give you half - No matter, wait here a moment in the shade. I am going back to speak to Kitty."

He sharply wheeled his horse as he spoke, and was gone. Dora looked after him in sorrowful perplexity, and then tears gathered in her eyes; but, before they could fall, the unswerving rectitude underlying her whole nature came to its relief, and she dashed them away, murmuring, -

"But I was right."

CHAPTER XXXV.

THE SECOND CHANCE.

REINING up her horse under the shadow of a clump of trees, Dora waited, as her cousin had requested, for his return; and so much pre-occupied was she with her own thoughts, that she failed to hear the quick footfalls of an approaching horse, until his rider slackened speed beside her, and Dora, looking up, saw that it was Mr. Brown.

She grew a little pale, divining, not only from the presence of the chaplain, but from a joyous and significant light in the eyes that encountered hers, what might be his errand; and though she had not failed to foresee this moment, no man, and surely no woman, is ever so prepared for the great crises of life that they fail to come at the last with almost as much of a shock as if they came quite unawares.

She turned her horse into the track, and rode on, her eyes fixed upon the wide prairie-view, which seemed to dance and shimmer before them as if all Nature had suddenly grown as strange and unreal as she felt herself. Her companion spoke, and in her ears his voice sounded as from some far mountain-cave, hollow, broken, and vague; and yet the words were far from momentous.

"Dora, I must leave you to-morrow."

"I am very sorry, sir," faltered Dora; and Mr. Brown, glancing at her face, could not but notice its unwonted agitation. His own wishes, and his sex, led him to misconstrue it; and, pressing, his horse closer to her side, he said joyfully, -

"And so am I sorry, Dora; but I need not be gone long if you wish for my return."

Dora did not speak; indeed, she could not: for the wild dance of sky and plain, of prairie and forest, grew yet wilder; and in her ears the voice of the chaplain mingled with a dizzy hum that almost drowned the words. She grasped the horn of her saddle with both hands, and only thought of saving herself from falling. The horse was halted, an arm was about her waist, her head drawn to a resting-place upon a steady shoulder; and that strange, far-off voice murmured, -

"My darling, my long-loved, long-sought treasure, calm yourself; be happy and secure in my love. Did you ever doubt that it was yours?"

He stooped to kiss her: but, at the motion, the virginal instincts of the young girl's nature rallied to the defence; and, with a sudden spring, Dora sat upright, her face very pale, but her eyes clear and steadfast as their wont.

"Oh, sir, indeed you must not!" cried she, as pleadingly as a little child, who will not be caressed, yet knows not why he should refuse.

"Must not, Dora?" persisted the lover gayly. "But why must I not kiss my own betrothed?"

"But I am not; I cannot be. Don't be angry, sir: I would have spoken sooner; but I could not. I believe I was a little faint;" and Dora's eyes timidly sought those of the chaplain, who, meeting them, remembered many such a glance when his pupil had feared to displease him by inattention or disobedience. Again he thought to have discovered the source of her refusal, and again he failed.

"Dora," said he gently, "you do not forget, that, some years ago, we bore the relation of master and pupil; and you still regard me with a certain deference and reserve, which, perhaps, blinds you to the true relation existing between us now. Remember, dear, that I am yet a younger man; and although my profession may have induced a certain gravity of manner, contrasting, perhaps unpleasantly, with your gay cousins joyous demeanor, I have all, or more than all, of his fervency of feeling; far more, I trust, of depth and steadfastness in my love for you."

"Please, Mr. Brown," interposed Dora, "do not let us say any thing about Karl. He is not concerned in this."

"You are right, Dora, and I was wrong," said Mr. Brown with a little effort of magnanimity. "But I was only trying to convince you that my love is quite as ardent, and quite as tender, as that of a younger and gayer man could be."

"Yes, sir," said Dora timidly, as he paused for her assent.

"Not 'Yes, sir,' child!" exclaimed the chaplain impatiently. "Don't treat me with this distant respect and timid reverence. I am your lover, your would-be comrade through life, as once through the less earnest battles of war. Call me Frank, and look into my face and smile as I have seen you smile on Karl."

A quick smile dimpled Dora's cheek, and passed.

"Not Karl, please, sir."

"Dora, if you say 'sir' to me again, I'll kiss you."

"Please not, Mr. Brown," said Dora demurely, "until you quite understand me."

"Well then, let me quite understand you very quick; for I think I shall exact the penalty, even without further offence."

"But I cannot promise, - I cannot be what you said," stammered Dora, half terrified, half confused.

"Nay, darling, - I am going to always call you that, as expressive both of name and nature, - it is you who do not quite understand either yourself or me. I do not expect, or even wish, you to profess a love for me as ardent, open, and pronounced as my own: that were to make you other than the modest and delicately reserved maiden I have loved so long. All I ask you to feel is, that you can trust yourself to my guidance through life; that you can place your future in my hands, believing me capable of shaping it aright; that you can promise to tread with me the path I have selected, sure that it shall be my care to remove from it all thorns, all obstacles that mortal power may control, and that my arms shall bear you tenderly over the rough places I cannot make smooth for you.

"Dora, years ago I resolved that you should be my wife, God and you consenting. I have waited until I thought you old enough to decide calmly and wisely; but, through these years of waiting, I have cherished a hope, almost a certainty, of success, that has struck deep roots among the very foundations of my life. You will not tear it away! Dora, you do not know me: you cannot guess at the ardor or the power of a love I have never dared wholly to reveal even to myself. Trust it, Dora: it cannot but make you happy. Give yourself to me, dear child; and I will account to God for the precious charge."

Never man was more in earnest, never was wooing at once so fervent and so lofty in its tone; and so Dora felt it. The temptation to yield, without further struggle, to the belief that Mr. Brown knew better what was good for her than she knew for herself, was very great; but, even while she hesitated, the inherent truthfulness of her nature rose up, and cried, "No, no! you shall not do such wrong to me who am the Right!" and turning, with an effort, to meet the keen eyes reading her face, she said, still timidly perhaps, but very calmly, -

"I am but a simple girl, almost a child in some things, and you are a wise and good man, learned in books and in the way of the world; but I must judge for myself, and must believe my own heart sooner than you in such matters as these. Years ago, as you say, I was your pupil, and you then nobly offered to adopt me as your child or sister."

"As my future wife, Dora. I meant it from the very first," interposed the chaplain impetuously.

"I did not know that: perhaps it makes a difference.

But, at any rate, I promised then, that if I went home with Capt. Karl, and you wanted me afterward, I would come to you whenever you said so."

"Yes, yes; that is quite true: well?" demanded Mr. Brown eagerly.

"Well, sir, a promise is a promise; and, if you demand it now, I will come and live with you, or you can come, and live with me, - not as your wife, however, but as your sister and child and friend."

"You will come and live with me, but not marry me!" exclaimed the young man, with a gleam of amusement at the unworldly proposal lighting his dark eyes.

"Yes, sir," replied Dora, without looking up.

To her infinite astonishment and dismay, she found herself suddenly embraced, and a hearty kiss tingling upon her lips.

"I am sorry if you don't like it, Dora; but I said I would if you called me 'sir' again; and you are so scrupulous about your promises, you cannot wish me to break mine."

"Then I am afraid I must promise, if you do so again, to go back and ride with Kitty all the rest of the way," said Dora, as, with heightened color and a decided pout, she drew her left-hand rein so sharply as to wheel Max to the other side of the road.

"Dora, I am afraid you are a little of a coquette, after all!" exclaimed the lover, gazing at her with admiration.

"Oh, no indeed, Mr. Brown! I wouldn't be for the world! I said just what I meant to you. I always do."

"But why, then, if you love me well enough to live with me as sister, child, or friend, can't you also live with me as wife?"

"Because, sir, - oh, no! I didn't mean sir, - because" -

"Frank, I told you to call me."

"Because, Frank, I don't love you that way."

The answer was so explicit, so unembarrassed, and so quiet, that, for the first time, Mr. Brown believed it.

"Not love me, Dora, when I love you so much!" exclaimed he in dismay.

"Not love you in a wife way, Frank, but a great deal in every other way. And then I don't think we should be happy together if we were married."

"And why not?" asked the young man, smiling in spite of himself at the quiet opinion.

"Because, as you said, you want me to put my life into your hands, and you will shape it; and you want me to set my feet in your path, and follow it with you; and you want me to trust my soul to you, and you will guide it: but I could never do that, Mr. Brown; never for any man, I think. I could never forget that God has given me a life, and a path, and a soul, all my own, and not to be judged except by Him and myself: and I am afraid I should always be asking if your guiding was in the same direction that I was meant to go; and, if I thought it was not, I should be very unhappy, and should try to live my own life, and not yours; and that would make trouble."

"Yes, that would make trouble certainly, Dora," said the chaplain gravely. "But are you sure that a young and comparatively unlearned woman like yourself would be a better judge of what was right and best than a man of mature years, who has made the care of souls his profession and most earnest duty?"

"No, Mr. Brown, not if I judged for myself: but I think God has especial care of those, who, like me, have none else to guide them; and I think this voice in my heart is the surest teaching of all."

The profound conviction of her tone was final; the simple faith of her argument was unassailable: and Mr. Brown, skillful polemic that he was, found himself silenced.

After a moment, he said calmly, -

"Dora, you will not forget that this is, to me at least, a very serious, indeed a vital matter. Is what you have just said the solemn conviction of your own heart? or have you suffered yourself to be misled by the tendency to self-esteem and perverseness I have sometimes had occasion to reprove in you? Have you thoroughly searched your own heart to its deepest depths? and is not your refusal tinctured by the natural reluctance of a determined nature to yield to a love, which, in woman, must bring with it some degree of dependence and deference?"

He looked almost severely into the pale face and

earnest eyes upraised to his, and read there pain, anxiety, an humble appeal, but not one trace of hesitation, not one shade of duplicity.

"I have searched my own heart, Mr. Brown; and I am sure of its answer. I never, never, can be your wife, so long as we both live."

"That is sufficient, Dora. I am rightly punished for building my hopes and my happiness upon the sandy foundations of an earthly love. They perish, and leave me desolate; but, among the ruins, I yet can say, 'It is rightly and justly done.'"

The bitter pain in his voice pierced to Dora's very heart, and wounded it almost as sorely as she had wounded his. The rare tears overflowed her eyes; and, pressing close to his side, she laid a hand upon his own, saying, -

"Oh, forgive me! - say you forgive me! Indeed, I must do and say what conscience bids me, at all cost."

"It is not for me to gainsay such a precept as that," said the chaplain.

"But I will come to you, and live as long as you want me. I will be everything but wife. Say I may do this, or I shall never forgive myself. Say I may make some amends for the pain I have given you."

The young man laughed bitterly, then, turning suddenly, seized both her hands, and looked deep into her eyes.

"My poor child," cried he, "my innocent lamb, who

turns from the shepherd because she will not be guided, and yet is all unfit to guide herself! Do not even you, Dora, guileless and unworldly as you are, see how impossible it would be for a young and beautiful girl to live with a man who admires and loves her openly, without such scandal, as should ruin both in the world's eyes, even if they saved their own souls unspotted?"

Dora snatched away her hands, and her whole face flamed with a sudden shame.

She was learning fast to-day in the book of human passion, suffering, and sin.

Without comment upon her embarrassment, the chaplain went on: -

"No, Dora: I must lay aside the dream of four sweet years, and take up my lonely life without disguise or embellishment. I cannot dispute your decision. I will not by one word or look urge you to change it; for I too deeply respect the truthfulness of your character to dream that it is capable of change. I do not say that I forgive you, for you have done nothing calling for forgiveness; and yet, if your tender heart should suffer, in thinking of my suffering, remember always that what you have to-day said has increased my respect and esteem for you fourfold: and, if it has also added to the bitterness of my disappointment, I will not have you reproach yourself; for I would rather reverence you as the wife of another than to claim you as my own, and know you untrue to yourself. And now, dear, the subject is closed utterly and forever."

CHAPTER XXXVI.

TREASURE-TROVE.

IT was a balmy September evening, some weeks after Mr. Brown's return to Ohio, when Karl, or, as he was now generally styled, Dr. Windsor, standing beside his horse, in the quiet Main Street of Greenfield, saw Dr. Gershom riding lazily into town, accompanied by a sturdy, good-looking lad, also on horseback, whom Karl failed to recognize.

"A new student, maybe," thought he, and, taking his foot out of the stirrup, waited to see.

"Hollo, Windsor, hold on a minute!" shouted Dr. Gershom as they approached. "Here's a young gentleman asking for you."

Karl bowed, and began hastily to review his half-forgotten army acquaintances; failing, however, to identify any of them with the young man now bowing to him, and taking a letter from his pocket-book.

"Mr. Brown favored me with this letter of introduction to you, sir," said he, holding it out.

Karl glanced hastily at the few lines, and remembered an allusion the chaplain had made to a particularly promising student of his, whom he thought of sending to travel a little in the West. So he frankly smiled, extended his hand, and said, -

"Ah, yes! I have heard Mr. Brown speak of you, Mr. Ginniss; and I am very happy to welcome you to our prairie life. I am just setting out for home; and, if you please, we will ride along directly."

"Better come in, boys, and have a glass of bitters to keep the night-air off your stomachs. Got some of the real stuff right here in the office," said the old doctor; but, both young men declining the proffered hospitality, he withdrew, grumbling, -

"You never'll make it work, Windsor, I tell you now! Such a dog's life as a country doctor's isn't to be kept up without fuel."

Karl laughed, and, turning to his new acquaintance, said, -

"So they told me in the army; but I got through without. I never tasted spirit but once, and then I didn't like it."

"I never have at all," said Ginniss simply. "I gave my mother a promise, when I was twelve years old, that I never would; and I never have."

Karl nodded.

"That's right," said he; "and all the better for you to have had such a mother."

"You'd say that, Mr. Windsor, if you knew what she'd done for me. There ain't many such mothers in any class," said the young man heartily.

Karl looked at his new acquaintance with increasing

favor, and found something very attractive in his open, manly face, and the honest smile with which he met his scrutiny.

"I hope you'll stay with us some time, Mr. Ginniss," said he heartily.

"Thank you; but, I believe, only for one day. The journey was my principal object in coming; and I must be at Antioch College again in a week, or ten days at the outside."

"Tell me about the life there. I was at old Harvard, and never visited any other college," said Karl; and the young men found plenty of conversation, until, in the soft twilight, they came upon the pleasant slope and vine-clad buildings of Outpost.

"Here is our house, or rather my cousin's house," said Karl. "You have heard Mr. Brown speak of Dora?"

"Yes, before he went away," said Ginniss significantly.

"But not since his return?" asked Karl eagerly.

"Very seldom."

"Hem! Seth, will you take our horses round? Jump off, and come in, sir. This is my sister Kitty, Mr. Ginniss. A scholar of Mr. Brown's, Kitty: I dare say you remember his speaking of him."

"Yes, indeed! Very happy to see you, Mr. Ginniss; walk in," said Kitty, who, if she had never heard the line, certainly knew how to apply the idea, of, - "It is not the rose; but it has lived near the rose."

"Where is Dora?" asked Karl, glancing round the room where the pretty tea-table stood spread, and Dora's hat and gloves lay upon a chair; but no other sign of her presence was to be found.

"Why," said Kitty, laughing a little, "Dolly took a fancy for rafting down the river on a log that she somehow managed to push off from the bank. Of course, she slipped off the first thing, and might have been drowned; but Argus got her out somehow, and Seth, hearing the noise, ran down and brought her home. Of course, she was dripping wet; and Dora has put her to bed."

"Is it a sanitary or a disciplinary measure?" asked Karl: "because, if the latter, we shall have Dora out of spirits all the evening. She never punishes Dolce half so much as she does herself."

"Well, I believe it is a little of both this time," replied Kitty. "I think she'll be down to tea. You had better take Mr. Ginniss right into your bedroom, Charlie. Perhaps he'd like to wash his hands before tea."

"Thank you; I should, if you please," said the guest, and left the room with his host.

When they returned, Dora was waiting to receive them, somewhat pale and sad at having felt obliged to refuse Sunshine's entreaties to "get up, and be the 'bedientest little girl that ever was," but courteously attentive to the guest, and ready to be interested and sympathetic in hearing all Karl's little experiences of the day. As for Kitty, her careless inquiry on seating herself at the table, of, -

"How has Mr. Brown been since he got home?" may serve as index to the course of her meditations.

"How in the world came Dolce to undertake the rafting business?" asked Karl, when his sister's inquiries had been amply satisfied.

"Why, poor little thing!" said Dora, laughing a little, "she thought she had found the way to heaven. She noticed from the window how very blue the river was, and, as she says, 'goldy all over in spots:' so she slipped out, and ran down there, forgetting for once that she is forbidden to do so. Standing on the brink, she saw the reflection of the little white clouds floating overhead, and was suddenly possessed with an idea that this was heaven, or the entrance to it. So, as she told me, she thought she would float out on the log till she got to the middle, and then 'slip off, and fall right into heaven.'"

"How absurd!" said Kitty, laughing.

"Not at all. She would certainly have reached heaven if she had carried out the plan," said Karl.

"Don't, please," murmured Dora, with a little shiver. "Don't talk of it."

"That is like a little sister of mine; a little adopted sister, at least. She was always talking of going to heaven, and planning to get there," said the guest.

Dora looked at him with pity in her honest eyes, and hastened to prevent Kitty's evident intention of questioning him further with regard to this "little sister."

"It seems to be a natural instinct with children," said she "to long for heaven. Perhaps that is the reason they bring so much of heaven to earth."

"I'm afraid mothers of large and troublesome families would say that earth would be better with less of heaven," suggested Karl slyly; and the conversation suddenly veered to other topics. But all through the evening, and even after he had gone to rest, the mind of Teddy Ginniss was haunted by the memory of the pretty child, so loved and mourned, and of whom this anecdote of the little heaven-seeker so forcibly reminded him.

"Whose child is this, I wonder?" thought he a dozen times: but, in the hints he had solicited from Mr. Brown upon manners, none had been more urgent than that forbidding inquisition into other people's affairs; and indeed Teddy's natural tact and refinement would have prevented his erring in this respect. So now he held his peace, and slept unsatisfied.

This may have been the reason of his rising unusually early, - in fact, while the rosy clouds of dawn were yet in the sky, - and quietly leaving the house with the purpose of a river-bath. Strolling some distance down the bank, until the intervening trees shut off the house, he plunged in, and found himself much refreshed by a swim of ten minutes through waters gorgeous with the colors of the sunrise-sky; and, as he paused to notice them, Teddy muttered, -

"The poor little sister! She'd have done just the same if she'd been here."

It was hardly time to return to the house when the

young man stood again upon the bank; and he strolled on through the wood, at this point touching upon the river so closely, that a broken reflection of the green foliage curved and shimmered along the fast-flowing waves.

Teddy looked at the water; he looked at the trees; he looked long and eagerly across the wide prairie that far westward imperceptibly melted its dim green into the faint blue of the horizon, leaving between the two a belt of tender color, nameless, but inexpressibly tempting and suggestive to the eye. All this the lad saw, and, raising his face skyward, drew in a long draught of such air as never reaches beyond the prairies.

"Oh, but it's good!" exclaimed he, with more meaning to the simple phrase than many a man has put to an oration. And then he muttered, as he walked on, -

"If it wasn't for the thought that's always lying like a stone at the bottom of my heart, there'd not be a happier fellow alive to-day than I. Oh the little sister! - the little sister that I never shall forget, nor forgive myself for the loss of!"

And, from the cottonwood above his head, a mocking-bird, who had perhaps caught the trick of grief from some neighbor whippoorwill, poured suddenly a flood of plaintive melody, that to the boy's warm Irish fancy seemed a lament over the loved and lost.

He took off his hat, and looked up into the tree.

"Heaven's blessings on you, birdy!" said he. "It's the very way I'd have said it myself; but I didn't know how."

The mocking-bird flew on; and Teddy followed, hoping for a repetition of the strain: but the capricious little songster only twittered promises of a coming happiness greater than any pleasure his best efforts could afford, and darted away to the recesses of the forest, where was in progress an Art-Union matin,e of such music as all the wealth of all our cities cannot buy for us.

Teddy followed for a while; and then, fearing that he should be lost in the trackless wood, turned his back upon the rising sun, and walked, as be supposed, in the direction of the house, his eyes upon the ground, his mind strangely busy with thoughts and memories of the life he had left so far behind, that, in the press and hurry of his present career, it sometimes seemed hardly to belong to him.

"God and my lady have been very good to me," thought the boy; "but I never'll be as happy again as when the little sister put her arms about my neck, and called me her dear Teddy, and kissed me with her own sweet mouth that maybe is dust and ashes now. No: I never'll be happy that way again."

He raised his eyes as he spoke, and started back, pale and trembling, fain to lean against the nearest tree for support under the great shock.

Not fifty feet from him, and bathed in the early sunlight that came sifting through the trees to greet her, stood a child, dressed in a white robe, her sunny hair crowned with flowers, her little hand holding sceptre-wise a long stalk with snow-white bells drooping from its under edge. Her arms were bare to the shoulder, and her slender feet gleamed white from the bed of moss that almost buried them. Still as a little statue, or a celestial vision printing itself in one never-to-be-forgotten moment upon the heart of the beholder, she stood looking at him; and Teddy dropped upon his knees, gasping, -

"It's out of glory you've come to comfort me, darling! and God ever bless you for the same!"

The child looked at him with her starry eyes, and slowly smiled.

"I knew you sometime," said she. "Was it in heaven ?"

"No: it's better than ever I'll be, you know, in heaven, little sister. Are you happy there, mavourneen?" asked Teddy timidly.

"Oh! I haven't gone to heaven yet. I never could find the way," said the child, with a troubled expression suddenly clouding her sweet face; and then she added musingly, -

"I thought I'd get there through the river last night; but I tumbled off the log, and only got wet: and Dora said I was naughty; and so I had to go to bed, and not have some supper, only" -

"What's that, then!" shouted Teddy, springing to his feet, and holding out his hands toward her, though not yet daring to approach. " It's not the spirit of the little sister you are, but a live child?"

"Yes, I'm alive; though, if I'd staid into the river, I

wouldn't have been, Dora says," replied Sunshine quietly.

"Oh! but the Lord in heaven look down on us this day, and keep me from going downright mad with the joy that's breaking my heart! Is it yourself it is, O little sister! is it yourself that's in it, and I alive to see it?"

He was at her feet now, his white face all bathed with tears, his trembling fingers timidly clasping her robe, his eyes raised imploringly to those serenely bent upon him.

"I knew you once and you was good to me," said the child musingly; "but I got tired when I danced so much in the street. I don't ever dance now, only with Argus."

"But, little sister, are you just sure, it's yourself alive? And don't you mind I was Teddy, and we used to go walking in the Gardens and on the Commons; and there was the good mammy at home that used to rock you on her lap, and warm the pretty little feet in her hands, and sing to you till you dropped asleep? Don't you mind them things, Cherry darling?"

The child looked attentively in his face while he thus spoke, and at the end nodded several times; while a light, like that of earliest dawn, began to glimmer in her eyes.

"Tell me some more," said she briefly.

"And do you mind the picture-books I used to bring you home, and the story of the Cock Robin you used to like so well to hear, and the skip-jack you played with, and the big doll that mammy made for you, and you called it Susan?" -

"O - h! Susan!" cried the child suddenly, and then stood all pale and trembling, while her earnest eyes seemed searching in the past for some dimly-remembered secret, which to lose was agony, to recall impossible.

"Susan!" said she softly again. "Yes, there was Susan, somewhere, and - Oh! tell me the rest, tell me who it was that loved me so!"

"Sure, it was Teddy loved you best of all," said the boy longingly: for, though her eager eyes dwelt upon his face, it was not for him or his that the depths of her heart were stirring; and, with the old thrill of jealous pain, he felt it so.

But then from the remorse and bitterness of the fault he had never ceased to mourn rose a nobler purpose, a higher love. He took the child in his arms, and kissed her tenderly, then released her, saying, -

"Good-by, little sister; for I never will call you so again, and you never more will call me brother. It's your own lady-mother, darling, that you're missing and mourning, - the own beautiful mother that lost you two years ago, and has gone to heaven's gates looking for you, and never would have come back if you had not been found. It's your own home, darling, that you have remembered for heaven; and it's waiting for you, with father and mother, and joy and plenty, all ready to receive you the minute you can get there."

But it was too much for the fine organization and sensitive temperament; and, as Teddy's words reached her heart in their full meaning, the child, with a long sobbing cry, fell forward into his arms, utterly insensible.

Teddy, not too much terrified for he had seen her thus before, raised the slender little figure in his arms, and carried it swiftly toward the house, now just visible through a vista of the wood, but, before he reached it, met Dora coming to look for her little charge.

"Good-morning, Mr. Ginniss. So you have caught my naughty runaway," cried she gayly; but coming near enough to notice Sunshine's drooping figure, and Teddy's agitated face, she sprang forward, asking, -

"Is any thing the matter with her? Where did you find her, Mr. Ginniss?"

"She's fainted, ma'am; but it's with joy, and will never hurt her. It's you and I that will be the sufferers, I'm afraid," said Teddy, with a sudden pang at his heart of love not yet cleansed of selfish jealousy.

"Bring her to the house, please, as quickly as you can. Poor little darling, she is so delicate!" said Dora, not yet caring to ask this strange news, but walking close beside Teddy, her hand clasping that cold little one which swung nervelessly over his shoulder, her eyes anxiously watching the beautiful pale face, half hidden in the showering curls.

CHAPTER XXXVII.

TEDDY'S PRIVILEGE.

To Mr. Burroughs, smoking his cigar upon the piazza of the Neff House, came a white-jacketed waiter with a card.

"The gentleman is waiting in the reception-room, sir," said he.

Mr. Burroughs paused to watch an unusually perfect ring of smoke lazily floating above his head; then took the card, and read in pencil, -

"Theodore Ginniss would be glad to see Mr. Burroughs a moment on important business."

"Indeed! Well, it is a republic, and this is the West; but only Jack's bean-stalk parallels such a growth." So said, in his own heart, Teddy Ginniss's former master, as he drew two or three rapid whiffs from the stump of his cigar, and then, throwing it into the grass, strolled leisurely into the reception-room.

"Ah, Ginniss! how are you?" inquired he of the pale and nervous young man, who stood up to receive him, half extending his hand, but dropping it quickly upon perceiving those of Burroughs immovable.

"I am well, sir, thank you."

"Want to see me on business, do you say?" continued the lawyer coolly.

"Yes, sir." And, as his true purpose and position came back to him, Teddy suddenly straightened himself, and grew as cool as the stately gentleman waiting with patient courtesy for his errand.

"I thought, sir, I'd come to you first, as it was to you I first had occasion to speak of my fault in hiding her. 'Toinette is found, sir!'"

"What! 'Toinette Legrange found! Teddy, your hand, my boy! Found by you?"

"Yes, sir," said Teddy, suffering his hand to be shaken.

"But what I wanted most was to ask if you think it safe to tell Mrs. Legrange."

"Oh! I'll see to that. Of course, it must be done very delicately. But where is the child now? and when did you find her?"

"If you please, Mr. Burroughs, I should like to tell the story first to Mrs. Legrange, and I should like to tell her all myself. It was I that hurt her, or helped to hurt her; and I'd like to be the one to give her the great joy that's waiting for her. Besides, sir," and Teddy's face grew white again, "though I did what was wrong enough, I never deny, I have suffered for it more, maybe, than you can think of; and this is all the amends I could ever want. Mrs. Legrange has been very good to me, sir, and never blamed me, or spoke an unkind word, even at the first."

"And I spoke a good many, you're thinking," said Mr. Burroughs keenly. "Well, Teddy, I am a man, and Mrs. Legrange is a woman; and women look at matters more leniently and less exactly than we do. But you must not be satisfied with pity instead of justice; for that will be to encourage your self-esteem at the expense of your manhood. I do not deny that I never have recovered from my surprise at finding you had so long deceived me; but the news you bring to - day makes amends for much: and, after I have heard the particulars, I may yet be able to forget the past, and feel to you as I used."

But Teddy's bow, though respectful, was not humble; and he only asked in reply, -

"Where shall I find Mrs. Legrange, sir?"

"She walked down to the glen about half an hour ago. You may follow her there, if you please; and, since you insist upon it as a right, I will leave you to break the news to her alone. But you will remember, I hope, that she is very delicate, - very easily startled. You will have to be exceedingly cautious."

"Yes, sir;" and with a ceremonious bow the young man left the room, and the next minute was seen darting along the path to the glen.

Mr. Burroughs looked after him appreciatively, and muttered, -

"A nice-looking fellow, and not without self-respect. I see no reason why, in half a dozen years, he should not enter his name at the Suffolk bar itself, and stand as well as any man on the roll.

But my little Sunshine! Confound the boy! why couldn't he have told me where to find her?"

So Mr. Burroughs went back to the piazza, and tried to quiet himself with another cigar, but was too nervous to make any more rings; while Teddy sped away to the glen, and presently found himself in a cool and cavernous retreat, which the sunlight only penetrated by dancing down with the waters that slid laughingly over a rock ledge above, and shook themselves into spray before they reached the pool below, then, after dimpling and sporting there for a moment, danced merrily away. At either hand, high walls of rock, half hid in trailing vines and clinging herbage, shut out the heat of day; and, through a thousand ever-changing peepholes among the swaying foliage, the blue sky looked gayly down, and challenged those who hid in the glen to come forth, and dare the fervor of the mid-day sun.

Under a tree near the foot of the fall sat Mrs. Legrange, her head leaning upon her hand, her book idle upon her lap, watching dreamily the waters that swayed and ebbed, and paused and coquetted with every flower or leaf that bent toward them; and yet in the end went on, always on, as the idlest of us go, until through the merry brook, the heedless fall, the sparkling stream, and stately river, we reach at last the ocean, calm, changeless, and eternal in its unmoved depths.

The lady looked up with a little start as she heard the approaching footsteps, and then rose with extended hand, -

"Theodore!" said she kindly. "I am very glad to see you; and so grown! You are much taller than in the spring."

"Yes, ma'am: I believe so. I don't think I shall grow much more," said Teddy, swallowing a great bunch in his throat that almost suffocated him.

"No? Why, you are not so very old, are you?" asked Mrs. Legrange, smiling a little.

"Nearly eighteen, ma'am."

"Oh, well! time enough for a good deal of growth, bodily and mental, yet. So you have been at the West?"

"Yes, ma'am, and have heard some curious things there, - some things that I think will interest you. Have you ever thought of adopting a little girl, ma'am?"

Mrs. Legrange sadly shook her head.

"No, Theodore: I never wished to do that. She never could be any thing like her to me, and it would seem like giving away her place. I had rather wait."

"I am sorry, ma'am; for I saw a little girl, where I have been, that I was going to speak of."

"Was she a pretty child?"

"Very pretty, and looked like" -

"Theodore, don't say that, because I shall think either you have forgotten or never learned her face. No child ever looked like her," said the mother positively.

"This little girl was very pretty though," persisted Teddy.

"How did she look?"

"She had great blue eyes (if you'll excuse, me, ma'am), just like yours, with long brown eyelashes, and a great deal of bright hair, not just brown, nor yet just golden, but between the two; and a little mouth very much curved; and pretty teeth; and a delicate color; and little hands with pretty finger-nails."

"Theodore!"

Teddy, for the first time in his description, dared to raise his eyes, but dropped them again. He could not meet the anguish in those other eyes so earnestly fixed upon him.

"She was the adopted child of the people I visited in Iowa," faltered he.

"Theodore!" said Mrs. Legrange again; and then, in a breathless fluttering voice, -

"Do not trifle with me; do not try to prepare my mind; and, oh! For God's sake, if it is a false hope, say so this instant! Is she found?"

"I think it may be so, dear Mrs. Legrange!"

"No, but it is so! you know it! I see it in your eyes, I hear it in your voice! You cannot hide it, you cannot deceive me! O my God! My God! - to thee the first praise, the first thanks!"

She fell upon her knees, her face upraised to heaven; and never mortal artist drew such a picture of ecstatic praise. And though in after-years Theodore Ginniss wandered through the galleries where the world cones-rves her rarest gems of art, never did he find Madonna or Magdalen or saint to compare with the one picture his memory treasured as the perfection of earthly loveliness, made radiant with the purest heavenly bliss.

"Now come!" exclaimed the mother, springing to her feet, and rapidly leading the way along the narrow path. "You shall tell me all as we go."

And the young man found it hard work to keep pace with the delicate woman, as she flew rather than walked towards her child.

"If you will wait here in your own room, I will bring her to you," said Teddy, as he and Mrs. Legrange approached the hotel again.

"Bring her! Where is she now? asked the mother, looking at him in dismay.

"I left them at the other hotel, thinking, if I brought her directly here, we might meet you before you were told," explained Teddy.

"Who is with her?"

"Dora Darling, the young lady who adopted her, - the one I told you of as living in Iowa."

"Yes, yes; and she has come all the way to bring my child to me! No, I cannot wait: I will come with you."

So Mr. Burroughs, still sitting upon the piazza, saw his cousin hastening by, and came to join her.

"Yes, come, Tom! come to-oh, to see Sunshine again!" and Mrs. Legrange turned her flushed face away, to hide the hysterical agitation she could not quite suppress.

"Take my arm, Fanny; and do not walk so fast. You will hurt yourself," said Mr. Burroughs kindly.

"No, no: nothing can hurt me now. I must go fast: if I had wings, I should fly!"

"Here is the house. Will you wait in the parlor till I bring her down?" asked Teddy, leading the way up the steps of the principal hotel at Yellow Springs.

"No: take me to the room where they are waiting. I want to see her without preparation," said Mrs. Legrange.

So the whole party followed Teddy up the stairs to a door, where he paused and knocked. A low voice said,-

"Come in!" and the opening door showed Dora seated upon a low chair, with Sunshine clasped in her arms, and fast asleep. She made a motion to rise upon seeing the visitors; but Mrs. Legrange, lifting her finger as imploring silence softly advanced, and bent with clasped hands and eager eyes over the sleeping child. Then, with the graceful instinct of a woman who knows and pities the wound in the heart of her less fortunate rival, she put her arms about Dora and the child, embracing both, and pressed her lips lightly upon Dora's cheek, devouringly upon Sunshine's lips.

Dora started as if she had been stung, and a sudden tremor crossed the rigid calm of her demeanor. She had schooled herself to indifference, to neglect or to civil thanks worse than either: but this unexpected tenderness, this sisterly recognition, went straight through all its defences to her quivering heart; and she looked up piteously into the lovely face bent over her, whispering, -

"I am so glad you have found her! but I have nothing left half so dear."

There was no reply; for Sunshine, without sound or movement, suddenly opened her eyes, and fixed them upon her mother's face, while deep in their blue depths grew a glad smile, breaking at last, like a veritable sungleam, all over her face, as, holding out her arms, she eagerly said, -

"I've come to heaven while I was asleep; and you're the angel that loves me so dearly well. I know you by your eyes."

"The mother clasped her own, - as who shall blame her? - and Dora's arms and Dora's heart were empty, robbed of the nestling they had cherished, - empty, as she said to herself, turning from the sight of that maternal bliss, of the best love she had ever known, or could ever hope."

Mr. Burroughs, who liked character-reading, watched her narrowly; and when, presently, the whole party returned to Mrs. Legrange's hotel, he quietly walked beside Dora, lingering a little, and detaining her out of hearing of Mrs. Legrange and Teddy, who walked on with Sunshine between them.

"Is virtue its own reward, Miss Dora?" asked he

abruptly, when almost half the distance between the two hotels was passed.

Dora looked at him a little puzzled; and then, as she read the half-sympathizing, half-mocking expression of his face, answered, -

"You mean I am not happy in bringing Sunshine back to her mother; don't you?"

"Exactly; and you told me once that no one ought to be rewarded for doing what is right, because it is reward enough to know that we are doing right."

"And so it is. I don't want any reward," said Dora rather hastily.

"No: but, if young Ginniss had not discovered the identity of the child, my cousin would not have been unhappier than she has been for two years; and you-would you not be at this moment better content with life?"

Dora's clear eyes looked straight into his as she wonde-ringly asked, -

"Do you want me to say I am sorry Mrs. Legrange has found her child?"

"If it is true, yes; and I know you will," replied Mr. Burroughs quietly.

"And so I would," said Dora, in the same tone; "but it is not true.

I am glad, not happy, but very glad, that Sunshine has

come to her mother at last, - her heaven, as she calls it. I do not deny that my own heart is very sore, and that I cannot yet think of her not being my child any more, without" -

She turned away her head, and Mr. Burroughs looked at her yet more attentively than he had been looking.

"But, if you could, you would not go back, and arrange it that Teddy should not come to your house? Word and honor now, Dora."

"Word and honor, Mr. Burroughs, I surely would not. Can you doubt me?"

"No, Dora, I do not; but, in your place, I should doubt myself."

Dora looked at him with a frank smile.

"I would trust you in this place, or any other," said she simply.

"Would you, would you really, Dora?" asked Tom Burroughs eagerly, while a slight color flashed into his handsome face. "Why would you?"

"Because I feel sure you could never do any thing mean or ungenerous, or feel any way but nobly" -

She paused suddenly, and a tide of crimson suffused her face and neck. Mr. Burroughs, with the heroism of perfect breeding, turned away his eyes, and suppressed the enthusiastic answer that had risen to his lips. He would not add to her confusion by accepting as extraordinary the impulsive expression of her feelings.

So he simply said, after a moment of silence, -

"Thank you, Dora. I hope you may never have occasion to regret your noble confidence."

Dora did not answer, but hastened her steps, until she walked close behind Mrs. Legrange; nor did her companion speak again, although, could Dora have read his thoughts, she might have found in them matter of more interest than any words he had ever spoken to her.

CHAPTER XXXVIII.

WHAT DORA SAID.

IT had been Dora's intention to return to Iowa immediately after leaving Sunshine in charge of her own
friends; but Mrs. Legrange insisted so urgently upon
her remaining with them for some weeks at least, and
the parting with the dear child she had so loved and
cherished seemed so cruel as it drew nearer and nearer,
that she finally consented to remain for a short time,
and removed to the Neff House, where Mrs. Legrange
had engaged rooms until the first of October.

To other natures than those called to encounter it, the
relation between these three might, for a time at least,
have been painful and perplexing; but Mrs. Legrange
was possessed of such exquisite tact, Sunshine of such
abounding and at the same time delicate affections, and
Dora of such a noble and generous temper, that they
could not but harmonize: and while 'Toinette bloomed,
flower-like, into new and wonderful beauty bathed in
the sunlight of a double love, Mrs. Legrange never
forgot to associate Dora with herself as its source. And
Dora joyed in her darling's joy; and, if her heart ached
at thought of the coming loneliness, the pain expressed
itself no otherwise than in an added tenderness.

"That is a noble girl, Fanny," said Mr. Burroughs one
day. "How different from our dear five hundred friends
at home! Put Mary Elmsly, or Lizzy Patterson, or Miss
Bloomsleigh, or Marion Lee, in her place, and how

would they fill it?"

"She is, indeed, a noble girl," replied his cousin warmly. "I never shall forget the tender and wise care she has taken of Sunshine in this last year. She has strengthened heart and principle as I am afraid I could never have done."

"Paul is coming out for you, isn't he?" pursued Mr. Burroughs after a pause.

"Yes: he will be here by the 20th. Why did you ask?"

"Because Dora cannot travel home alone, and I think of accompanying her. I may stay a while, and study prairie life."

Mrs. Legrange looked at him in surprise a moment; and then a merry smile broke over her face, for such a smile was possible now to her.

"Capital!" exclaimed she. "I never thought of it. But why not?"

"Why not spend a few weeks in Iowa? Well, of course, why not?" asked Mr. Burroughs a little grimly, and presently added, -

"That is a pernicious custom of yours Fanny, - that rushing at conclusions."

"Men never rush at conclusions, do they?"

"No: of course not."

"Very well, then: arrive at your conclusion as leisurely

as you like. It is none the less certain."

"Pshaw!" remarked Mr. Burroughs; and as his cousin laughingly turned to bend over Sunshine, and help her read her story-book, he took his hat and went out, turning his steps toward the glen.

Not till he reached its deepest recesses, however, did he find Dora; and then he stood still to look at her, himself unseen. But what a white, dumb look of anguish upon the sweet face! what clouds, heavy with coming showers, upon the brow! what rainy lights in the upturned eyes! what a resistless sorrow in the downward curve of the lips, ordinarily so firm and cheerful! Even the shapely hands, tightly folded, and firmly set upon the knee, told their story, - even the rigid lines and constrained attitude of the figure. Mr. Burroughs's first impulse was artistic; and he longed to be a sculptor, that he might model an immortal statue of Silent Grief. The second was human; and he longed to comfort a sorrow at whose cause he already guessed, and yet guessed but half. The third was less creditable, but perhaps as probable, in a man of Mr. Burroughs's temperament and education; for it was to study and dissect this new phase of the young girl's character. He quietly approached, and seated himself beside her with a commonplace remark, -

"A very pretty bit of scenery, Dora."

"Yes," replied she, struggling to resume her usual demeanor.

"I am afraid, however, it does not satisfy your eye, accustomed to the breadth of prairie views. Confess that you are a little weary of it and us, and longing for home."

"I shall probably set out for home to-morrow," said Dora, turning away her head, and playing idly with the grass beside her.

"I thought you were homesick. I am sorry we have so ill succeeded in contenting you."

"Oh, don't think that! I have been so happy here these two weeks! That is the very reason I ought to go."

"How is that? I don't see the argument."

"Because this is not my home, or the way I am to live, or these the people I am to live with; and the sooner I am away, the better."

She did not see all the meaning of her words, poor child! but her companion did, and smiled merrily to himself as he said, -

"You mean, we do not come up to your standard, and you cannot waste more time upon us; don't you?"

Dora turned and looked at him, her suspicions roused by a mocking ring beneath the affected humility of his tone; and, looking, she caught the covert smile not yet faded from his eyes.

"It is not kind, Mr. Burroughs, to laugh at me, or to try to confuse me in this way," said she steadily. "No doubt, you know what I mean; and why do you wish to force me into saying, that the more I see of the life and thoughts and manners of such people as Mrs. Legrange and you, and even my own little Sunshine, now so far away from me, the less fit I feel to associate with them? And, just because it is so pleasant to me, I feel that I ought to go back at once to the home and the duties and the people where I belong. I am but a poor country-girl, sir, hardly taught in any thing except the love of God, and the wish to do something before I die to make my fellow-creatures a little happier or more comfortable than I find them. Let me go to my work, and out of it I will make my life."

Perhaps never had the self-contained heart of the young girl so framed itself in words; certainly never had Mr. Burroughs so fully read it: and when she finished, and, neither turning from him nor toward him, steadfastly set her eyes forward, as one who sees mapped out before him the path he is to tread through all the coming years, he took her hand in his with a sudden impulse of tenderness, -

"Dora, you will love some one yet; and love will make you happy."

"I have loved two people, and lost them both. I do not mean to love any one else," said Dora, quietly withdrawing her hand.

Mr. Burroughs stared at her in astonishment; and, with a directness more natural than conventional, exclaimed, -

"You have loved twice already!"

"Yes. Three times, indeed. I loved my mother and Picter, and they are both dead. I loved Sunshine and she is lost to me. O my little Sunshine! who was all to me, and who, I thought" -

And then-oh rare result of all these days of suffering, and hidden bitterness, and a lingering relinquishment of the sweet and tender hope of her future life! - Dora gave way all at once, and, covering her face with her hands, burst into a passion of tears; such tears as women seldom weep; such tears as Dora herself had shed but two or three times in her short life.

Mr. Burroughs sat for a moment, looking at her with a yearning tenderness in his eyes, and then folded her suddenly in his arms, whispering, -

"Dora, Dora Darling! I love you, and I will be to you more than all these; and no time nor chance shall rob you of my love, if only you will give me yours instead."

But Dora repulsed him vehemently, sobbing, "No, no, no! you shall not say it! I will not hear it!"

"Not say it? Why not? It is God's truth; and you must have known it before to-day."

"No: it is only pity, because you think I want to stay, and because - No, I will not have it! I will not hear it! You are quite wrong, Mr. Burroughs: you do not know" -

She stopped in confusion. She had done sobbing now; but she did not uncover her face, or look up. Mr. Burroughs regarded her with a strange expression, and then, taking her hand, said softly, -

"Dora, I have not dared, as you fear that I have, to fancy that you cared for me. A moment ago, I should not have dared to ask you as I now do; and remember,

Dora, that I ask for the solemn truth, - do you love me?"

Dora tore away her hand indignantly, and attempted to rise. She had not spoken, or looked at him. Over the pale face of the lover shot a gleam of triumph. But he only said, -

"Dora, it will not be like you to leave me in this way. It is unjust and untrue."

"It is you who are unkind and ungenerous," said the girl passionately.

"Why, Dora? Why is it ungenerous to ask for a confession of your love, when I have already told you that all my heart is in your hands?"

"You fancied that I-that I-liked you; and you knew I did not want to go home, and you pitied me: and I won't have it, sir. I do not need pity, and I do not" -

Her voice died away, killed by the falsehood she could not speak. Mr. Burroughs no longer pressed for an answer to the question he had asked, but grasped at a new argument.

"Pity and kindness!" sadly repeated he. "Dora, if you only knew how much more I stand in need of your pity than you of mine, if you only knew what kindness your life has already done mine, you would not treat me in this manner."

"You need my pity!" exclaimed Dora, forgetting herself, and turning to look at him in naive astonishment; "and for what?"

"For a purposeless and weary life; for an empty heart and a corroded faith," said her lover bitterly; "for an indifference to men, amounting almost to aversion; for a trifling estimate of women, amounting almost to contempt; for wasted abilities and neglected opportu-neities, - for all these, Dora, I need your pity, and have a right to claim it: for it is only since I loved you that I have recognized my own great needs and deficiencies. Complete the work you have unconsciously begun, dearest. Reverse the fairy fable, and let the beautiful princess come to waken with her kiss the slothful prince, who else might sleep forever."

"How can you know so soon that I am the princess?" asked Dora shyly.

"So soon! I felt the truth stirring blindly in my heart that first night, now a year ago, when I saw you in the old home, and read your candid eyes, and heard your clear voice, and marked your steady and serene influence upon all about you. I hardly knew it then; but, when I was away from you, I was myself surprised to find how vivid your impression upon my mind remained. When my cousin asked me to accompany her here, I silently resolved, that, before I returned home, I would see you again; would study as deeply as I might the character I already guessed. Then, Dora, when I saw you, as I have seen you in these last weeks, struggling so nobly to render complete the sacrifice you came hither to make; when I saw the sweetness, the power, the loftiness, and the divine truth, of your nature, shining more clearly day by day, and yourself the only one unconscious of the priceless value of such a nature, - then, Dora, I came to know for truth what I tell you now, God hearing me, that you are the woman of all the world whom I love, honor, and undeservingly long to make my own. Once more, Dora, - and you cannot now refuse to answer me at least, - once more I ask, do you or can you love me?"

He grasped her hands in both his own, and his keen eyes read her very soul. She raised hers as steadily to meet them; and, though the hot blush seemed to scorch her very brow, she answered, -

"I did not know it, quite, until to-day; but I believe - I think-I have cared about you ever since a year ago. That is, not love; but every one else seemed less than they had been: and since I knew you here, and since I thought I must go home, and never see you any more, it was" -

She faltered and stopped, drooping her head before the tender triumph of his glance. Truth had asserted herself, as with Dora she must have done in any stress, but now of a sudden found herself silenced by a timidity as charming as it was new in the strong and well poised temperament of the girl who, a moment before so brave, now stood trembling and blushing beneath her lover's gaze.

He drew her to his breast, and pressed his lips to hers.

"Dora, my own wife!" whispered he. "God so deal with me here and hereafter as I with you, the best gift in his mighty hand!"

And Dora, hiding her face upon his breast, whispered again, -

"I was so unhappy an hour ago! and now, as Sunshine, says, I have come to heaven all at once!"

Her lover answered by a mute caress; for there are moments when words are all too weak for speech. And so he only clasped her closer in his arms, and bent his head upon her own; while all about them the hundred voices of the summer noon whispered benediction on their joy; the eddying stream paused in its whirl to dimple into laughter at their feet; the sunlight, broken and flecked by the waving branches, fell in a shifting golden shower upon their heads; and Nature, the great mother, through her myriad eyes and tongues, blessed the betrothal of her dearest child.

CHAPTER XXXIX.

A SURPRISE FOR MRS. GINNISS.

"SURE an' it's time they was a-coomin'," said Mrs. Ginniss going out upon the door-stone, and shading her eyes from the level rays of the sunset as she looked steadfastly down the road.

"An' who'll they all be, I'm woondherin'? The missus says fove bids was wanted; an' faith it's well she said no more, for sorra a place 'ud there be to stand anudder in. An' tay ready for eight folks, at sax o'clock. That's it, I belave; though all thim figgers is enough to craze me poor head."

She took a little note from her pocket as she spoke, and, unfolding it, looked anxiously at the delicate letters.

"Sure an' it's all there if on'y I had the sinse to rade it. An' feth, it's the tail uv it I'm howldin' to the top, as I'm a sinner! No' thin: it looks as crabbed this way as that. I'd niver be afther makin' it out if it towld of a fortin coomin' to me for the axin'. Shusin, Shusin, I say!"

"What is it, Mrs. Ginniss?" asked a pleasant voice from within; and Susan, looking a little thinner and paler than when we first met her, came out of the parlor, where she had been picking a few scattered petals from beneath the vases of flowers upon the mantle-shelf.

"An' would ye be plazed to read the missus's note to me wonst more? Me owld eyes are that dim, I can't make it out in the gloamin'."

Susan, with unshaken gravity, took the note, turned it right side up, and read aloud, while her companion craftily glanced over her shoulder to note the position of the words as they were spoken: - "DEAR MRS. GINNISS, -

"We shall be at home on Wednesday evening, at six o'clock, and shall bring some guests. You will please prepare tea for eight persons; and make up five beds, three of them single ones. Tell Susan to make the house look as pretty as she can; and send for any thing she or you need in the way of preparation. "F. LEGRANGE"

"An' faith it's this minute they're coomin!' Look at the jaantin' - cars fur down the road!"

"One's a carryall, and the other's a rockaway," said Susan sententiously.

"Musha, an' what's the odds if they're one thing or the other, so they bring the purty misthress back halesomer than she wint? That's her in the first car: I know her white bonnet with the blue ribbon."

"Yes, there's Mr. and Mrs. Legrange, and a strange lady and gentleman; and the other carriage are all strangers, except Mr. Burroughs. Those young ladies are pretty; ain't they?"

But Mrs. Ginniss was already at the gate, courtesying and beaming: -

"Ye're wilcoom home, missus and masther; an' it's in health an' pace I hope yees coom."

"Thank you, Mrs. Ginniss. We are very well indeed, I believe," said Mr. Legrange, rather nervously, as he jumped from the carriage and helped out his wife, and then Kitty and Mr. Brown. From the other carriage, meantime, had alighted, without the good woman's observation, Mr. Burroughs, Dora, Karl, and another, who, the moment her feet touched the ground, ran forward, crying, -

"O mamma! I've been at this home before."

At the sound, Mrs. Ginniss turned, dropping the shawls, bags, and parasols she held, in one mass at her feet, and then dropping herself upon her knees in their midst; while her fresh face turned of a ghastly yellow, and her uplifted hands shook visibly, -

"Glory be to God, an' what's that!" exclaimed she in a voice of terror.

"Oh, it's mammy, it's mammy! that used to rock me in her lap, and hold my feet, and sing to me! I 'member her now, and Teddy said so too. O mammy! I'm so glad you've come again!"

The sobbing woman opened wide her arms; and Sunshine leaped into them, shouting again and again, -

"It's the good old mammy! and I'm so glad, I'm so glad!"

"O Mrs. Legrange! is it?" exclaimed an agitated voice; and Mrs. Legrange, turning, found Susan standing beside her with pale face and clasped hands, her eyes fixed upon the child with a sort of terror.

"Yes, Susan, it is 'Toinette, her very self. I would not write, because I wanted to see if she would know you both, and you her."

"Oh, thank God! thank God! I didn't believe I'd ever forgive myself for not minding her better; but now I may. Miss 'Toinette, dear, won't you speak to Susan?"

"Susan!" exclaimed the child, struggling out of Mrs. Ginniss's embrace, and leaving that good woman still exploding in a feu-de-joie of thanksgiving, emotion, and astonishment. "Are you Susan? Why, that was a doll!"

"A doll?" asked the nurse in bewilderment, and pausing in act of kissing her recovered charge, not with the rapturous abandonment of the Irish woman, but with the respectful tenderness of a trained English servant.

"She named a doll after you, Mrs. Ginniss says, although she did not remember who you really were," explained Mrs. Legrange. "But come, my friends: we will not wait longer out of doors. Dora, you and Kitty know the way even better than I; and Mr. Windsor" -

"It isn't Mr. Windsor, it's Karlo, mamma," persisted Sunshine, dancing up the narrow path in advance of the party.

"Yes, Karl, if you will be so kind," said Dr. Windsor, offering Mrs. Legrange his arm.

"Then Karl will feel himself as much at home here as

he ever did, I trust," said the lady cordially.

"It was peeping out at that window I saw you first, Dora; and I thought it must be the sunrise," whispered Tom Burroughs to the lady he escorted.

"I am sorry I should have so put you out of countenance. Perhaps that is the reason you never have seen straight since, - so far as I am concerned at least," replied she.

"One does not care to look straight at the sun: it is sufficient to bask in its light," whispered the lover.

"Oh! very well, if that is what you want - Here, Sunshine! Cousin Tom wants you."

The little girl came bounding toward them; and Dora, with a wicked little laugh, slipped away, and up the stairs, to the room that had been Kitty's, now appropriated to the use of the two young girls.

Soon the happy party assembled again in the kitchen, where stood a tea-table judiciously combining the generous breadth of Mrs. Ginniss's ideas with the more elegant and subdued tastes inculcated upon Susan by a long period of service with her present mistress.

"Mind you tell 'em there's more beyant, on'y you wouldn't set it on all to wonst," whispered the Irish woman hoarsely, as she rushed into the scullery, leaving Susan to receive the guests just entering the kitchen.

"Mrs. Ginniss thought we should arrive with appetites, I suspect," said the hostess, laughing a little apologetically as they seated themselves; and Susan did not think it best to deliver her message.

"And so we have, some of us at least; and I do not believe even the ladies will refuse a bit of this nice tongue, or some cold chicken. What do you say, Dora?" asked Mr. Legrange gayly.

"No tongue for her, please; she is supplied," remarked Mr. Burroughs sotto voce; and Dora, with a little mutinous glance, passed her plate with, -

"A slice of tongue, if you please, Mr. Legrange."

"Never mind: wait a few days, and we will see," murmured Burroughs threateningly; and Dora did not care to retort, but, blushing brightly, began an eager conversation with Sunshine, who had nestled a chair in between those of her mother and Dora, and made lively claims upon the attention of both.

An hour or two later, Mrs. Legrange went to seek her housekeeper, and found her seated upon the step of the back door, her hands clasped around her knees, and softly crooning a wild Irish melody to herself as she rocked slowly backward and forward, her eyes fixed upon the little crescent moon, swimming like a silver boat in the golden sea of sunset.

"An' isn't it a purty sight, you?" asked she, rising as Mrs. Legrange spoke to her. "Sure an' its the hooney-moon for Misther Booros an' the swate young lady that's to marry him."

"Yes, it's their honey-moon; and I believe it will be as bright and as long a one as ever shone," said Mrs.

Legrange, smiling tenderly, as happy wives will do in speaking of the future of a bride.

"I came to ask you to go up stairs with me, Mrs. Ginniss," continued she with a little agitation in her sweet voice. "There is something for you to see."

"Sure an' I will, ma'am. Is it the chambers isn't settled to shute yees?"

"Oh, no! every thing is admirable, except that we must contrive a little bed for 'Toinette upon the couch in my room."

"An' faith, that's asy done, ma'am. There's lashin's o' blankets an' sheets an' pillers not in use at all, at all. We've plenty uv ivery thin' in this house, glory be to God!"

Mrs. Legrange smiled a little at the satisfaction with which the Irish woman contemplated a superfluity, even when not belonging to herself; and led the way to her own chamber, where sat Dora, as she had sat many a time within those four walls, holding Sunshine upon her lap, and, while loosening her clothes for the night, telling her one of the stories of which the child was never weary.

"See here, Mrs. Ginniss!" said the mother hastily, as she stripped the frock from the child's white shoulders, and showed a little linen bag hung about her neck by a silken cord. "Did you ever see that before?"

"Sure an' what would ail me owld eyes not to seen it, whin me own fingers sewed it, an' me own han's hoong it aboot the little crather's nick?"

"You are quite sure it is the very same?"

"Quite an' intirely; for more by token the clot' is a bit uv the linen gownd that my mother give me whin I wor married to Michael, an' the sthring wor to a locket that my b'y give me one Christmas Day."

"And what is in it?" asked Mrs. Legrange eagerly.

"The bracelet, uv coorse. Whin Teddy brought her to me the black night he foun' her sinseless in the strate, she had it clinched in the little hand uv her; an', whin she got betther, there wor nought she loved so well to have by her, an' tooch, an' look at. So when she roomed about, an' I wor thinkin' it might be laid asthray, or she might lave it out the windy, or some place, an' not find it, I sewed it in the bit bag, an' placed it round her nick, and bid her niver, niver, niver let it be took off till she coom to her own agin.

"'That manes hivin, mammy, don't it?' axed the darlint in her own purty way; an' so I says, 'Yis, that manes hivin; an' don't ye niver be lettin' man, woman, nor child, be knowin' to it, till ye git to hivin'.' For sure I knowed she must be some person's child that 'ud one day give their hearts out uv their buzzums to know for sure that she wor their own."

"And that is the reason she never would let me look at it, or open it," said Dora. "She always said, when I asked about it, that it was to go to heaven with her; and, when she got there, she'd open it. So I supposed it was a charm or relic, such as some of our soldiers used to carry about their necks; and I never meddled with it."

"And I, although I knew what it must be, wanted to hear Mrs. Ginniss say that it was the very same bag and all, that she put about the darling's neck soon after she went to her. But now" -

The quick snip of the scissors finished the sentence, and the bag lay in Mrs. Legrange's palm. Sunshine's little hand went up rather forlornly to her bosom, robbed of what it so long had cherished; and Dora clasped her tighter, and kissed her tenderly: but neither spoke, until Mrs. Legrange drew from the bag, and held before them, the coral bracelet, with its linked cameos, broken at one point by the force with which Mother Winch had torn it from the child's shoulder, and with the clasp still closed.

Mrs. Legrange opened it, touched the spring, causing the upper plate to fly up, and silently showed to Dora the name "Antoinette Legrange" engraved within.

"Not quite two years since it was engraved, and what a life of sorrow!" said she softly.

Then, going to her jewel-case, she took out the mate, saved as a sacred relic since the day it had been found upon the floor in the drawing-room after 'Toinette's flight, and handed it to the child, saying, -

"Here is the other one, darling; and you may, if you like, give it to Dora for your wedding-present. This one, that has showed the wanderings of my poor little lost lamb so long, I shall keep for myself."

"Will you take it, Dora, and some love, ever so much love, along with it?" said Sunshine, trying to make her little offering in somewhat the form she had heard from older people, but finishing with a sudden clasp of her arms about Dora's neck, and a shower of kisses, among which came the whispered words, -

"I love you ever and ever so much better than Cousin Tom does, Dora. Be my little wife, and never mind him; won't you?"

CHAPTER XL.

THE WEDDING-DAY.

"MAKE haste, Mr. Sun, and get up! Don't you know it is my birthday, and, what is better, it is Dora's wedding-day? So jump up, pretty Sunny, and be just as bright as glory all day long!"

And the sun, hearing the appeal, stood suddenly upon the summit of the distant hills, shooting playful golden arrows into the child's merry eyes, and among her floating hair, where they clung glittering and glancing; while to her mind he seemed to say, -

"Oh, yes, little namesake! I know all about it; and I promise you sha'n't find me backward in doing my share towards the entertainment. As for a glare of light, though, I know a trick worth two of that, as you shall see. But, first, here is my birthday-kiss. Don't you feel it warm upon your lips?"

"O papa!" shouted Sunshine, as the fancy whirled through her busy little brain, "it seems just as if the sun were kissing me for my birthday."

"If the sun does, the father must; and it ought to be twice over, because last year he lost the chance. Eight! Bless me! where shall I put them all? One on the forehead, two on the eyes, one on the tip of that ridiculous little nose, two on the rose-red cheeks, one in that little hollow under the chin, and the last and best square on the lips. Now, then, my Sunshine, run to mamma, who is waiting for you."

The sun meantime, after a brief period of meditation, took his resolve; and, sending back the brisk October day that had prepared to descend upon earth, he summoned, instead, the first day of the Indian Summer, and bade her go and help to celebrate the bridal of one of his favorite daughters, as she knew so well how to do.

So, summoning a south-west wind, still bearing in his garments the odors of the tropic bowers where he had slept, the fair day descended softly in his arms to earth, and, seating herself upon the hills, wove a drapery of golden mist, bright as love, and tender as maidenhood. Then, wrapped in this bridal veil, she floated, still in the arms of the gentle wind, through the forests, touching their leaves with purer gold and richer crimson; over the harvest-fields, whose shocks of lingering corn rustled responsive as her trailing garments swept past; over wide, brown pastures, where the cattle nibbled luxuriously at the sweet after-math; over lakes and rivers, where the waters slept content, forgetting, for the moment, their restless seaward march; over sheltered gardens, where hollyhock and sunflower, petunia and pansy, dahlia and phlox, whispering together of the summer vanished and the frosty nights at hand, gave out the mysterious, melancholy perfume of an autumn day.

And from forest and field, and pasture and garden, and from the sleeping waters, the dreamy day culled the beauty and the grace, the perfume and the sweet content, and, floating on to where the bride awaited her coming, dropped them all, a heavenly dower, upon her head; wrapped the bright veil caressingly about her;

and so passed on, to lie reclined upon the hills, dreaming in luxurious beauty, until the night should come, and she should float once more heavenward.

But the south-west wind lingered a while, kissing the trembling lips of the bride, fanning her burning cheek, and dallying with the floating tresses of her hair; then, whispering farewell, he crept away to hide in the recesses of the wood, and sigh himself to sleep.

"Dora, where are you, love? Do you hide from me today?" called a voice; and Dora, peeping round the stem of the old oak at whose foot she sat, said shyly, -

"Do you want me, Tom?"

"Want you, my darling? What else on earth do I want but you? And how lovely you are to-day, Dora! You never looked like this before."

"It never was my wedding-day before," whispered Dora; and, like the summer day and the west wind, we will pass on, leaving these our lovers to their own fond folly, which yet is such wisdom as the philosophers and the savans can never give us by theory or diagram.

As the fair day waned to sunset, they were married; Mr. Brown saying the solemn words that barred from his own heart even the unrequited love that had been a dreary solace to it. But Mr. Brown was not only a good man, but a strong man, and one of an iron determination; and so it was possible to him to say those words unfalteringly, and to look upon the bride-lovelier in her misty robes of white, and floating veil, than he had ever seen her before-with unfaltering eyes and unchanging color. No great effort stops short at the end for which it was exerted; and the chaplain himself was surprised to find how calm his heart could be, and how little of pain or regret mingled with his honest admiration and affection for Thomas Burroughs's wife.

The carriage stood ready in the lane, and in another hour they were gone; and let us say with Mrs. Ginniss, - radiant in her new cap and gown, -

"The blissing of God go with 'em! fur it's thimsilves as deserves it."

To those who remain behind when an absorbing interest is suddenly withdrawn, all ordinary events seem to have lost their connection with themselves, and to be dull, disjointed, and fatiguing.

Perhaps that was the reason why Kitty, as soon as the bridal party was out of sight, crept away to her own chamber, and cried as if her heart would break; but nothing except the natural love of mischief, inherent in even the sweetest of children, could have tempted 'Toinette, after visiting her, to go straight to Mr. Brown, - strolling in the rambling old garden, - and say, -

"Now, Mr. Brown! did you say that you despised Kitty?"

"Despise Kitty! Certainly not, my dear. What made you think of such a thing?"

"Why, she said so. She's up in our room, crying just as hard! And, when I asked her what was the matter, she hugged me up tight, and said nobody cared for her, and nobody would ever love her same as Cousin Tom does

Dora. And I told her, yes, they would, and maybe you would; and then she said, 'Oh, no, no, no! he despises me!' and then she cried harder than ever. Tell her you don't; won't you, Mr. Brown?"

The chaplain looked much disturbed, and then very thoughtful; but, as the child still urged him with her entreaties, he said, -

"Yes, I will tell her so, Sunshine, but not just now. And mind you this, little girl, - you must never, never let Kitty know that you told me what she said. Will you promise?"

"Yes, I'll promise. I guess you're afraid, if she knows, she'll think you just say so to make her feel happy. Isn't that it?"

"Yes: that is just it. So remember!"

"I'll 'memberer. Oh, there's Karlo! I'm going to look for chestnuts with him to-morrow. Good-by, Mr. Brown!"

"Good-by, little Sunshine!"

And, for a good hour, Mr. Brown, pacing up and down the garden-walk, took counsel with his own heart, and, we may hope, found it docile.

The next day, he said to Kitty, -

"I have been telling your brother that he had better let you board at Yellow Springs this winter, and attend the lectures at the college. Should you like it?"

"Oh, ever so much!" exclaimed Kitty eagerly. "But we

were to keep house together at Outpost."

"Karl thinks it will be as well to shut up the house and leave farm-matters to Seth and Mehitable, until spring, when Mr. and Mrs. Burroughs return. He will prefer for himself to spend the winter in Greenfield, perhaps in Dr. Gershom's family. If you are at Antioch College, I can perhaps help you with your studies. I take some private pupils."

Mr. Brown did not make this proposition with his usual fluency. Indeed, he was embarrassed to a considerable extent; and so, no doubt, was Kitty, who answered confusedly, -

"I could try; but I never shall be fit for any thing. I never-I never shall know much; though, if you will try to teach me" -

"I will try, Kitty, with all my heart. You have excellent abilities, and it is foolish to say you 'never can be fit' for almost any position."

"O Mr. Brown! it seems to me as if I was such a poor sort of creature, compared with almost any one!"

"Dora, for instance?"

"Yes. I never can be Dora: now, could I?"

"No, any more than I could be Mr. Burroughs. But perhaps Kitty Windsor and Frank Brown may fill their places in this world, and the next too, as well as these friends of theirs whom they both admire."

"O Mr. Brown! will you help me?" asked Kitty,

turning involuntarily toward him, and raising her handsome dark eyes and glowing face to his. He took her hands, looked kindly into her eyes, and said both tenderly and solemnly, -

"Yes, Kitty, God helping me, I will be to you all that a thoughtful brother could be to his only sister; and, what you may be to me in the dim future, that future only knows."

And Kitty's eyes drooped happily beneath that earnest gaze, and upon her cheeks glowed the dawn of a hope as vague as it was sweet.

CHAPTER XLI.

KARL TO DORA. GREENFIELD, IOWA, March 15.
MY DEAR COUSIN, -

YOURS of the 10th duly received, and as welcome as your letters always are. So you have seen the kingdoms of the world and the glory thereof, and find that all is vanity, as saith the Preacher. Do not imagine that I am studying divinity instead of medicine; but to-day is Sunday, and I have been twice to meeting, and taken tea with the minister besides.

But to return to our mutton. Nothing could be more delightful, or, on the whole, more probable to me, than your decision to return to Outpost, instead of settling in Boston or New York. I can hardly fancy my cousin Dora changed into a fine lady, and fretting herself thin over the color of ribbon, or the trail of a skirt; and I am not surprised that she finds what is called "society" puzzling and wearisome. Your life, Dora, began upon too wide a plan to bear narrowing down into conventional limits now; and I feel through my own heart the thrill with which you wrote the words, -

"I long for the opportunity of action and usefulness; I long for the freedom of the prairie, and the dignity of labor; I long to resume my old life, and to see my husband begin his new one."

But, to be quite frank, I was a little surprised that Mr. Burroughs should enter so heartily into your plan of resuming the farm. To be sure, I suppose the land-agency, and the practice of his profession, will occupy most of his time; and his principal concern with the estate will be to admire your able management of it. You and he, my dear Dora, seem to form not only a mutual-admiration, but a mutual-encouragement and mutual-assistance society; and I wish my partnership with Dr. Gershom was half as satisfactory an arrange-ment.

Yesterday, after receiving your letter, I rode directly to Outpost, and communicated your wishes to Seth and Mehitable. The former threw the chip he was whittling into the fire, and said, -

"Miss Burroughs coming back? Waal, then, I'll stop; but I own, doctor, I wouldn't ha' done it ef she hadn't. It's took all the heart out o' the place, her bein' gone so."

And Mehitable and he joined in a chorus of praises and reminiscences, which, pleasant though I found it, I will not put you to the blush by repeating. Both, however, promised faithfully that the house and farm should be ready for you by the middle of April; and Seth says he can take hold "right smart" at helping put up the new house, as he was "raised a carpenter," in part at least.

You ask about me, my dear cousin; but what have I to tell? I work hard at my profession, and take nearly all the night-practice off Dr. Gershom's hands; so I have very little leisure for any thing besides: and you say to be useful is to be happy; so I suppose I am happy; but, if I may be allowed the suggestion, it is rather a negative kind of bliss, and will be decidedly augmented when Outpost is once again open to me as a second home (I assure you I shall be a frequent visitor), and when Burroughs comes to occupy an office beside my own.

As for the rumor of my engagement to Sarah Gershom, it is quite unfounded. I am not thinking of marrying at present.

A letter from Kitty, received a few days since, brings very satisfactory accounts of her progress in learning and in life. She is as happy as possible in her engagement to Frank Brown, and improves, under his tuition, beyond my wildest hopes. She has a strong nature and a deep heart, has Kitty; and I believe Brown understands and can guide them both. Kitty tells me, also, that Theodore Ginniss is taking high honors in his class, and is one of the most promising fellows at Antioch College. He will yet become man of mark, and Mrs. Legrange may well be proud of her prot,g,. Give her my regards, please; and a thousand kisses to Dolce, whom I thank most humbly for her kind message to her poor old Karlo. I hope to see her again in my little vacation next summer. Remember me, too, most kindly to your husband, upon whose coming to Greenfield I am depending a good deal, as I do not suffer, like you, from too much society; and I shall be glad to associate with one man who does not chew tobacco, or sit in the house with his hat on.

And now, dear Dora, good-night, and good-by for a little while.

Always your affectionate cousin,

KARL.